CITY OF GHOSTS

VIOLET FENN

First published by Harker House Publishing 2023

Cover design by GetCovers.

This book is dedicated to

Li Zakovics

We never did get that chicken-inna-basket...

"Liverpool, set in its ways, at the end of the line, at the beginning of time, with its back to the land, its feet in the water, its head in the clouds, its heart on its sleeve, hearts in its mouth."

Paul Morley, *The North*

DARK SHADOWS

"**Y**ou get your idiot ratty backside out of here right this second or I will come over there and move you myself!" I shouted across the crowd in the bar. The vampire I was yelling at either hadn't heard me or was too carried away with wowing the crowd with his surprisingly good rendition of Miley Cyrus's *Wrecking Ball* to even care. The pub was jammed with punters, all of whom seemed to be thoroughly enjoying the spectacle of a bloke dressed all in black singing as though his life depended on it. Of course, they weren't to know that the vocalist in question was a three-hundred-year-old vampire and the sunglasses he was wearing indoors were to hide his weird black eyes. Although I strongly suspected he was the type who'd have worn them as an affectation anyway, even if he hadn't been a member of Liverpool's very own Club Dead. Coopers Town House is tucked away on Cases Street in the entrance to the Clayton Square shopping centre, and you could be forgiven for walking straight past without noticing it—if it's closed. If it's open, however, you'll be able to hear the noise from the other side of Ranelagh Street. "Leave him alone, you mardy cow," said a woman sitting at the table beside me. I turned to give her a Look, but she grinned back. "Come on, love," she said, "we don't get punters like him in here very often." She nodded towards the corner where the vampire was finishing his performance with a dramatic sprawl across a table. "Let us enjoy it for a bit, aye?" I caught the vampire's eye just as the karaoke machine launched into *Wuthering Heights*, and was so fascinated as to whether he'd actually be able to manage the top notes that I forgot to drag his stupid carcass out of the pub before he started singing again. Sighing, I dropped down onto the bench seat next to the woman. "He's a regular," the woman confided, whispering it into my ear at such volume that it was lucky I was dead already and therefore incapable of suffering hearing loss. "All the girls fancy him." The 'girls' appeared to have an average age of about fifty and were all several sheets to the wind despite it being four o'clock on a Wednesday afternoon. I sat with my arms folded across my chest to show that I was indeed still pissed off with him and he'd better shift his ass the second he'd finished his Kate Bush impression. In return, the vampire upped his armography—yeah, I watch *Strictly Come Dancing*, what of it?—and swung happily around as the crowd hollered along with him.

"You've beaten me to it, I see," said a voice in my ear.

I turned to the vampire who'd sat down next to me. "Again," I said. "You're going to have to keep better control of your minions if you don't want to be found out, Aiden."

"Aah," said Aiden, "let him have his fun. He's spent decades in those cold, damp tunnels—it's good for him to get out in the open air a bit." I squinted at the head of the local vampire society to check whether he was being serious. "They need to integrate, Lilith. Not hide away. Was it not yourself who said we were going to be more open about our existence?"

"By which I meant that those of us who belong to the nether-fucking-weird could perhaps try to subtly join in with human life," I said. "Pretty sure I did not suggest bouncing straight out of the coffin and into one of the busiest bars in the city centre." The singing vampire was coming to the end of the song and glanced over to make sure I was watching. When he saw who I was with, his voice faltered and he dropped the arm he'd been flailing around in the air. Aiden made a polite gesture that I interpreted as 'do carry on, we'll discuss this later' and the vampire immediately stopped singing. Putting the microphone down on the table and waving apologetically at the disappointed women, he wriggled through the crowd like a thin black snake and was out of the door before anyone could stop him.

"Ohhhh," I snarked, "he does what *you* tell him. What happened to me being Queen Of All She Surveys?"

"Lilith," said Aiden kindly, "you ruin that for yourself by being far too reasonable and loath to use violence. Whereas Stefan there knew very well that if he hadn't left when he did, I might possibly have ripped his head off when I got back to the tunnels."

"Would you, though?" I asked. "Would you really rip someone's head off just because they were doing a bit of karaoke when they shouldn't have been?"

"I might," said Aiden. "And I might not." He winked at me. I don't know if you've ever had a vampire wink at you, but it's quite unnerving. Even to me, and I am a certified member of the undead underworld. Aiden is, however, one of the few vampires I've met who's aesthetically pleasing to look at, so the effect is softened slightly. He's not exactly handsome—at least, not in a conventional way—but at least he doesn't resemble an elongated humanoid rat, like the rest of them. Although Rachel who lives in the flat below me is also a vampire and actually mostly just looks like an underfed goth, so clearly there are exceptions to the rule. "That's the trick, Lilith," Aiden went on. "They can't be sure whether or not I'd actually carry out any threats, and it's enough to keep them under control. Most of the time, anyway."

"How's work going on the tunnels?" I asked, changing the subject. Aiden's vampire coven lived in the old Wapping rail tunnel, up in Edge Hill. Joe Williamson had been hiding them there for a good while before I found out about it, and things were still frosty between us. Not least because I'd cut Joe out of the equation and begun dealing with Aiden directly, in the hope of simplifying the undead politics that takes up so much of my (after)life these days. It had been agreed that the vampires could stay in the tunnels and make some home improvements, on condition they a) didn't upset the locals; and b) promised not to eat any of the urban explorers that liked to wander the remains of the tunnels. I'd had to explain live streaming to a very confused Aiden, who'd struggled to grasp the concept of the entire world potentially being able to witness him chowing down on someone via a video link. He'd asked to look at my iPhone in order to satisfy his curiosity and it still had visible teeth marks on the back of its case.

"Work goes well, thank you," he said politely. "But we need to talk about something else, Lilith. I fear there may be a problem developing in this paradise we call Liverpool." Oh, how fucking brilliant. Just as I was beginning to think that herding vampires was going to be the most difficult part of my daily life, the madness was clearly about to kick off yet again. Cynical of me, I know. But when you've just been through the kind of year I have—involving death, murder, and serious damage to several major city landmarks—you learn to expect the worst. I got up to leave and Aiden stepped outside with me.

"Go on then," I said as we walked past the fruit and veg stall that still seemed to be doing brisk business, even on a January afternoon, "hit me with it. What kind of batshittery am I being landed with now?"

"You use some very strange words at times," said Aiden, "I'm sure I don't understand some of them at all."

"Making up inventive curse words is my hobby," I said. "Sometimes it's all that gets me through the day."

"I see," said Aiden in a serious tone of voice. "Well, I'm sure you know best how to deal with the stresses of a position as lofty as your own."

"Cut the crap, Aid, and just tell me what the fuck's going on. I've promised Izzy I'll go to the cinema with her tonight," I lied, "and I've still got paperwork to do." Turns out being dead doesn't cut admin out of your life. That discovery has been one of my biggest disappointments so far, I don't mind telling you.

"Aah," said Aiden, "the moving pictures! Such a delight." I coughed loudly. "Yes, yes, of course you're busy. I shall take leave of you in the briefest of moments. I just thought you'd want to know that a body's been found just off Great Homer Street."

"Is that in Everton?" I might have been living in this city for well over a decade now, but like many people I mostly just know the bits I, well, *know*. I rarely had much cause to go any further north than Leeds Street, so mostly didn't bother.

"It is indeed," said Aiden. "And a very curious case it is, too. The unfortunate chap was found inside a large piece of metal piping. He had clearly been there for some time."

"And you think it has something to do with us?" I hadn't had to deal with a murder for a while. I should have known the peace and quiet was too good to be true.

"Not directly, no," said Aiden. "It's believed he somehow made his own way into the tube and got stuck. Probably suffocated, the poor chap."

"Well that's all very sad and everything," I said, "but why are you telling me about it? Horrible things happen to people by accident all the time."

"Aah well," said the vampire, stopping so I had to turn and face him. "There's the thing, you see. We already know the details of what happened, because it was investigated a very long time ago."

"How could it have been investigated ages ago if he's only just been found?" I frowned at him. "You're talking in riddles now."

"Actually," said Aiden, "the body in the pipe was found in nineteen-forty-five. And it was eventually decided by the coroner that it had been there some sixty years before it was discovered during clearances after a bomb raid. This supposedly new discovery is, in fact, a very old one."

"Nope," I said, "I got nothing. You're going to have to explain this again, but in shorter sentences."

Aiden gave me a small, sad smile. "Lilith," he said, "the time slips are back."

Most Liverpudlians already know the legend of the time slips. The stories usually begin with someone stopping to look in a shop window, only to realise either the stock on display or their price tags seem suspiciously out of date. A woman once went into a branch of Mothercare and tried to pay for her bargain purchases with a credit card, only to be met with confusion from shop staff, who didn't seem to know what it was. Which was unsurprising, because the shop in question had actually closed down years before she stood at the counter trying to buy gifts for her new niece. A man whose wife had walked ahead of him into the

Bold Street branch of Waterstones made to catch her up, only to suddenly find himself in the late nineteen-fifties. Crossing the road and dodging a van that was at least three decades past being liable for road tax, he headed to the bookshop only to discover its window was displaying shoes and handbags, rather than the latest Stephen King novel. When he stepped inside, he was once again in Waterstones in the present day. And then there was the even stranger tale of the modern-day shoplifter who ran down Hanover Street with a security guard hot on his tail so turned into Brookes Alley in the hope of escape. Which should have been a lucky move from the security guard's perspective, because Brookes Alley is a dead end. But when the guard made it round the corner after his prey, the alleyway was empty. The thief, in the meantime, was walking out of the same alley and wondering where the security guard had disappeared to. Which was when he realised the street looked very different. Not only that, but his mobile phone was refusing to work. Panic really began to set in when our would-be Fagin spotted a newspaper kiosk and, heading over to check, discovered he was somehow walking round Liverpool city centre in May 1967—thirty-nine years earlier than when he'd got up that morning. As he ran to the end of the street, his phone pinged back into life—but when he turned to look behind him, the street in the distance was still set in the nineteen-sixties. The first stories were pretty easy to write-off as overdramatic urban myths. But the one involving the shoplifter had always fascinated me, because the security guard involved had backed up the lad's story. He gave chase and saw his target veering into what he knew was a dead-end. Turning the corner with anticipatory glee at the prospect of such an easy catch, he was shocked to discover the lad had apparently disappeared into thin air.

And now Aiden was telling me that not only were the stories true, they were happening again. "Why?" I asked, already marking it down as one of the stupidest questions I'd ask all year. And it was only January.

"Who knows the whys and wherefores of these things?" Aiden shrugged elegantly. It randomly occurred to me that if he trained some of his underlings in clothing and deportment, they might be less noticeable on the city streets. As it was, the *Echo* had recently run an article about how goth was clearly on the rise again in Liverpool and several of the student club nights had put the Sisters of Mercy back on their playlists in anticipation. "But as we ourselves know, Lilith," he caught my elbow to guide me politely around a woman attempting to clean up the mess her small poodle had made in the middle of the pavement, "this, aah, shall we say, *upsurge* in activity has been growing exponentially since you decided to, aah, join our merry band."

"No." I stopped in my tracks and Aiden lurched slightly as he lost his determined grip on my arm. "Not again. I am *done* with everything being down to me, Aiden. Yeah yeah," I stepped backwards to let Poodle Woman walk between us, the little dog eyeing us suspiciously as he went, "I was the catalyst, the netherworld is rising, all that jazz. I accepted it, I took control, it's old news."

And now the city is rising with you, said the voice in my head.

You know how some people have an inner voice that they kind of hear but don't really? I have a real, sentient voice in my head, made up of all the long-gone residents of Liverpool who made this city what it is today. And sometimes that voice is *really* annoying.

You can stay out of this, I said silently, *I'm doing my bit*. Which was true—sort of. Despite still owning Flora's, the coffeeshop below my flat on Harrington Street, I'd long ago given up the idea of actually working there. The only real input I had was covering days off for my best friend Izzy, who now pretty much ran the place. She had help from Todd, who'd started out as an occasional extra pair of hands but was now all but full-time. And I'd been demoted to sitting in the staff kitchen behind the café, sighing over boring paperwork whilst occasionally gazing longingly out into what seems to me an attractively tedious, normal human world. This was partly because being Queen of the Underworld is a full time job in itself and doesn't leave much time for hanging out in cafes with friends. But it was also because Izzy got fed up with repairing things I'd accidentally broken with my superhuman speed and strength, and told me to 'just sit down and look pretty'. I could manage the sitting, at least.

"What does the city think?" asked Aiden politely.

"It thinks it ought to stay out of my business, is what it thinks," I said, glaring at him. Everyone and his undead hellhound seemed to know about me being able to talk to the city, and none of them appeared to find it remotely weird. Which says a lot about the level of what counts as normal background weirdness in the undead section of Liverpool society.

"Is that so?" Aiden was suppressing a smile, I could *hear* it. "Then I'm sure it trusts you to do whatever you think best in regards to this new and emerging threat." Fuck*sake*. There really was no rest for the wickedly undead.

"Fine," I sighed, "I'll find out what's going on and get back to you."

"Excellent," said the vampire, "I look forward to hearing of your adventures." And with that, he disappeared in a brief flurry of dark shadows.

See? Something ridiculous happens, it gets left to me to sort it out. Me, a thirty-something cafe owner who has better things to do with her time than investigating endless mysteries like an undead Miss Marple. Everyone else just sits back and waits for the entertainment to start. *I could do with some entertainment of my own*, I thought, trudging sulkily down Church Street.

You could always call that king of yours, said the city.

Fuck off. I crossed over to Lord Street and nearly knocked a cyclist off his bike because I wasn't looking.

So much for undead superpowers. You'd perhaps be less noticeable if you looked where you were going.

So much for you being a helpful and supportive companion, I snarked back, *instead of some weird combination of judgmental nanna and terrible advice.*

Charmed, we're sure, said the city, but it didn't sound too offended. I guess it's hard to take insults seriously when you're the ethereal embodiment of thousands of separate souls and you only have one person to talk to. *We hear Ivo Laithlind is back in his own territory.*

Good for him. I hadn't seen the divine Mr L since he'd turned up at Flora's a few months earlier to inform me he was going away but would be watching from a distance because—and I quote—I might be 'dangerous'. As if. Okay, so danger did seem to find me on a regular basis. But it was usually me who was at risk, not the people around me. Although to be fair, the last time things had kicked off my best friend, her boyfriend and my potential boyfriend had all ended up in hospital. And by potential boyfriend I mean Sean Hannerty—yes, *that* Sean Hannerty, the award-winning crime writer—who had made it very clear he would like to be more 'definite' than 'potential'. But they were all very fragile humans who were going to get hurt if they hung around me too much, as I kept trying to explain to Sean. He'd started writing a new paranormal series and his agent was very excited about it. It apparently had 'Netflix potential' which all sounds very exciting and cool to most people. But as Sean's stories were actually based on stuff that had happened in my own real (after)life, I just found it unnervingly weird. Not weird enough to stop me insisting on a share of the royalties, mind. I might be dead, but I'm not entirely stupid.

Maybe you should give in to the inevitable and take Mr Hannerty up on his eager offers of intimacy, suggested the city. ***He already knows the truth, after all. And it certainly doesn't appear to be quelling his ardour.***

Well it bloody well should! I said, stalking around a busker who was taking up way too much room for someone with only a small amplifier and a plastic ukulele. *It's too dangerous.* I wasn't even being overly dramatic. It was still less than twelve months since I'd woken up dead in the car park outside Flora's, and in that time Sean had come face to face with a feral mermaid, had his memory sucked out of him *and* narrowly avoided being killed by an immortal brat with mommy issues at the top of the Radio City tower. The fact that his life had been saved by William the Conqueror and the brat in question had gone on to be dinner for said feral mermaid and her friends wasn't even the strangest part of the shit Sean had been caught up in since he'd first taken a shine to me.

The king, then, said the city. ***William is as immortal as you and as keen as Hannerty. A match made in heaven.***

Or hell.

That too, it said happily. ***The joy is that, as you cannot ever die in the human sense, neither of you will ever discover whether either truly exists. Probably best to just make the most of it.***

Ugh. I'd spent way too much time over the past few months pondering immortality, and the prospect was truly terrifying. I sometimes struggle to get through a single day in Liverpool without losing my unholy shit with people—god knows how I was supposed to survive forever with my sanity intact.

For god to know, offered the city, **he or she would have to exist. We've certainly never met them.**

I think the gods gave up on Liverpool a long time ago, I said. *Probably got scared off by the place. It's stronger than any god I can imagine.*

True enough. Perhaps that's why Chester dislikes us so much.

Yeah, I said, spotting an opportunity to get to the bottom of something that had been bugging me for ages, *about Chester*—

"Red!" My internal conversation was interrupted by a lanky man with floppy hair and a guitar slung across his back. "How's it going?"

"Hey Ifan," I grinned despite myself. It was impossible to dislike Ifan Davies—not that I'd known anyone ever try. Why would you? Fully human—and very famous, if you know your music—Ifan had dropped from public view a few years earlier. He now split his time between busking in Liverpool city centre and fighting off the endless pretty students who'd like to get to know him better. *Much* better, if you catch my drift. I had no idea how or why a renowned musician had ended up living on the city streets, and I'd long decided it was better not to ask. What was more impressive was that—so far, at least—Ifan hadn't been recognised by any of his fans. As far as I knew, his records still sold and the music magazines still referenced him occasionally, yet not one person had so much as done a double-take at him playing his guitar with his eyes closed on Mathew Street. And he was often playing his own songs. Maybe he had some kind of force field around him that stopped people recognising him.

Stranger things have happened, said the city. **All we know is that he belongs here. For now, at least.**

"Gonna come to my gig next week?" Ifan asked with a shy smile. "See me play properly?"

"An actual gig?" I asked. "Where?"

"In the Cavern," he grinned. "Thought I'd keep it traditional." The original Cavern Club is long gone, lost to the developers' wrecking ball by way of some terrible town planning decisions. I knew from personal experience that its spirit lived on, deep beneath Mathew Street, and I just had to hope the literal cavern I'd had the misfortune to find down there the previous year had now been properly fortified. But the original club is way too big a part of Liverpool history to stay buried for long, and a reproduction of it now exists as a popular club just a little way up from the original site.

"I thought you didn't play gigs?" I said. "Too mainstream, and all that."

"Yeah," he said, "I did say that, didn't I?" He shuffled slightly in embarrassment. "But, well, Missy suggested it." Missy Leschi lived up at Anfield Cemetery, in the old groundskeeper's house that's tucked away in the trees just off Priory Road. She'd been suspicious of me when we'd first met, but had gradually warmed to the insanity that was my life and now spent as much time in Flora's as she did up in Anfield. It's hard not to bond when you've been forced to band together to fight the evils of darkness (or at least, those evils of darkness that aren't ourselves or our friends). And Missy was one of the few friends of the undead variety who weren't interested in either beheading or dethroning me, which was a major plus point in my book. I sometimes think she likes Izzy more than me, but then most people do. I've got used to it over the years.

"Isn't Missy in London?" Originally from Italy by way of a sixteenth-century move to Britain, Missy had friends all over the place and no desire to explain who any of them were, however many times I asked.

"Got back late last night," said Ifan. "Gave Alan a shock, by all accounts. Apparently he was practicing his stage moves on the kitchen table when she walked through the door and started yelling at him." Alan is, well, I suppose he's Missy's housemate, of a sort. They've been friends for decades, ever since Alan died too young and found himself wandering Anfield in the sharp stage suit he hadn't actually worn in years. He's now dating the shy vampire who lives downstairs from me and seems to be thoroughly enjoying being back in Liverpool society. Even if he does have to keep fielding curious questions from older women who are sure they recognise him from somewhere. Missy's reappearance at least explained why Mapp had been missing in action. I'd called in at his shop on Renshaw Street first thing, only to find the closed sign on the door and no signs of life. The one revenant I really would trust with my undead life, Gaultier Mapp was also Missy's closest friend. He'd have shot up to Anfield the second she got home and not left until he'd wrung every last ounce of gossip out of her.

"And she's come back filled with the urge to become a music promoter?" Missy hadn't struck me as the musical type. If she'd decided to go into events management I'd have expected it to be more the 'arts festival based out of the Walker Gallery' type of thing, not tiny gigs in even tinier basements.

"She got chatting to someone in London who used to be involved with music up here. Brian something-or-other, I think it was. Anyway, he told her it was a shame the old clubs had lost their way a bit, and you know how Missy doesn't like anyone criticising her city." Missy might have been as much of an incomer as me—although a much longer established one—but this city gets into your soul. You become very defensive of it, very quickly. "So she decided to give it a go," he went on, "and dragged me into it."

"And the Cavern are just letting her do it? Without any previous experience?" Having attempted to put on my own events whilst at university, I knew how difficult it was to get venues to take a chance on unknown promoters. I'd ended up running occasional indie nights at the Student Union bar, and felt lucky if I got enough punters to cover the costs. And here was Missy, dipping her toe in the entertainments water with a debut night at the most famous club in town.

"This Brian bloke called in a few favours, by the sounds of it," said Ifan. "Think he was a big shot up here, way back when." Recognition was starting to prickle at the back of my neck, but I decided to ignore it. When you're dead and unburied, you learn to turn a blind eye to all manner of strange coincidences.

"I'll be there," I promised. Ifan gave me a little salute and an enormous grin, and headed off towards Derby Square. No doubt his fan club were already waiting for him.

~

As a fully paid-up denizen of the darker side of life, I could walk away from most injuries without much more than a few pained squeaks as my undead body knitted itself back together. I'd heard rumours of revenants like me actually surviving being beheaded, simply by scrabbling round for their lopped off skull and wedging it back on before the cuts had time to heal. Humans, not so much. I sighed heavily, and accidentally breathed in just as a pair of well-dressed businessmen walked past. The shock of inhaling a sudden cloud of human emotions—aggression, determination and just a hint of fear—made me stop dead in my tracks and a woman behind me ploughed straight into my back.

"Oh god," I said, spinning round a bit too fast, "I'm so sorry!"

The woman was middle-aged, with faded blonde hair and narrow green eyes. Tall and painfully thin, she had a slight stoop that made me suspect she was mocked for her height as a child. "Fucking hell," she said, "can you not mind where you're going?" She stalked off down the road without waiting for a response, shaking her head as she went.

See what we mean?

Please shut up, I said silently. *I'm not in the mood for a lecture.* In the early days I'd often forget I was the only one who could hear the voice in my head and I'd reply out loud. Having convinced too many people that I maybe wasn't in complete control of all my faculties, I've learned to keep it silent. It's a bit weird when your brain has to divide itself between general thoughts and actual conversation with someone/something else, but I mostly managed. Although I did worry that one day I'd maybe think about it all just a tiny bit too much and would finally go stark raving mad.

No one would notice, said the city helpfully. I growled under my breath and stalked off. Hopefully Flora's would be quiet and Izzy would have time to sit and listen to me moan for a while. That would make things better.

THE CAROUSEL

"**A**'right, dead girl?" Izzy grinned as I walked into Flora's. It was quiet enough for the few customers to hear what she said, and more than one turned to look curiously at me.

"Will you stop calling me that?" I hissed as I joined her behind the counter. "People will talk."

"People already talk," she said, turning to lean back against the till as she watched me make an espresso. "'There's some weird people in that Flora's place', is what they say. Lean into it, I reckon." She shrugged. "If everyone already expects us to be a bit odd, they're less likely to notice the genuinely weird shit that goes on."

"Ooh, pour me one, Lil," said Aunt Kitty, appearing out of nowhere at the table in the little staff kitchen. "I'm parched."

"See what I mean?" said Izzy. "Weird shit like ghosts appearing in the kitchen and demanding coffee. How's tricks, Kitty?"

"Tricks are very good, thank you," said Kitty. I sighed and reached for a second cup. My late lamented great-aunt was wearing a black mini dress with white daisies on it and had her long blonde hair pulled back with a black Alice band. It had a matching daisy perched jauntily on one side. Her bare feet were tucked up underneath her and you'd have to look closely to realise she was sitting partly *in* the chair, rather than on top of it. She looked all of twenty years old, rather than the thirty-five she'd been when she'd died, back in the mid nineteen-sixties. "Jonny's visiting later," she went on. "We're going out on the town."

"Is he staying over?" Jonny Mytton was an absolute rogue, but a likeable one. It helped that a couple of centuries of immortality had knocked most of the old-money entitlement off him. He'd lived a short but very eventful human life, before dying in a debtors' prison back when Queen V's uncle was still on the throne. I had no objection to Kitty having visitors, but I liked to have a bit of notice so that I didn't have to sit in my own living room trying to ignore my aunt smooching with her boyfriend. If they were going to spend the evening gazing into each other's eyes, then I'd just have to go hang out with the mermaids down at Otterspool prom.

"I'll probably go back to Shrewsbury with him for a couple of days," Kitty said, "if that's okay with you?"

"I keep telling you," I said, "you don't have to ask my permission. You're a grown up, Kitty. You can do what you please with your time."

"I don't like leaving you home alone so much," said my aunt. "You should go out more."

"I tell her that," said Izzy, "but will she listen?"

"Whenever we go out together," I said to Izzy, "something ridiculous happens. Every time."

"Ridiculous things have happened all our lives," said Izzy in a reasonable tone. "Why worry about it now?"

"Why worry about what?" We all turned to look through the kitchen doorway at Nikolaus Silverton, who'd appeared as if by magic at the counter behind Izzy. I looked across at the customers sitting by the window, who seemed oblivious. Nik slid past Izzy to join me and Kitty in the kitchen.

"Anything," I said. "Although I've just been informed that this absurd town of ours is now growing time slips. Which I do think counts as slightly unnerving, by any standards." Izzy and Kitty both gaped at me, but Nik looked annoyingly unperturbed.

"The very thing I have come to discuss," he said happily, sitting down at the table with us. "What luck!"

"Can anyone use these time slips?" asked Kitty, a distinct note of hopefulness in her voice.

"Sadly not," said Nik. "They only appear to certain people and generally disappear as quickly as they arrive. And there's only the one this time, thankfully."

"Is this Bold Street again?" asked Izzy. "I always assumed that was a hoax."

"Some of it undoubtedly was," said Nik. "But other incidents were all too real. Caused Eadric no end of sleepless nights, last time it happened."

"Eadric doesn't sleep," I pointed out. Eadric Silverton—Nik's brother in name, if not blood—is *de facto* head of the north-west division of Undead United. I might have the crown and the supposed power, but Eadric's the one with the paperwork and fancy offices. He keeps offering to let me take over the lot and I keep politely turning him down, because what's the point in being immortal if your time's taken up with admin? The only duties I'm happy to carry out up at the Liver Building are those involved with keeping the birds happy. The liver birds might look small when you're on the ground looking up at them, but you don't want to be next to Bella's enormous feet when she's stamping them in a tantrum, is all I'm saying.

"You understand the metaphor though," said Nik patiently. "Or did you miss out on the English language section of your history degree?" I scowled at him. I'd actually got a First in History way back when. Sadly, it had turned out to be fairly useless in the face of your actual, genuine history becoming an all too real part of my daily life.

"Why is it our problem?" I asked. "Let the *Echo* have its fun. They haven't managed any really ridiculous headlines in a while."

"What about *'Killer Mermaids in the Mersey?'*?" said Nik. "That was a good one."

"You leave Daisy out of this," I said. "She was just helping out."

"She's developing a taste for humans, more like," said Nik. "You need to keep an eye on her, Lil. It's one thing her polishing off your dumped corpses and taking out supernatural threats, but what if she starts on innocent humans?"

"Daisy wouldn't do that," I said indignantly. "She's got morals."

Nik made a disbelieving noise under his breath. "She has, though," I insisted. Daisy might have some unsavoury habits, but she'd saved my bacon on a couple of occasions, and I owed her a bit of defence.

"Anyway," said Nik, changing the subject before it turned into an argument, "the mermaids aren't our problem right now. The time slips are. How did you know about them?"

"I bumped into Aiden," I said. "Up at Cooper's."

Nik's brow furrowed into a delicate frown. "Dare I ask why the pair of you were frequenting that den of absolute iniquity?" he asked. "Or am I better off not knowing?"

"Turns out vampires have good singing voices," I shrugged. "Some of them, anyway."

Nik considered this for a moment, then wisely decided not to pursue it. "That particular portal appears to have closed itself," he said, "at least for now."

"Excuse me," Izzy was waving her hand in the air like a kid in a classroom, "did you just say *portal*? Have we dropped into a video game now?"

"Oh, I like video games," Kitty piped up, "Jonny's been teaching me how to play them. I think you'll find the cake is a lie."

Nik looked utterly nonplussed. "It's a geeky reference," I explained. "There is no cake."

"Exactly!" said Kitty happily. "It's so funny." The customers from the window table were getting up to leave, and Izzy walked back into the cafe to clear their table. I heard them saying their goodbyes, and Izzy latching the door behind them and turning the sign to show we were closed. I checked my watch and was surprised to find it was almost six o'clock. The weather had been so gloomy this past week that it felt as though daylight hardly broke before it started fading away again.

"If the—" I struggled with the ridiculousness of the word 'portal' and decided I really couldn't manage it, "—*time slip* has closed again, then what's the problem? Obviously, I would prefer it if we did not develop fucking great chasms in the fabric of reality right in the middle of Liverpool city centre. Mostly because I absolutely do not wish to experience my teenage years ever again. But it isn't actually the strangest thing to happen round here, is it?" That honour was probably jointly awarded to either my discovery that the afterlife was not only real, it was actually pretty bloody crowded; or to the recently acquired knowledge that there'd been a pack of werewolves lurking in Sefton Park for the last few hundred years. Eadric had mentioned it casually in conversation, and seemed confused by my concern. As if Sefton Park isn't already weird enough. Anyway, Eadric kept insisting no one had spotted a werewolf in years and it probably wasn't worth worrying about, but I'd made absolutely sure to accompany any humans I was even remotely fond of if they wanted to walk any further south than Warwick Street. You can't be too careful when it comes to creatures of the undead night. As if reading my thoughts, a large grey face appeared at the back window. If Grimm had been hoping to give us a fright he was disappointed, because no one so much as flinched. I got up with a sigh and went over to let him in. The big grey cat plopped casually down into the kitchen, before padding across to the table and leaping up onto it with an elegance disproportionate to his size. He looked round at us all in turn, then stretched a back leg high into the air. With a happy sigh, he set to licking bits of himself I didn't need to know about.

"If there's one," said Nik, "there'll be more. That's how it always happens. Can you *not*?" This was to Grimm, who was making horribly enthusiastic slurping noises. I gave the cat a shove and he unrolled himself enough to glare at me, before giving in and flumping down onto the table like a beanbag that didn't have quite enough filling. "That dratted animal," Nik went on. "I'm sure he does these things purely to irritate people."

"He likes playing games," said Kitty, reaching over to stroke Grimm's ears. He purred happily, despite me knowing damn well he'd make a good attempt at taking my fingers off if I tried the same move. "He's just a big baby. Aren't you, Grimmy?" He rolled his head backwards and blinked slowly at Kitty in acknowledgement.

"I'm sure he's not hygienic," fretted Nik.

"So don't lick him then," I said. "Anyway, what do you mean by 'how it always happens'? You're not telling me this is a regular occurrence?"

"I'd quite like to walk down Bold Street in the sixties," offered Izzy. "I bet it was interesting."

"Rough as fuck, more like," I said. "Same as all cities were in the sixties. Swinging or not."

"True," said Nik. "You certainly wouldn't have wanted to walk down Harrington Street alone at night back then." He thought about it a bit. "Or anytime, really."

"Well, it's a good job it's gone upmarket these days then, isn't it?" I said, just daring anyone to say something. Nik looked as though he might, but I cut him off. "Focus, grasshopper," I said. "What's with the wibbly-wobbly, timey-wime-y shit?"

"Don't ask me to explain it," said Nik. "I'm all about the poetry and romance. Quantum makes my head hurt."

"Quantum makes *everyone*'s head hurt," said Izzy. "Mine more than most. Damon likes to talk about it. Usually in the early hours when all I want to do is roll over, fart and go to sleep." Izzy was the last person in the world I could imagine farting, but I was trying not to get sidetracked and managed not to say anything.

"You don't have to give me a scientific explanation," I said to Nik, "but I'm going to need more than *'oh yeah the time slips are real better add that to the list of weird shit you have to deal with'*. If you don't mind."

He sighed and draped himself backwards over the chair. I think he was going for drama, but it actually just looked bloody uncomfortable. "So, there's this theory," he said, "that everything happens at the same time. Time isn't a linear thing that's always moving forwards—rather, it's all here at once. Everything that ever happened and everything that ever *will* happen. We just never have to acknowledge it because we generally 'walk'" he made air quotes with his fingers towards the ceiling, "through it in one direction. But sometimes it gets thin in places. And that's when the trouble starts."

"Block theory?" I said. Nik pulled himself upright and looked at me. "Time's just one amorphous lump of everything and we're moving through *it*, rather than it moving along its own rail, sort of thing." I frowned. "I think my grandad showed me a book on it once."

"Your grandfather was clearly an interesting chap," said Nik, tilting his head as he gazed at me thoughtfully. "But yes," he sat forward suddenly and slapped the table, making both Grimm and Kitty jump, "that's about the sum of it. Or so I'm told by those more scientifically inclined." He shrugged.

"And these thin patches are in Liverpool right now?" I asked. Nik nodded. "What about Manchester?" He looked confused. "Why does Liverpool get the stupid quantum bollocks?" I went on. "Can't it go annoy Salford instead?"

"You wouldn't last long in Salford if you insisted on describing it as part of Manchester," said Nik. "Anyway, I don't know and there's no point wondering about the whys and wherefores of it all. The port—sorry, time slips—are back, and it's up to us to deal with them."

"Where?" I asked him. "The only one I've heard about is the bloke on Great Homer Street."

"Well," said Nik, "that's the thing. There hasn't been anything else as yet. Although," he looked thoughtful, "I did spot a dashing chap in Derby Square the other day who looked as though he could have come straight out of the Regency period. Maybe something's going on there."

"That was probably just Mapp," I said. "He's got a new winter coat and is insisting on wearing it everywhere." It was a really impressive coat, to be fair. It fitted him perfectly and was long and swishy, with fancy gold buttons. He'd been into Flora's a few days earlier to show it off to me and Izzy. We had a table of stray tourists in at the time and I was pretty sure they'd assumed he was part of a cosplay group.

"Whatever," Nik said, with the tone of a mardy teen. "If it's started, it'll keep happening. For a while, at least."

"How do we stop it?" Izzy asked.

"Oh, my sweet summer child," said Nik, "we cannot stop the march of time. Not even when it's marching in the wrong direction. No," he stood up and made a show of brushing cat hair off his moleskin trousers, "we merely observe. And make sure no humans walk into it, of course. That's your job, Lil." He smiled brightly at me.

"The fuck?" I said. "How am I supposed to babysit the population of an entire city?"

"You're not babysitting," soothed Nik, "you're just watching over them. Like a guardian."

"Maybe guard *dogs* would be better," said Izzy. "Hire the werewolves, give them something productive to do with their time."

"Do you tell your friends *everything*?" said Nik, looking at me. "Humans aren't supposed to know about these things, Lilith!"

"Izzy's not a human though, is she," I pointed out. "Well, she is a human, obviously. But not *just* a human. She's my friend. And I tell my friends whatever I need to tell them in order to keep them safe."

"Uh huh," said Iz. "I'll not be walking down Princes Avenue on my own anytime soon."

"Anyway," I went on, "I'm in charge, remember? Eadric might still technically be the head of this area, but you all wanted me to take over and I did and now you have to live with my decisions. Whether you're actually alive or not. Soz like." I shrugged.

Nik shook his head. "You will be the death of me, Lilith O'Reilly," he said. "If I wasn't dead already." There was banging from outside at the cafe door and Izzy went to see who it was.

"Heard the latest?" Missy was already talking as she came banging through the cafe and into the kitchen. "Oh sorry," she said to Nick, who was getting up to leave and nearly went flying as she barrelled in. She hopped up onto the worktop that runs along the kitchen wall and swung her legs as she looked at us.

"Don't tell us," said Izzy, "Alan's trying out for *Britain's Got Talent*."

"Huh," said Missy, "he's better than any of them on there and you know it. No, it's bigger than that."

"I'm so terribly sorry to miss out on such excitement," said Nik, "but there are terrible, terrible novels back in my rooms, just waiting for me to read them." He looked at me. "Do try not to cause any catastrophes in the meantime, Lilith." I flipped a middle finger at his retreating back as he let himself out through the cafe. Izzy followed him and put the latch back on with a sigh.

"So," said Missy, when Izzy was back in the room, "do you want to know, or not?" She looked at us both in turn, and we dutifully stared back at her. "The time slips are back," she said, clearly waiting for a reaction that didn't come. "Come *on*," she said, "you can't tell me this isn't mad stuff. Even by our standards!"

"Sorry to spoil your fun," said Izzy, "but we already knew about it.

Bloke in a tube, up Everton way, happened decades ago. Old news, mate."

"Not him," said Missy, "this is something else. Haven't you heard about the drama down at the dock this morning?" Uh-oh.

"No," I said, "we haven't. Which dock?"

"Albert," said Missy. "A little kid went missing. More kids should go missing in my opinion," she looked thoughtful, "they're mostly really annoying. But anyway, yeah. Kid gets on the carousel and rides round while the parents or whoever try to look like they're interested. The ride stops, and everyone gets off—except one. Nowhere to be seen, disappeared into thin air. Panic everywhere, police get called, full-scale search begins. Cos obviously, everyone assumes the bratling got off on the other side where she couldn't be seen and somehow fell into the Salthouse Dock, right? How have you missed all this?"

"We've been busy," I shrugged. "Some of us have to work for a living."

"Ha ha," said Missy. "As if it isn't work enough keeping an eye on the shit that goes on up in Anfield. Anyway, so the search and rescue boat turns up and there's divers and everything and they're trawling the dock, but no sign of this kid. The mum's hysterical by this point and the other woman with her—who turned out to be the kid's nan—isn't much better. Both white as sheets and convinced their girl's either drowned or kidnapped. Guess what happened next?"

"The kid turned out to be standing behind them all the time?" asked Izzy.

"Not quite," said Missy, "but not entirely wrong, either. The kid *was* behind them, but she hadn't been before. Reappeared right out of nowhere, eating a packet of sweets and happy as a pig in muck. And she looked like a pig in muck, as well. Really grimy, like she'd been up a chimney or something."

"So where had she been?" asked Izzy.

"That's the thing," said Missy, who was enjoying the drama hugely, "it wasn't so much where she'd been, as *when.*"

"What?" I asked stupidly.

"That's what I said when Jenny told me about it," said Missy. Jenny was a member of Mapp's knitting club. A human one, and a part-time

22

special constable with the local police. Jenny was also very good at passing on interesting information, and I suspected she knew things weren't always entirely as they seemed. But she didn't seem inclined to ask questions and none of us was in a hurry to fill her in, so we all pretended everything was perfectly normal and the world kept turning.

"She was walking to work and got caught up in it," Missy went on. "I bumped into her just now, and she filled me in."

"Filled you in on what?" said Izzy impatiently. "Bloody hell, Missy, you're going to have to get quicker than this at spilling the beans. I'll be claiming my pension by the time you get to the end of this story."

"It's worth the wait," said Missy, who didn't look remotely put out by Izzy's snark.

"You said 'when', not where," I said to Missy. I was pretty sure I knew what was coming next, and I didn't like it one tiny bit.

She nodded. "Yup," she said, "she didn't disappear on the dock—she disappeared on the *clock*." By the look of satisfaction on Missy's face, I suspected she'd been rehearsing that line all the way to Flora's.

"How do they know that?" asked Izzy, intrigued now. "Was this a really little kid? Or a tween looking to cause a bit of drama?"

"It was a six-year-old girl," said Missy, "on a day trip over from Runcorn. She was very clear about what had happened, but vague on the actual detail."

"And?" I raised an eyebrow. "What *had* happened?"

"God," said Missy, "you're no fun sometimes. Okay so, basic details. According to the kid, she gets off the ride but everything is different, and she can't see her mum or nan. Then a 'nice lady'—her words, not mine —says she'll help her find them. They walk round for a bit and the lady gives her a packet of sweets. Then the lady tells her to stay where she is for a minute and disappears. The girl turns around to look for her, realises she's standing behind her mum. Taps her on the back, mum turns and screams with relief, frightens the kid half to death."

"How do you know she was in a different time?" I asked Missy, but she looked blank. "She might have just wandered off for a bit. Kids do that all the time."

"Aah now," said Missy, "that's what you'd think, isn't it? And that's what everyone assumed—right up until the point a police officer asks the kid if he can see the sweets the lady gave her. Cos they were obviously worried about what the kid might have been eating, you know? Anyway, after a fair bit of persuasion she finally handed them over, and that's when the confusion started. The sweets she was holding were discontinued about thirty years ago. And that's not all," Missy went on, "she was filthy, as well. But she swore she'd just walked round the docks with this lady. Thing is, she was insisting that the docks looked different. Dirty, she said. And no water in them, just mud."

"The silt was taken out decades back," I said slowly. "When they were regenerating the place."

"Exactly," said Missy, a triumphant tone in her voice. "But according to Jenny, no one believed what the girl was saying. Because why would they?" She shrugged. "It's a little kid, and they have good imaginations. But Jenny knows the story of the time slips. And she remembered the sweets—Spangles, they were called—because her dad used to talk about them when he was feeling nostalgic. So, she decided to cross-reference the existence of Spangles with the time the dock spent silted up and looking particularly grim. Which is how," Missy practically bounced with glee, and the worktop creaked ominously, "she worked out that the girl hadn't disappeared at all—she'd just been walking around in the nineteen-seventies." The Royal Albert Dock—then just the Albert Dock, the regal honorific only being added in 2018—was the very heartbeat of nineteenth-century industrial Liverpool. It was secure and all but fireproof, two things that were vanishingly rare in the days before formal health and safety legislation, and thus an important staging post for the most valuable of the endless cargo that came into Britain via the Mersey. But the development of steam ships and the associated need for open quaysides meant that Albert Dock and its surroundings fell slowly out of favour, until by the early twentieth century the docks were almost entirely disused and their buildings used mainly for storage. A brief rebirth as the base of the British Atlantic Fleet during the Second World War only added to its appeal as a target for German bombers, and the damage caused was greater than anyone could afford to fix during the period of post-war austerity. By the seventies, the docks were silted up and their buildings nothing more than the skeletal remains of a once glorious past. It was only when Margaret

Thatcher's government finally realised the locals weren't going to go down without a politically damaging fight that money was found for regeneration. And now here we were in the twenty-first century with docks filled with art galleries and world-class museums and an authentically retro Victorian carousel that was, apparently, running a side gig as Liverpool's answer to the TARDIS. "Oh," said Missy, "I almost forgot to tell you the other thing that's been happening."

"Isn't there enough going on already," I said, "without adding any more drama to it?"

"Not my fault the city's kicking off, is it?" Missy squinted at me. "Winding cities up to the point they start playing silly beggars is more your domain, I reckon."

"Don't you—" I started, but Izzy cut me off.

"Children!" she said sharply. "Behave yourselves, or I will send you both to bed without any supper." Missy and I both turned to look at her. "I don't give a shit," Izzy went on, "who's responsible for the ridiculousness that keeps happening around here. What I *do* care about," she slapped a tea towel hard down onto the table for emphasis, "is that it bloody well stops. And while we're here, what about the cats in Toxteth?"

"What cats?" I'd been spending a lot of time feeling very confused about the world around me over the last few months. It clearly wasn't going to be getting simpler any time soon.

"That," said Missy, "is what I'd forgotten to tell you about."

"Would someone like to tell *me* about the cats?" I asked. "Or do I have to bring out the voice?" The voice—or *The Voice*, as Izzy likes to call it, usually complete with a terrible attempt at a doom-laden tone—is what I use when I really need people to do as I say. I'd finally learned how to control it better, but it still had a tendency to pop out when I wasn't expecting it. Sometimes I make small children cry and dogs start barking in terror, but that's a small price to pay if it ensures people actually bloody well listen to me occasionally.

"It doesn't work if you warn us in advance," shrugged Izzy. "But you can try, if you like."

"No thank you," said Missy. "It just makes me want to disagree with you even more, just for the hell of it."

"Fucksake," I said, "will one of you just tell me about the bloody cats?"

"There's been sightings in Toxteth," said Missy.

"As far up as Edge Hill now," added Izzy. "Overheard a customer talking about it earlier. She'd been walking her dog on the Crown Street park, and he'd gone nosing in the bushes along the edge. She called him back but he didn't reappear—she was just beginning to panic she'd lost him when he came flying back out of the bushes faster than she'd ever seen him run before. Too overweight to bother running normally, she told her friend. Anyway, he nearly ran straight past her, but she managed to grab his collar, said he was shaking with fear. So she picked him up, and walked towards the hedge, with the dog proper quaking in her arms, by the sound of it. Apparently, he was whimpering and scrabbling to get away, she had to hold on tight."

"This was quite a long story you managed to accidentally overhear," I said.

"Cleaning the other tables, wasn't I?" said Izzy blithely. "You want the story or not?" I pulled an apologetic face. "So yeah," she went on, "this woman's staring at the bushes and wondering what on earth could be in there that's so scary. Figured it must've been a fox or whatever. But just as she was turning away—" Iz leaned forward for emphasis.

"—a bloody great big cat walked out," finished Missy.

Izzy looked outraged. "I was *telling* a *story*," she growled. "I'd just got to the good bit!"

"Yeah," said Missy, "the bit where a bloody great big cat walked out of the hedge. Like I said. Anyway," she turned to me, "that's not the only sighting. They're mostly Toxteth way, but as well as the one Izzy has just so eloquently informed us about," Iz flipped her middle finger at Missy, who ignored her completely, "there's at least two down in Dingle."

"If there's at least one in Edge Hill," I said faintly, "two in Dingle, and they're still 'mostly'," I even did air-quotes for emphasis, "in Toxteth, how many are there? And how big?" They both looked blankly at me. "The cats," I went on, "how big are they? Are we talking feral cats with attitude, here? Or are fucking great pumas wandering round Princes Park?" This was just fucking brilliant. As if unexpected time lord bollocks wasn't enough, now we had giant cats on the loose? *Fuck me, Liverpool*, I thought, *you don't do things by halves.*

Never did, said the city. **And never will.** I swear I could hear it grinning.

"Oh," said Missy happily, "they're definitely big. *Big* big cats. The sort you get in Wales." People regularly spot cats of varying exotic species in the Welsh countryside and the government is always keen to stress how unlikely it is. Must just be a particularly large tomcat, maybe the spotter needed their eyes testing, etc. All I'll say is that once you've seen the damage those 'tomcats' can do, you'll never question their existence ever again. Also FYI, the puma that lives in the forest just outside Llangollen is really cute and friendly, *if* you're careful not to startle him and make sure you've got plenty of sausage-meat about your person. He likes a treat as much as the rest of us. "I don't think there's actually that many, though," Missy went on, "so don't worry too much."

"How many," I said, "is not many?"

"Oh," she said airily, "maybe five or six? Nothing we can't cope with. They just need a telling."

"How, exactly," I said slowly, "does one give a puma a telling?"

"I've no idea," said Missy, "I was planning to leave that up to you. Where are you going?" I'd got up from the table quickly, and the chair crashed to the floor behind me. Bending to pick it up, I thumped it back down too hard. We all heard the wood crack.

"I am going for a lie down," I said, my teeth gritted so tightly it was difficult to speak. "And when I get back up, I expect everything and everyone to be doing their best to be LESS FUCKING RIDICU-LOUS." With that I stalked out, leaving all three of them staring after me. *Yeah*, I thought as I slammed out of the door, *the voice still works.*

Nova Scotia

I was floating on my back down a river. The water was warm and and the sun shone down, glittering off the grassy banks. Bobbing on the surface around me were endless leaves, each one carrying a note. *When will people realise I don't know what I'm doing?* said one. *I wonder what's really in those old locked cases down at the bottom of the Mersey*, read another. The one with *I really need to get my love life in order before I turn into the sort of mad old bat who lives alone in the Anfield catacombs* on it had already spun away from me on an eddy of water and disappeared satisfyingly into the distance. I could feel my hair billowing like a cloud around my head, twisting into watery ropes and glowing like an unearthly Ophelia. Hadn't Elizabeth of London been the model for Millais' *Ophelia*? Thoughts of reality broke the spell, and suddenly I was back lying on my bed in the darkness of my flat. I stared up at the cracked plasterwork on the ceiling and cursed my flittering mind. I'd got better at meditating and these days I could lie for hours in a literal world of my own, oblivious to whatever madness happened to be going on outside. It was just unfortunate that the real world always broke back through eventually. And there clearly *was* something going on outside in the real world, because I could hear Rachel having a muffled argument with someone in the car park. Now, I know some people think vampires don't make good tenants, but I'd had Rachel living below me for months now and she was no trouble at all. Okay, so she did occasionally leave drained rat corpses on our shared fire escape, but only if she and Grimm had had one too many the night before and forgotten to clear up after themselves. Plus she always apologised—and it did at least mean Flora's never had a rodent problem. Rachel and I both used the fire escape as our main staircase because the internal one went down through the cafe, and using it out of hours meant making sure the shutters were locked up each time. And those shutters creak horribly, so we leave them alone as much as possible.

I'd been collecting plants again, and the top platform of the metal fire escape stairs that sat outside my kitchen door was a veritable oasis of greenery in the middle of the city. I stepped out carefully past the big fern that was doing its best to block the exit and glanced up to where tonight's vampiric security guard perched on the roof. Aiden was still insisting on sending one over every night, despite my assertions that I could look after myself in an emergency. I kept saying it and he kept smiling and nodding and then he'd send one anyway. I chose not to argue because it clearly made him feel better about my insistence on staying put in my flat rather than moving down to the relative safety of the Albert Dock, as both he and Eadric would have preferred. Putting a finger to my mouth to shush the guard—a small female who did regular shifts and was actually good company on boring nights—I peered down into the gloom of the carpark. Rachel had her back to me and appeared to be arguing with Grimm. He was sitting in the farthest corner of the car park and gazing up at her with polite disinterest. My hearing's really good these days, but even so it was a struggle to make out what she was saying. Something about something or someone who shouldn't be in town, and she didn't care what Grimm thought, he needed to move them on right now. I could see Billy, our resident rough sleeper, in his usual spot on the street out front. He was curled up inside his blanket burrito and either not hearing or ignoring whatever was going on. There was movement in my peripheral vision and I turned back to see something behind Grimm in the shadows. It was far bigger than him, but appeared to be hunching down to make itself look small. For a second, I panicked that the werewolves had started coming into town. Then I realised there was no way my cat would be defending a dog, no matter how sentient it might be. "Anyone want to tell me what you're up to down there?" I said loudly. Rachel jumped and spun round, a guilty look on her face. I doubted she'd actually done anything wrong— Rachel just looks guilty by default. It's as though she worries everything that's wrong with the world is somehow down to her and she's just waiting to be found out. Grimm, on the other hand, gazed up at me with an implacable expression that suggested *everything* could be his fault and he still wouldn't waste energy on feeling guilty about it. The shadow behind him just shuffled further backwards into the darkness until it was up against the high brick wall at the very back of the car park. I glanced over to where my beloved Beetle was parked, and saw the trail of muddy footprints right across Basil's roof and down over the bonnet. The trail led towards where the cat and vampire stood half hidden in the corner of the car park. "Who the fuck did that?" I demanded, already bouncing my way crossly down the fire escape. When I got to the first floor I took a shortcut, jumping over the railing and landing on my feet next to the car. Before I could say anything else, there was a scuffle in the corner and I turned to see the shadow leap up over the wall and disappear into the night. I looked at Rachel and Grimm, then back at the prints all over what *had* been my lovely shiny car. I didn't used to be so precious about Basil, but I very nearly lost him a few months back. Eadric's then-wife had gone on a rampage, during which a void had opened up under the street and swallowed my beloved car. As with most things in my life, it's a long story. Anyway, Eadric had put a lot of guilt money into the repair job, so Basil is a thing of four-wheeled beauty these days and I give him the valeting treatment he deserves. Which had just been spoiled by muddy paw prints. Very big muddy paw prints. "Was that," I gestured to where the mystery visitor had casually hopped over the extremely high wall, "a *cat*?" Grimm's gaze didn't flicker, but Rachel was shuffling uncomfortably and looked very much as though she'd rather be anywhere else than caught in the full beam of my quizzical glare. "A *giant* cat?"

Rachel broke first. "Sorry-sorry-Lil," she mumbled. Her speech is much better these days, but she still has a tendency to run her words together. Most vampires do it, probably to avoid people noticing their teeth. Which do not include fangs, in case you were wondering. I think it's more that vampire teeth are yellow and pretty horrible-looking, and they get self-conscious. Anyway, it makes them really difficult to understand at times. "Not-expected-not-welcome."

"Too right it's not bloody welcome," I said. "What the fuck was it doing climbing on my car?" It was lucky whatever it was had been light on its paws, because I liked the new, un-dented Basil and would be having strong words with anyone who changed that status.

"Scared-it," said Rachel. I walked towards her and Grimm and she took an involuntary step backwards. "Jumped-up-told-it-I-told-it."

"I'm not cross with you, for heaven's sake," I said. "Stop panicking. You, on the other hand," I glared down at Grimm, "have some explaining to do." The cat tilted his head slightly, then lifted a paw up in front of his face. After inspecting it for a long minute, he began to wash himself methodically. "So, *was* it a cat?" I asked him. "One of the giant fucking cats people are talking about?"

"Big-cat," said Rachel. "Big-cats-coming-back."

"But are they actual cats?" I asked her. "Normal cats, just big? Like the Welsh pumas?"

"Human-cats," said Rachel. "Human-changing-cats."

I looked from the vampire down to the cat, then up at the wall our mystery visitor had scaled with ease. Then I looked back at Rachel. "Are you telling me," I said slowly, "we've got an infestation of were-cats? No," I put up a hand to stop Rachel speaking, "actually don't tell me. I really don't want to know. I'm going back to bed." I looked at the vampire and the cat in my car park and sighed. "If you're going to have visitors," I said to them, "at least make sure they wipe their feet."

"I need to nip out for half an hour," said Izzy, sticking her head through the door into the back kitchen. "Think you could cover for me?"

"Course," I said, putting down my pen. "This is going to take forever, anyway. Give me a minute to tidy away and I'll be through." Eadric had asked me to go through the records for Silverton Properties and make a list of everything they owned. When I'd pointed out they clearly owned too fucking much if they couldn't remember it all, he'd pointed out that he'd been around a very long time and it was easy to let these things slip. So far I'd found twenty-four houses, all similar in that they were generally old and big. Twenty-two were in Liverpool city centre, one was Chester and the last turned out to be a big old manor house over the river in Oxton. The properties in town included a massive place up on Canning Street that was next door to one I knew damn fine had recently sold for just over a million. Like many people, I have a property-porn addiction. Eadric had discovered this one day after spotting me gazing covetously at the online details for a three-storey Georgian place on Mount Street, opposite the old Liverpool Institute. I suspect it's what made him assume I'd take up his offer of an Albert Dock apartment. But what Eadric hadn't considered was that my habit of window-shopping for houses was along the same lines as people looking at incredibly valuable paintings or jewellery that come up for auction—they appreciate the aesthetics, but have zero intention of forking out the necessary cash to actually make the dream a reality. Anyway, that's how I knew the current market value of most of the buildings scattered within the paperwork. And that current market value was a *lot*. As well as the houses, there were sixteen commercial properties, each with residential space above. I was surprised to find the deeds for Mapp's Renshaw Street shop in the pile. For some reason, I'd always assumed he owned it himself. But then he was open about having lived in Dingle for decades, so maybe he owned that house and leased the shop in town. Not that it was any of my business what they all got up to in private. *But*, said a little voice in the back of my head, *it is your business now. You're technically in charge of them. All of them.* Ugh. I mostly tried not to think about the fact that I was, indeed, the supposed head of all undead realms. Well, those north of Hereford, anyway.

One day, said the city, **you will rule it all.**

I mostly try not to think about it, I replied silently.

Uh huh, it said. **How's the not thinking working out for you so far?**

Badly, I admitted. *I'm terrified at the thought of the responsibility, given that some days I struggle to even get dressed properly.* I was currently wearing a pair of very odd socks, as if to prove my point. I didn't have to look under the table to know one foot was in a pink trainer sock whilst the other was wearing a white ankle sock with a red stripe around the top. I'd got dressed in a hurry after realising I'd been sitting at the laptop all night and not taking any notice of the time. Not that anyone's forcing me to work set hours these days, but I like to be in Flora's before Izzy arrives at least a couple of times a week. If I didn't, she'd assume I wasn't interested in the cafe anymore and nothing could be further from the truth. I genuinely loved sitting out back at the battered old table watching the comings and goings of the customers. If Todd was working, he'd come to see me for a quick catch-up before putting on his apron and starting the strenuous task of arranging pastries behind the glass of the front counter. And I really liked it when Iz asked me to help out, like today. I dumped the paperwork back into the plastic bag I was currently using as a very unglamorous briefcase, and hung it on a peg next to the sink before going through into the cafe proper.

"What are you up to?" I asked, as Izzy wiped down the serving counter and pulled her apron off over her head.

"Don't get excited," she said, "it's nothing very interesting. Me and Damon went to an exhibition down at Mann Island a while back and he really liked a print that was on display. I said I'd buy it him for Christmas, but they couldn't take it down off the wall til the exhibition was over so I didn't bother. What he doesn't know is that I secretly bought it anyway, and they just texted to say I can go pick it up."

"Awww," I said, "that's so sweet!"

Izzy glared at me. "Don't be assuming I'm going soft in my old age," she said. "I just thought he'd appreciate a little surprise."

"He'll be thrilled," I said. "And quite right, too. It's a lovely thing to do." Izzy made a muffled harrumphing noise, but she pinked up slightly with pleasure just the same.

"Anyway," she said, "that's all I need to do. Won't be long."

"Perfect timing!" announced Gaultier Mapp, coming through the door behind Izzy. "I need to talk to you two about this year's knitting club schedule." Izzy rolled her eyes, but Mapp ignores any and all negativity. He says it messes with his chi. "We are going to be *busy*, ladies!" He leaned onto the counter and looked at each of us in turn, a gleefully conspiratorial expression on his face. "What do you think," he said, "about doing a display at Southport Flower Show?" We both stared blankly at him. "Oh, come *on*," he said, "it'd be fun! We just need to find out what this year's theme is, then everyone makes a little contribution. And we'll have months to do it in, so no panicking. Not like last time." Mapp had decided at the last minute that he and his crafty cohort would make a gigantic knitted flower arrangement for the craft section of Knowsley Flower Show, and had been openly peeved when they were beaten to first place by a display of self-portraits made by the nursery class from a local junior school. "We'd have won if we'd had longer to prepare."

"You were competing against five-year-olds," said Izzy. "Five-year-olds making pictures out of potato prints."

"All the more reason to beat them next time," shrugged Mapp. "I have a reputation to uphold."

"Your reputation is absolutely scandalous," I said, "and not to be exhibited anywhere near small, impressionable children."

"Ooh, Lilith O'Reilly," shrieked Mapp happily, "I cannot *begin* to imagine what you might possibly mean!" He grinned and leaned in closer. "Their teacher liked me, though."

"Too much," I scolded him. "And that is why you are not allowed to compete against schoolchildren. Their responsible adults are way too vulnerable."

"Much as I am *fascinated* by all of this," said Izzy, "I need to go pick up this parcel. Back in twenty." With that, she headed out onto Harrington Street and banged the door closed behind her.

"Pour us an espresso, girl," said Mapp, settling happily into one of the two high stools we keep tucked up against the counter. "I'm parched." The only people allowed to call me 'girl' are Mapp and Alan, because they're both locals from way back and that makes it an affectionate term. If anyone else had tried it, they'd have got a supernatural kick in the soft bits.

Which reminded me. "Heard from Liam at all?" I tried my best to sound casual, but Mapp wasn't fooled.

"Nope," he said. "Sorry, like. I ask around and my spies are usually pretty good, but no one seems to know what he's up to. Of course," he went on, "he might just be paying people to keep their mouths shut. Good at financial incentives, is our William."

"Huh," I said, "that figures. He's such a fucking creep."

34

"Uh huh," said Mapp. "Such a terrible creep, yet you keep asking if I've heard from him." I stayed silent, but felt my face reddening. "What makes you think I'd hear from him over anyone else?" he went on. "He's more likely to get in touch with you, I reckon."

I hadn't heard a word from Liam since he'd taken a bullet for Sean up in the Radio City tower last autumn. He'd left the city by the time I'd got back to the Liver Building, and I suspected Eadric had made sure that happened. "Well, I haven't heard from him," I said. "And I'm only asking because it's better for all of us if someone keeps tabs on the little scrote." I began loading the dishwasher.

"And you'd be best suited to keeping those tabs, you're thinking," said Mapp. "Mind you don't break those cups, they're not designed to cope with your temper." I slowed down my attempt at crockery Tetris, discreetly dropping a cracked mug into the waste bin before Mapp noticed. "Nah, love," he leaned back on his stool and swung round to smile beatifically around the cafe. The small group of art students at the window table smiled back, but looked faintly nervous. "I've no idea where your man is."

"Liam is not my man," I said firmly, straightening up. "And nor is anyone else, before you start."

"I'm not starting anything," shrugged Mapp. "You brought it up. Although," he said conspiratorially, leaning towards me for emphasis, "maybe you should be starting something with that Sean. He's a decent bloke, everyone says so. And I reckon he can cope with your, uh, differences." He tilted his head as though inspecting me. "You're a good catch, Lilith," he said. "Shame to waste the opportunities, I'm thinking."

"Says the man who's never wasted an opportunity in his life."

"Got to find your jollies wherever you can when you've been around as long as I have." Mapp grinned at me. "You'll learn soon enough."

"Got a minute, Lil?" said Izzy, walking in through the front door less than fifteen minutes after she'd left. She headed past us without waiting for a reply. Mapp and I both watched as she stalked into the back room and dumped her coat and bag onto the table with an audible thump.

"What's going on there, then?" said Mapp in a low voice.

"How am I supposed to know?" I looked round the cafe. Three tables were currently occupied. One by the students, who appeared to be competing as to who could make a flat white last longest; another by Roger, a regular who never spoke other than to confirm his order. His name almost certainly wasn't Roger—we'd just taken to calling him that because it was what he said every time anyone said 'the usual?' to him. "Stay here," I said to Mapp, "and keep an eye on things. If anyone comes to the counter, just shout me. And do not seduce my customers." Mapp flapped a hand at his chest in mock horror.

"As if I'd do a thing like that," he cackled.

"Pretty sure you said that just before the incident with the traffic warden," I said. "You're on a warning."

"But no one gets a parking ticket down this street anymore," said Mapp. "So you should probably be thanking me for my service to the community." I gave him one last sharp glare before heading after Izzy.

"Have you been down to Pier Head recently?" she asked as I walked in. She was pacing the tiny kitchen and looked as flustered as I'd ever seen her.

"No," I said, "why? I haven't done anything I shouldn't. I don't think so, anyway."

"I didn't mean you'd done anything wrong," said Izzy, picking a mug up from the table and gazing at it. "It's the bloody city that's going wrong, not you." She stared blankly at the cup in her hand and put it down again, as though unsure where it had come from.

"What happened? Did you pick up Damon's present?"

"Oh shit," said Izzy, "I was so confused that I forgot all about it and just came back here! I'll have to go back down later."

"Can you at least tell me what's happened?"

"Okay," she said, "but you have to promise you won't think I'm losing my mind."

"As if," I laughed. "You put up with enough weirdness from me, it's about time you balanced it out a bit."

"I don't like this, Lil," she said, looking at me with frightened eyes. "It's going way beyond normal levels of weird now. This is fully-batshit-level weird."

"I can't help if I don't know what's happened," I said. I was beginning to get nervous myself now. "But I promise I won't tell you that you're losing your mind. Or laugh."

"Okay," said Izzy, finally sitting down. "So I went down to Mann Island like normal, right? Walked down James Street and crossed the main road, nothing to worry about. Except that when I walked across to the gallery, it wasn't there." The art gallery at Mann Island is inside one of two enormous, black glass buildings that people either love or hate with an absolute passion. Relatively new additions to the waterfront, they're impossible to miss and everyone seems to have an opinion about them.

"Eh?" I couldn't think of anything else to say.

"Exactly," said Izzy. "Impossible, right? But honestly Lil," she began twisting a stray napkin into a thick paper rope, "it just wasn't there. Neither of them. Nor the museum. The port building was on my right as normal, but I could see straight down to the river in front of me." The tissue ripped, and she dropped it onto the table. "But there were houses. I was right up by them before I even noticed. How the hell can *that* happen? It looked like a narrow street with really shonky old houses along it. Like, *really* old. Proper slums. Half falling down and hard to tell where one ended and the next began. And there were people walking around."

"There's always people around there," I said, worried now. The time slip stories had always been, well, *small*, somehow—silly little tales that probably weren't true. Not my best mate telling me about entire massive buildings disappearing in front of her eyes.

"Not these people!" Izzy was wide-eyed. "These were like, I dunno, from another time or something." A cold feeling began making itself at home in the pit of my stomach. "They all looked, well, *poor* is the only way of describing it. Not like modern poor, though. These were proper raggedy poor people. Like you see in the background of period dramas."

"That might be it," I said hopefully. "Perhaps they're filming something down there." Liverpool's quite the go-to place for filming these days. Eadric once confessed to doing quite well out of hiring out his section of the Liver Building to film crews. I could only assume he went up and had strong words with the birds beforehand, in case Bella got bored and decided to take a chunk out of a fictional superhero, just for funsies.

"Then it disappeared again," said Izzy, blowing my theory right out of the water. Oh well. No one can say I don't at least try. "And I was so freaked out that I just turned round and came straight back here."

"Did you look behind you at all?" I asked. "Maybe it was a trick of the light or something."

"For fuck's *sake*, Lil," Izzy's voice had gone up an octave, and she was clearly struggling not to shout. "Everything was normal and then suddenly I was in the, I don't know, seventeen-fucking-hundreds or something! Then I scarpered back over the road and it all looked normal again. That's some trick of the bloody light, mate."

I know Izzy's really stressed when she calls me mate. I gazed at her for a long minute, then sighed. "Why don't you stay here," I said, "and I'll go pick up the package for you. If there's something going on down there, I'd better find out what it is."

"Doesn't that voice in your head have anything to say about it?" she asked. "It's mouthy enough the rest of the time."

Charmed, we're sure, said the city. ***Anyway, this is nothing to do with us.***

Oh well, that's okay then, I replied silently. The city said nothing, but I was pretty sure it was giving me a silent shrug. The inner voice that 'talks' to me made it clear from the start that it's made up of the people who've made Liverpool their home over the centuries, rather than the city itself. Having felt the power of the city's spirit on several terrifying occasions, I was just grateful I only had its smaller sibling inside my head.

Cheers, it said sarcastically. ***We'll remember that next time you need our help.***

What you should *be remembering*, I replied, *is that I'm the only one who can hear you. We're stuck with each other. And I'm no happier about it than you are, believe me.* There was a barely discernible harrumphing noise in the very back of my brain, then it fell quiet.

"It doesn't know anything about it," I said to Izzy, who's learned to wait for me and my mental passengers to get our thoughts in order. "I think this might be the city itself kicking off. I'd better go see what it wants."

"Lilith," called Mapp in a singsong voice, "you have a visitor!"

"Well hello, ladies," came a second voice. "Any chance of a brew round here?"

Izzy moved to get up, but I waved her back. "I'll go sort him out," I said.

"I just bet you will," said Izzy with a weak smile.

"That's my girl." I went out to the counter and started the coffee machine running. Sean has the same every time he comes into Flora's, which is pretty much every day of the week. Plain black Americano. He used to have it with a single sweetener, but weaned himself off as a new year's resolution. "Hey you," I said, as I put his drink on the counter. "How's tricks?"

"Tricks would be better if you'd let me take you out sometime." He was grinning and his hair had flopped over one eye. Sean Hannerty was seriously one of the cutest men I'd ever met. He was also wealthy, thanks to his thrillers spending years on the bestseller lists, as well as genuinely sweet and kind. Pretty much the perfect man. Right there in front of me, and desperate for me to agree to date him. Sometimes dreams really do come true. Unfortunately for both of us, there was the whole 'fragile human versus potentially lethal immortal' thing going on. I certainly wasn't short of fantasy material in the dark and boring early hours when everyone else was asleep, put it that way.

"Yeah, yeah," I said, "whatever." This was a regular conversation between us. Sean just grinned. "Anyway, I'm nipping out for a minute. Izzy's out back if you need her."

"She's here," said Izzy, appearing beside me. "Back to the real world. You go sort the spooks out, I'll be fine."

Sean's face lit up. "What's going on in the Scouse netherworld this week, then?" he asked. I silently cursed Izzy and her filterless mouth. "Anything good for my notebook?" He waggled his pen at me in what I suspected he thought might be a suggestive manner.

"Nothing for you to worry your pretty little head about," I said. "I won't be long." Unfortunately for me, Sean was a step ahead. He reached into his satchel and pulled out a shiny steel travel mug. With an air of triumph, he opened up the mug and tipped his fresh coffee into it.

"I'll come with you," he said. "It'll be nice to get you to myself for once."

"You're just looking for story material," I pointed out. "Which is actually quite shallow of you."

"Nah, it's your delightful company I'm after," said Sean. "The royalties are just an added bonus."

I sighed. There was no point arguing with Sean when he was like this, it always felt like kicking a puppy. "You are *not* to walk into anything weird," I said firmly. "Understand?"

"Aye aye, cap'n," he saluted. "See you in a bit, Iz. Mapp," he nodded to where Gaultier Mapp was grinning at us both like a maniac. I gave Mapp a warning look, which he obviously chose to ignore.

"Good luck," said Izzy. "I hope you don't need it."

ADULTHOOD IS A TRAP

"Spill the beans, then," said Sean, as we headed down towards the river. I was walking at the fastest pace I can get away with without people noticing, but Sean was annoyingly adept at keeping up. He didn't seem to even notice the speed, let alone be struggling with it. I decided to be honest, because he always finds out the truth anyway. I suspect Mapp's got a bit of a soft spot for him and gossips more than he should.

"The time slips are back," I said as we crossed the Strand. "Everyone assumed they were silly stories made up for the papers years ago, but they're here and they're real."

"Is that what the hoo-hah up at Everton was about?" The Mann Island monoliths stood in front of us, as real and solid as any building made almost entirely of glass could ever hope to be. I eyed them suspiciously as we got closer. Just because something looks real, it doesn't follow it actually is.

"Yeah." We reached the art gallery and I half expected it to disappear at my touch, but the door felt reassuringly solid as I pushed it open. "But Izzy had a weird experience just now, so I thought I'd better come look. Everything seems normal enough, though."

"That's a shame," said Sean. "It would be cool to be a time traveller, don't you think? Mate of mine had a sonic screwdriver back when we were at school. He swore it was real, but you could see he'd made it out of bits of plastic and gaffer tape. I'm a bit of a geek on the quiet," he said in response to my raised eyebrow. "Shame I wasn't born a bit later, really. They didn't start making commercial toys for it til the nineties, and I was a full-grown adult by the time the first official sonic screwdriver came out."

"You could buy them now, you know," I said, as we headed into the gallery. "There's no rules about what you spend your own money on."

"You'll have to come over to my place some time," said Sean. "Then you'll see why I can't start collecting any more memorabilia."

"Get a cleaner to do the dusting for you?" I offered.

Sean laughed. "It would take a long time," he said. "They'd have to get past all the Munsters miniatures first."

We picked up Izzy's parcel without any sign of a ghost street or its inhabitants, then took the scenic route back to Flora's. I figured I'd better check out the rest of the riverfront while I was at it, just in case Izzy's time slip had moved somewhere else. It was cold and drizzly, and there was hardly anyone around as we walked behind the Museum of Liverpool to the little lock-bridge, then over to Albert Dock. The glass doors of the Tate were steaming up with condensation, and I could just about make out a large school party inside. "We should go back there some time," said Sean. "That was a good day."

"Yeah," I said, "until it all went horribly wrong."

"Things go wrong all the time," he said with a shrug. "If you keep worrying about something awful happening then it's more likely to actually happen, I reckon."

"Try living in a world where all the terrible things *do* happen," I said, "often on a daily basis. That tends to knock the optimism out of you after a while."

"Get on with you," said Sean, "you just need to make space for more fun in your life, is all. And," he stopped in his tracks, "here's a prime opportunity."

"What," I said, "to get pissed?" We were outside the Pump House pub, which looked practically deserted. "Not going to work for me, I'm afraid."

"No," said Sean, "I meant over there." He pointed to the Victorian carousel that sits on the corner of Salthouse Quay. "Let's go pretend to be kids, just for five minutes. It'll be fun."

"I really ought to get back to Izzy," I said. Sean clearly didn't know about the carousel's adventures through time and I wasn't about to give him any more book ideas. "She's had a proper fright. And I can't help feeling it might be my fault."

"Not everything that happens is because of something you've done," said Sean. "The world doesn't revolve around you entirely, you know."

I knew he meant it as a joke, but it stung all the same. "I wasn't implying it did," I said. "But I can't help feeling responsible for you all."

"If we were that worried," said Sean reasonably, "we wouldn't still be hanging out with you. Would we?" I gazed at him silently, feeling my chin jutting out slightly like a grumpy child who's finding the world a bit much. "Come on Lil," he went on, "just for me? I've always fancied a go on it, but felt daft doing it on my own with kids and families all over the place. There's no one on it now, it'd just be us two. And it would be fun." I looked over to where the carousel horses were slowly looping round in an endless circle, repetitive music playing out of tinny speakers. A bored-looking man in his twenties was standing on the ride, gazing blankly out at nothing as it spun him slowly round and round.

"Go on, then," I said finally. At least this way I could be sure the carousel was behaving itself again. "If it'll make you happy. But after that, I'm heading straight back to Flora's."

"Absolutely," said Sean, grinning from ear to ear and already setting off towards the carousel. "One spin and we're done." I sighed and followed him. Hopefully no one I knew would walk past whilst we were on the bloody thing. By the time I climbed up onto the ride, Sean had already paid for both of us. "Hop on," he said, "let's see where Dobbin and friends are going to take us today." Smiling despite myself, I climbed onto the horse next to Sean, Izzy's painting still wedged under my arm. "Here," said Sean, "give me that. Saves you hanging onto it." He took the painting from me and tucked it into the satchel he always had slung over his shoulder. He'd taken the inside horse, so the only thing between me and the view of Mann Island was a tree that had moulted most of its leaves. I eyed the glass buildings suspiciously as the ride clunked into life, just daring them to disappear each time they came back into view. As we rolled round past Salthouse Dock and the back of the giant brick warehouses yet again, I looked across at Sean. He was beaming with happiness, one hand holding the horse's pole and the other down by his side. He looked like a metrosexual cowboy, surveying the horizon.

"Enjoying yourself?" I was smiling, despite myself.

"Yup," he said happily. "I'll tell you a secret, Lil." He winked. "Never grow up, is my advice. Adulthood is a trap."

Before I could reply, the ride gave a jolt and slowed down. We did one last bumpy circuit, and I was relieved to see the buildings were all still present and correct. The ride finally ground to halt and we slid off the horses, Sean waiting for me to get off the ride first. "There you go," I said to him, "you were right. It *was* fun."

He grinned at me. "Told you," he said. "Come on then, let's get back to Flora's." I stepped down off the ride—and fell face-first into cold and filthy water.

To Live And Die In L8

I t was bloody lucky I didn't need to breathe, or I'd have been a goner. I floundered in a panic and finally bobbed to the surface, spitting frantically. Treading water, I looked around me and realised I was in the river. This wasn't the Mersey, though. There were buildings along the water's edge, but they were low down and nothing like Liverpool's famously towering skyline. Small boats bobbed around between me and the shoreline. They were old fishing boats, the type you usually only see as models in the maritime museum. The current was already pulling me away from the shore and I twisted round in the water to see where I was headed. The river widened in front of me, opening out into what looked horribly like the sea. The weather was gloomy and grey, and I could just about see a faint light in the distance on my left, where the opposite bank of the river gave out into the water. Even supernatural eyesight struggles in fog—no one's seen fit to give immortals x-ray vision yet, which I personally think is rude—but I squinted enough to make out the tall post that held the lantern I'd spotted. My stomach clenched in horror as I realised what I was looking at. It was the Old Rock Perch.

. . .

A 'perch' was a tall pole that carried a lantern at the top and was supported by a wooden tripod at the base. They were installed at danger points along the coastline as a precursor to modern-day lighthouses. I knew all this from reading information boards on day trips over the water. The Old Rock Perch had been erected in the late seventeenth-century and replaced by the more efficient Perch Rock Lighthouse in eighteen-thirty. Which meant I was definitely still in Liverpool, but at least two centuries into the past. I twisted back round to gaze in horror at the undeveloped waterfront that was rapidly disappearing into the distance. Just as my brain started registering that I should maybe start swimming back to shore, something hit me hard in the stomach. It was big, and travelling fast. Before I even had time to shriek, something that felt suspiciously like a human arm hooked itself under my chin and began dragging me back upriver. I tried not to panic—whoever or what-ever it was that had hold of me, they were at least heading in the right direction. I concentrated on staying as flat as possible on the water's murky surface and definitely did not open my mouth. Although if I'd travelled as far back as I suspected, it was at least to a time before the Industrial Revolution turned the Mersey into a giant disposal system for the cotton and chemical industries. I risked tilting my head slightly to the right, and recognised the shape of Liverpool Castle rising from where the Queen Victoria monument would sit centuries later. By now I had a fair idea what was dragging me along, and just hoped it was friendly. Asrais had become nothing more than a distant myth by the time I'd met one in the present day, so I couldn't be certain the OG version would be as tame as those I knew. Whatever it was, it was now aiming diagonally across the current towards the shore, and I could feel occasional sandbanks bumping up against my feet. We were still a good way out from the riverbank when we finally ground to a halt and the creature below me spun around in the shallows and jumped to her feet. I stared up at her in astonishment. "Daisy?" My very own Mersey mermaid grinned down at me, her wide mouth not quite hiding the rows of tiny sharp teeth. I pushed myself up to sit on the wet sand and turned to look towards where the city should be. We'd travelled a fair distance upriver and the buildings around the mouth of the old pool itself had disappeared round the bend in the river. The bank to my right climbed up towards what looked like farmland, and across on the other side of the water I could see the low-level buildings of what I thought might be Tranmere. I looked up at Daisy. She was jiggling her elongated limbs on the spot and looking very pleased with herself. "This is why you didn't try to eat me when we first met, isn't it?" When one of Joe Williamson's ratty little vampires 'rescued' Daisy almost a year earlier, after finding her wandering around on dry land, she'd been all but feral and potentially very dangerous. But she'd taken to me from the second we met and no one had ever been able to figure out why. I'd assumed it was down to my delightful personality and consummate grace, but there was clearly more to it than that. "Had you already met me?" I asked her. "Centuries earlier?" Daisy just shrugged. "Fuck me," I said. "This is more confusing than *Donnie Darko*."

So anyway, it turns out that supernatural powers don't make it any easier to get out of muddy quicksand. Even Daisy struggled with the river silt as we floundered across to the shoreline. I tried not to think about what might happen to someone who sank beneath the surface but didn't need to breathe and couldn't actually die. Presumably I'd just have to hang out down there until the industry of the nineteenth century kicked in and cleared the waterways a bit. It would be quite amusing to rise from the deep and clamber up onto an unsuspecting ship. My clothes were filthy and soaked, but the 'I STILL BLAME THATCHER' logo was clearly visible across the front of my t-shirt. Maybe they'd just assume I had a beef with the local roofers. When we finally scrambled up onto the bank, Daisy jumped up and down and hugged me briefly, before turning and running back to the river. I watched her skip lightly across the wet sand and wondered whether I'd have found it easier had I simply run at full speed across the surface. And if so, was there anything to stop me 'walking' on water? Maybe I could convince people I was the Second Coming. Go skipping across the bay and become the Crosby Christ. It definitely had a ring to it. On the other hand, life was complicated enough without making myself even more notorious. I made my way up onto higher land, and looked over to where Liverpool should have been. There was *something* there—a vague and shifting idea of buildings and boats—but it refused to stay in focus. Ahead of me was farmland, with old buildings dotted around. Although, I realised, they were probably new buildings right now. Sighing, I set off to see whether the tiny embryo of a great city contained any handy time portals. I really hoped so, because I didn't fancy spending several centuries hanging out with Daisy and her underwater crew. Not to mention my clothes wouldn't last that long. I'm not one to care much about looks, but I draw a line at wearing literal sackcloths. The implication that Daisy already knew me when we first met was troubling me, and it wasn't hard to figure out why. I walked at a careful human pace along the track towards the harbour, scared I might accidentally end up in some horrific dystopian future if I was running too fast to notice a time slip. Could the slips move people forward as well as back? The sixteen-hundreds were going to be difficult enough, but at least I had a rough idea of how the proto-city would be laid out and what the local customs might be. But what if I found myself in the twenty-fourth century? Would Liverpool even still exist? If it did, would it finally have those flying cars we've been promised for decades?

I dragged my thoughts back to Daisy. That I was in a much earlier time than my own was evident. And that the Asrai already knew exactly who I was, was also clear. But how? "Block time, remember?" said a voice next to me. I whipped round to face the man who was suddenly walking with me. He didn't seem entirely solid, and I wasn't sure he was really there. Perhaps my poor frazzled brain was simply making him up. "Time is everywhere and everything. Everything, everywhere, all at once. We're not pushing time forwards," he gestured at the grassy path ahead of us, "we're walking through it. And sometimes we lose our way."

"Who are you?" I started walking again, and the strange man kept pace at my side. I glanced sideways and saw a long, well-rounded face topped with a wig that I suspected had once been both expensive and ornate, but was now dirty and fraying around the edges. He was about my height, and wore a long frock coat over baggy breeches that had definitely seen better days. His stockings were droopy, and, like the rest of his outfit, his shoes had clearly once been expensive, but had now been worn into a look of ingrained shabbiness. Although he was obviously from a very different era to mine, he didn't seem to be finding anything odd about walking through the ghost of a city that hadn't even been built yet.

"I ask myself that quite often," said the man. His tone was polite enough, but there was a tone of sad regretfulness to it. "Who am I, what is the reason for my still being here so long after my sad demise, that sort of thing. But this isn't a day for melancholy." He turned to me as we walked, a surprisingly cheeky smile on his face. "This, Lilith O'Reilly, is a day for recognising just how inconsequential we are in the greater scheme of things."

"Oh brilliant," I sighed, "I'm going to get a philosophy lesson to go with the history one."

The man gave a polite chuckle. "My name is Jonathan," he said, "and it is long past due that we met."

"Why?" The path had become more defined now, and buildings were becoming visible in the distance. A church faded into view on our right, its bricks and slates materialising before my eyes like the sketchiest of visual tricks.

"Because there are few who can traverse the worlds in this manner," he said, "and we two are amongst them. I myself was not yet born at this point in time, but now I'm a mere shadow of my long-gone self. And yet still I walk with you."

"Don't you dare tell me we're time travellers," I said, "because I have dealt with enough bullshit this past year to send anyone into an early grave. Not that I'm even being allowed the luxury of actually dying and being left in peace. And," I added sharply, "if you so much as *begin* to utter the word 'quantum', I will not be held responsible for my actions, so help me."

"Understood," said Jonathan amiably. "Perhaps it would be easier if you merely accepted that I—as in, this weak version of myself—exist in the same time as you. That is, what you would call the present day. I am, of course, much older than you, having been tied to this mortal coil for nigh on three centuries. But as I say, I am also of your own time."

"So, we're walking through time together?" I glanced across at Jonathan, and he nodded. "And everything that's ever happened and ever *will* happen is going on around us? All at once?" Another nod. "So how do I stop it?" I said, coming to a halt on the grassy path. Jonathan continued on for a few paces before realising I wasn't with him. Turning, he looked at me quizzically. "I need to stop it," I said again. "Because if I don't, this city is going to run utterly out of control. And I don't think even the combined efforts of Ivo Laithlind and Liam the Lying Conqueror could help me then. Not that they'd join together to help me, anyway. Maybe I'll have to write a list of pros and cons, figure out which one of them would be the best bet in a pinch," I trailed off. Jonathan was still looking at me patiently.

"You perhaps underestimate both your suitors," he said, waving his hand to stop me even as I opened my mouth to indignantly deny suitor status of any of the undead idiots of my acquaintance. "I suspect they would indeed work together if it was for the benefit of all. But that," he went on, "is something for the future. Right now, you need to get this city of yours in hand. Have you tried talking to it?"

"I talk to it all the time," I said, realising as I said it that I hadn't actually heard from the city in my head since I first landed in the water. "It just goes quiet when it's scared, I think."

"That one isn't here yet," said Jonathan kindly. "I meant the *real* city, Lilith. Not its people. The city itself, in all its ragged and ancient glory. Have you spoken to it at all?"

"I, erm," I floundered, "I think I kind of just assumed it wasn't interested in humans." Jonathan tilted his head inquiringly. "That it was above that sort of thing, you know? Like a monarch who knows about their people in theory, but wouldn't want to actually touch one."

"Then you underestimate the city, too," said Jonathan. "I suspect it is even now wondering why you haven't tried talking to it about your problems. It's very protective of its people. I know this from personal experience."

"What sort of personal experience?" Jonathan shifted uncomfortably. "Come on," I said, "you can't just appear in front of me like this and talk like you know me, then refuse to tell me anything about yourself in return. Who are you, Jonathan? Who are you really?" He opened his mouth to speak, but then something made him turn sharply in the direction of where the city should be.

"I have to leave you now," he said.

"Why?" I turned to follow his gaze, but couldn't see anything out of the ordinary. Other than the fact I was walking through seventeenth-century farmland that lay across where I was pretty sure Toxteth ought to be.

"I shouldn't have come," said Jonathan. "But I wished to meet you, and he wouldn't let me."

"Who wouldn't let you?" I asked. "Who's 'he'?"

"The person who controls my life," said Jonathan sadly. "I wish for death, but he will not allow it."

"But you're a ghost," I said helplessly. "You're already dead." Jonathan shook his head.

"I am a mere shadow of my former self," he said, "and I dearly wish to be allowed to rest. I deserve that much, I think. After so many years of working for him. But until he gets what he wants, I cannot be free. Perhaps not even then."

"Who?" I grabbed Jonathan's arm. He was solid enough, but I felt something like a static shock as I touched him. "You have to tell me who's controlling you, Jonathan!"

"You already know," he said quietly. "He tries to control you, also." He stepped backwards, bowing deeply as he went. "I'm sure we'll meet again, Lilith," he said. "And then, perhaps, we can save each other."

"Don't you dare!" I reached out a hand to grab him, but he was already fading away. Finding myself clutching at thin air, I almost lost my balance. "Fucksake." A gull wheeled overhead and screeched in response.

For want of any better plan, I kept walking along the track towards the city—slowly, in case my surroundings decided to change again. The land around me was still mostly rough and grassy, with just an occasional rudimentary fence to break things up. But my surroundings flickered occasionally, as though still undecided as to what form they ought to take. At one point I thought I'd spotted the enormous tower of the Anglican cathedral, but I blinked, and it was gone. There were occasional clouds of smoke, puffing up from invisible industrial chimneys, but as soon as I tried to focus on them, they dissipated and became indistinguishable from the clouds in the sky above. It was sunny now, and the sound of gulls carried on the breeze. The ground suddenly shuddered beneath my feet and I stumbled. Ahead of me, dark shapes flitted across the sky. They appeared to be dropping something onto the city, but the distance was too far even for my undead eyesight to see clearly. It was only when the ground below them began exploding upwards after each drop that I realised what I was watching. This was the Liverpool Blitz of 1941. Or, more accurately, the ghost of it. I could feel the shockwaves under my feet and hear the muffled boom of bombs landing on the helpless city below, but the city itself wasn't there—yet. I broke into a run, heading towards the almost soundless death and destruction. My clothes were nearly dry, but my sneakers still made horrible sucking noises against my feet as I ran. I stopped for long enough to pull them off, flinging them into the undergrowth before setting off again. The grass felt absolutely real underneath my bare feet, but it couldn't be—at least, not in my world. And my world—the twenty-first-century one, complete with flat and cafe and cat and collection of wonderful yet ridiculous friends—was the one I needed to get back to. If I could put myself back in the correct time, maybe I could stop this awful cycle of ingrained memories rising up and overpowering my beloved city.

Buildings were sprouting up around me now. First came the large merchants' houses, set along wide streets dotted with trees. Carriages rolled silently past, drawn by well-kept horses. As I ran, the houses unfolded themselves down towards the old pavements, then rebuilt themselves back up into endless rows of terraced housing, each one narrower and darker than the last. Small ragged children wandered the filthy streets, their bare feet unprotected from the rough surfaces. What smelled horribly like literal shit wafted out from the darkest corners. I could still feel the grass under my own feet and hoped I really was still on farmland, rather than the grimy tracks that were snaking in all directions around me. Just when I thought I was going to be stuck in this hell hole forever, the terraces began dropping away again, brick by brick. Any initial relief was trodden firmly down when I saw the bricks rebuilding themselves directly in front of me. 'Rebuilding' was too literal a word to describe what was happening—in reality, the bricks were merely flying off the disintegrating houses and dropping into a growing wall of rubble that blocked my route back into the city. Even as I closed the gap, the barricade grew higher until it was choking off the light and the world began to turn dark grey around me. *Oh well*, I thought to myself, *here goes nothing*. I built up speed and launched myself at the rubble. The bricks raced me as I scrabbled upwards, determined to keep growing higher than I could climb. Just as I got a hand on top of the makeshift wall, other bricks below me dropped out and I lost my footing. This was all too reminiscent of last year's panicked climb up the Radio City tower —although at least the tower hadn't dropped segments out of its middle in an attempt to shake me off. Gritting my teeth, I pushed hard against the bricks and random boulders and somehow scrambled up the misshapen blockade quicker than it could grow. Wedging a bare foot into a narrow gap, I managed to lever myself up and over the top of the wall.

It was a hard landing, and when I opened my eyes, I realised why. I was on the pavement of Upper Parliament Street, my back against the stone front wall of a house and legs splayed across the pavement. A man wearing dirty tracksuit bottoms and a sweatshirt that hung from his thin frame was staring down at me over the top of a can of Special Brew. "Y'aright, girl?" he asked, his words slurring together. "Come from nowhere, din'tcha?" He waved the can at me, and beer slopped out over my jeans. The man quickly put the can to his mouth, making an unholy slurping noise as he sucked at it. Satisfied he'd saved what he could, he held the can out to me. "Wanna drink?"

"I'm okay," I said, clambering to my feet, "but thanks anyway." I glanced around me and was relieved to see the more familiar version of Liverpool stretching out in front of me. A car drove past—a two-year-old Fiesta, rather than the horse and cart I'd been half-expecting. "Thank fuck for that," I muttered.

"Too right," said man-with-a-can, holding his hand out towards me. I stared at it stupidly for a few seconds before realising he was trying to fist bump me. I politely tapped knuckles.

"What day is it?" I asked him. I had no idea how the time thing worked—for all I knew, I could have been gone five minutes or five years.

"Don't ask me, love," the man said, already turning away. "I gave up worrying about time a long while back." I watched as he made his way slowly up the hill, occasionally taking a staggered step to the side and then overcompensating and nearly falling the other way instead. Sighing, I crossed the road and headed down towards the riverfront, my bare feet slapping on the pavement. Eadric had some explaining to do.

TOXTETH IS A
WEREWOLF-FREE ZONE

"What on earth happened?" Eadric got up as I stalked into the room, eyebrows disappearing up into his hairline. I'd managed to get back to the Liver Building without attracting too much attention, by the simple method of running too fast for humans to register anything more than an unexpected breeze blowing past. It had worked well—right up to the point my bare feet had slipped on the wet stone of George Parade and I bounced sideways down the steps by the canal, finally coming to rest wrapped around the metal barrier fence. It was such a dramatic entrance that the few people around on such a miserable day had steadfastly ignored me the minute they'd seen me get to my feet and were reassured I wasn't actually dead. Well, I *was* dead, obviously, but they didn't know that. Limping slightly as my joints discussed between themselves whether they really could ignore such indignities, I'd walked the rest of the way with my eyes resolutely forward so I wouldn't have to speak to anyone. Unfortunately, my hair makes me quite recognisable, and I was pretty sure I heard a man sitting outside the Fab4 Cafe telling his companion I was 'that bird from the weird cafe up on Harrington Street'. By the time I made it up to the Silverton's floor via the private lift, I was in the kind of temper that historically ends with the fall of entire civilisations.

"Get me clean clothes and a brandy," I said, "and I'll tell you."

"I'll sort you out," said Nik, coming into the room behind me. "Follow me, m'lady." I dutifully followed him into his private rooms, where he furnished me with purple silk pyjamas, a pair of thick, hand-knitted socks and a large fur throw that looked worryingly real. "It's ancient," he said, seeing me eyeing the fur. "And I didn't kill the wolf myself, before you ask."

"I wasn't planning to ask," I said, pulling the fur around my shoulders. It was warm and comforting and smelled surprisingly of patchouli oil. "You've never struck me as the hunting sort."

"Oh, I'd have hunted anything when I was alive," said Nik happily. "Pheasants, rabbits, the occasional rogue footman. But we didn't have wolves in London. Mapp got that," he nodded at the fur, "in a job lot of house clearance stuff." That at least explained the patchouli. By the time we went back into the main room, Eadric had lit a fire and pulled three armchairs into a semi-circle around it. I curled up in the nearest chair, wrapped the fur around myself as tightly as possible, and gratefully took the large glass of brandy Eadric offered me.

"Can I borrow your phone?" I said to Eadric, as he sat down in the chair opposite me. Both the Silvertons owned mobiles, but Nik's was the type that people buy their elderly parents after one too many missed emergencies. It was about as light and elegant as a house brick and had huge buttons with the old-style letters underneath the numbers. Trying to send a text on it was like attempting the Times crossword armed only with a chunky crayon and the intellect of a five-year-old. Eadric reached over to where his iPhone lay on the floor next to the fire and tossed it towards me with the casual air of someone who has enough money to not have to worry about breaking things. At least, that's what it looked like. He considered phones to merely be a necessary evil, and I suspected he was always hoping it might get accidentally broken. Sadly for him, I caught it in mid-air and used it to send Izzy a quick message to confirm I was, if not actually alive, then at least still kicking. As an afterthought, I sent a second message, asking her to let Sean know I was okay. I passed the phone back over to Eadric with an air of careful consideration and he dropped it onto the floor.

"Come on then," he said, looking at me. "Out with it." Nik poured himself a glass of brandy and, instead of taking the third chair, threw himself down onto the battered old chaise that sat next to the fire. I screwed my face up and looked at both of them in turn, unsure of quite where to begin. In the end, I went for the straightforward approach.

"I fell in the river," I said. "But when I got out I was in the seventeenth-century. Ish. Toxteth, from what I could make out. There was a noticeable lack of wolves, by the way," I shook the fur for emphasis, "of the were-variety or otherwise."

"What on earth were you doing running round in the past?" asked Eadric. "More to the point, *how*?" He looked alarmed. "I told you not to mess with such things, Lilith."

"As it happens," I said, "I didn't do anything at all. One minute I was here, the next I was...then."

"How?" Nik asked eagerly. "I've always wanted to try it, but I've somehow never been in the right place at the right time."

"Wrong place at the wrong time, you mean." I pulled a face at him. "Honestly Nik, it was bloody awful! I fell in the river, and would have had to swim back from bloody Formby if Daisy hadn't given me a tow. The city had disappeared, but the castle was there."

"The actual castle?" asked Eadric. "The one that's been gone these three hundred years?"

"Yup," I said, "that one. Anyway, Daisy towed me to the bank further down and I got out of the water and went for a walk in Toxteth. Only it was farmland, not houses. Actually, it did turn into houses later on, but not to begin with. And *then* I met a ghost who looks a bit like a judge. Pretty sure he isn't a judge like, but the clothes were similar. So, yeah," I trailed off, "it was really fucking weird."

"How did you get back?" asked Nik. "To the present, I mean." So I told them about the ghost disappearing and me running towards the city, and how the surroundings had constantly flickered. "As if they were trying to be real, but couldn't quite manage it." By the time I got to the bit about the self-building wall, they were both looking at me as though they weren't entirely sure I hadn't just banged my head really hard.

"Then I jumped off the wall but landed on the pavement up on Upper Parliament Street. And then I had to walk home through town in wet clothes. Which was embarrassing."

"Daisy helped you?" asked Eadric.

"Yeah," I said. "Weird, huh?"

"When did you meet her?"

"I told you," I said. "Earlier today."

"Not when in the context of our time," said Eadric. "I mean *when*. What year do you think it was?" I told him about the Old Rock Perch.

"That's got to be around seventeen-hundred," said Nik. "Especially if the castle was still here."

"And when—how—did you get back to the present day?" Eadric asked.

"By falling off a sentient wall and landing on the pavement," I said. "Like I said."

"But Toxteth was farmland?" Eadric persisted.

"Yesss," I said patiently. "But more just plots of rough land, not fields like you get in the countryside today."

"Who was the man?" asked Eadric. "The one who looked like a judge."

"Well," I said, "he disappeared without warning , so I didn't actually spend much time getting to know him. Got the impression he was hiding from something. Or someone." I stopped myself. Jonathan had suggested someone was trying to control me, but hadn't specified who. I very much doubted it was either of the Silvertons, going by their equally confused expressions. But if there's one thing I know from endless episodes of *Murder She Wrote*, the bad guy is usually the last person you'd expect. "His name was Jonathan," I went on. "That's all I know. Oh, and he's from a later time than we were in then, but earlier than we're in now. Why did no one warn me the afterlife was this complicated?"

"Because it usually isn't," said Eadric. "This complicated, I mean. Hardly anyone survives the process of human death. And of those that do, the vast majority take the option of disappearing elsewhere for a century or so and just, I don't know, hang out or something."

"Hang out?" I stared at Eadric. "You never say things like that. You'd say something like 'Perchance we could meet for refreshments and perhaps some delightful pianola entertainment'," I could see Nik trying not to snigger out of the corner of my eye. "Not 'hey, let's hang.

Bro.'" I narrowed my eyes. "Have you been *hanging* with Ifan, by any chance?"

"I enjoy his stories," said Eadric defiantly. "We *hang* quite often, if you must know." This was news to me. I hadn't been aware that Eadric and Ifan even knew each other, past the occasional wave of acknowledgement. Plus, Eadric rarely comes down from the tower if he can help it, so even waving's a bit thin on the ground. And all this time Ifan had been coming up here and not telling me?

"Which bird likes him best?" I demanded. Nik and Eadric both looked confused. "Which bird," I repeated, "likes Ifan best. Is he friends with them?"

"Bella isn't two-timing you, Lilith," said Eadric, comprehension dawning. "Her adoration is for you, and you alone." I puffed up slightly, but tried not to let it show. "Ifan usually sits with Bertie. Apparently, he's an excellent audience for trying out new songs."

"I'm not jealous," I lied. "I just like to be careful with the birds, is all. They're sensitive, bless them."

"There is nothing sensitive about those ridiculous creatures," said Nik. "They're tough as old boots."

"Regardless of birds and social circles," said Eadric, "I don't like the sound of any of this. We need to shut it all down before outsiders get wind of it." He looked at me and Nik. "This cannot become public knowledge."

"Well, you'd better go tell that to the *Echo*," I said, "because they've started running a series about the time slip legends and the best places to go if people fancy their chances in the past. It's mostly just repeats of the Bold Street stuff for now. But according to their social media, they've interviewed the mother of that girl who went missing at Albert Dock yesterday, so god only knows what else is going to come out."

"Good," said Eadric. And then, in response to my confused expression, "No one believes anything that gets printed in local newspapers, Lilith. Hopefully, people will assume it's just another tall tale and forget about it. Nevertheless, we need to ensure it doesn't happen again. Can you remember exactly where you were and what you were doing when you passed into another time?"

"Yeah," I said. "I was riding the carousel down on the dock." Nik raised an eyebrow. "With Sean Hannerty." His other eyebrow shot up to join the first.

"So this happened in full view of a human?" asked Eadric.

"One who already uses your life as the basis of his stories," said Nik. "Stories that are no doubt going to join his other titles on the bestseller lists before too long. Well *done*, Lilith."

"Oh shut up," I said, rounding on him. "It's hardly my bloody fault if this stupid city is throwing a hissy fit and chucking people into the wrong centuries, is it? Oh no you don't," I'd seen Eadric open his mouth to speak, but beat him to it. "This time it is absolutely nothing to do with me. I think this is the city itself, Eadric. The actual city—the one that's been here forever."

"How do you know that?" he asked.

"Because *my* city says it's not to blame," I said. "You know—the version that lives in my head like a particularly annoying squatter." There was a faint grumbling at the back of my skull. Oh, *now* it felt safe to reappear. "The one that keeps getting me into trouble that I then get blamed for," I went on, just daring it to interrupt me. There was a bit of quiet muttering, but it knows when it's wrong-footed. "The one in my head is the spirit of the people, but the one that's kicking off now is its big boss. I think," I said slowly, "it's the spirit of the land itself. The heart of the city. Its core, or whatever. It's always been here, but now it's had enough."

"Of what?" asked Eadric. "Does it want to vote? Is it going to expect to pop in here for a coffee and discussions about future development of industrial land? Perhaps I should book it a seat at the next city council meeting?" He looked weary.

"Of everything, I think." I screwed my face up. "I get the impression it's a bit, well..." I gave it some thought. "In all honestly," I said eventually, "I think it's just thoroughly pissed off."

"Who can blame it?" We both turned to look at Nik. "Think about it," he said. "It's been here literally eons—since way before even our ancient friend here," he nodded at Eadric, "was so much as a twinkle in the old squire's eye. People eventually pop up and start growing on it, like endless tiny carbuncles. They use both its land and its water for their own ends, and make themselves stronger and bigger along the way.

By the time this spirit of this city has finally got round to realising it's got a terrible case of human dandruff, they're choking its waterways and building stone embankments to stop it escaping." He reached across and picked up one of his endless tatty paperbacks from a nearby occasional table. "I'd be pretty cheesed off at the discovery as well, to be honest."

"Well, it's taken an awful long time for it to get round to actually doing something about it," I said. "If it was that cross, wouldn't it have started kicking off a couple hundred years back, when they were digging holes in it and cutting railway lines through its middle? In fact," I went on, "why hasn't it had words with Joe Williamson? He'd be the most annoying, I reckon. All that tunnelling under its surface without so much as a by your leave."

"It doesn't matter who's done what in the past, Lilith," said Eadric. "What matters is how we deal with it now. Too many things are happening for it to all be coincidental."

"What sort of things?" I asked. "Aren't time slips enough? What other fresh hell are we having to deal with?"

"I mean everything that's happened over the past year," said Eadric, carefully not saying 'since you died'. "Things were relatively quiet before that, and had been for a long time."

"True," agreed Nik. "Can't deny that one. Sorry, Lil." I glared at him and he made a point of opening his book.

"But now," Eadric went on, "we've got vampires living openly in the city centre and werewolves supposedly making a comeback."

"I *told* you," I said, "there were no werewolves in Toxteth. Just weird ghosts. And walls with a mind of their own. Okay," I went on, "things are weird. And I think the werewolves might actually be cats. But that doesn't mean it's my fault."

"No one said it was your fault, Lilith," said Eadric.

"You were both thinking it," I said. I waited for them to deny it, but they didn't bother. Rude. "So," I said eventually, "what's the plan?"

"Well I," said Nik, waving his book at me, "have the last few chapters of *Fanny Hill* to get through. It is absolute filth." His voice was gleeful. "I cannot believe it's from before even my own time."

"You didn't invent scandal, Nik," I pointed out.

"Tell that to the tabloid press," he said darkly. "Wagatha Christie's got nothing on the stuff that used to be made up about yours truly."

"It's a shame we can't tell people who you really are," I mused. "I reckon you'd be excellent on *Big Brother*."

"Have some taste, woman," Nik said archly. "It's *Strictly* or nothing for me. I fancy myself in sequins and a decent spray tan." He did a little tap-dance on the carpet with his toes.

"Children, children," said Eadric, "can we get back to the point?"

"There's a point?" I asked. "Wow. I'd assumed we were back to floundering around trying to keep a lid on everything and just hoping for the best."

"It's worked so far," shrugged Nik.

"It works," said Eadric, "because I sit here keeping an eye on it all and making sure nothing goes too far off the rails. But there's a limit to how many crises one person can manage. And if the city itself is waking up, we could all be in serious trouble."

"I could ask Liam what he thinks?" The words were out before I even realised what I was saying. Dad used to accuse me of putting my mouth into gear before my brain was properly engaged and although I'd pretend to take offence, I couldn't ever deny it. I like to think that my absolute lack of filters was part of my charm. Neither Eadric or Nik were looking particularly charmed right now, though. "Just a thought," I said meekly.

"We cannot let the other territories know this is happening," said Eadric. "It's bad for our image."

"We have an image now?" I raised my eyebrows at him. "Wow," I said, "if I'd known, I'd have got my hair done."

"You insist on turning everything into a joke, Lilith," said Eadric, "which makes me suspect you still don't take the netherworld entirely seriously."

"Netherworld, netherweird," I said, "what's the diff? Come on," I held my hands out in supplication, "I'm just trying to lighten things up, is all. You might have spent centuries quietly desiccating up here, but I haven't. Hang on," I frowned at him, "where *did* you live before moving here?" Eadric's been around for a millennium, give or take, but the Liver

Building didn't welcome its first tenants until the early twentieth-century.

"We've been over this before," he said. "I had a place in town."

"What about you?" I said to Nik. He looked up from his book, a confused expression on his face.

"What about me?" asked Nik.

"Where did you live before here?" I asked. "You died in the early eighteen-hundreds, and from what I know, you almost immediately travelled back to Britain." Nik had died in Greece—of natural causes, although he was also nursing a broken heart after an ill-advised romance with a young man who was more interested in Nik's money than either his looks or intellect. After terrifying a priest with his unexpected resurrection, he'd popped a handy dead pauper into the coffin in his place and travelled home on the same ship as 'his' body. Unless the history books had things badly wrong, Nik had been dead since before a young Victoria had so much as sniffed at the British throne.

"True enough," nodded Nik. "I spent some time at my mother's place, out in the sticks. Luckily," he winked, "mother dearest was long dead herself by that point. So I was thankfully saved from an eternity of dealing with her frankly shameful behaviour."

"You and your mother," said Eadric, "were as bad as each other."

Nik shrugged. "I'm sure a psychoanalyst would thoroughly enjoy teasing apart the," he coughed politely, "*difficult* relationship I had with my mother. And the relationship she, in turn, had with my father. And he with his father. Personally," he looked at Eadric, "I consider blaming one's behaviour on one's upbringing to be rather crass. Don't you think, Lil?"

"Don't bring me into it," I said. "You still haven't explained where you spent your time before coming to Liverpool."

"And why should I?" Nik's voice was light, but there was an edge to it. "This might be a newer, more open time in which to be living, Lilith, but that doesn't gift you entitlement to people's personal history."

"I'm sorry," I said. "I didn't mean to pry." I looked from one Silverton to the other. "I'm just interested, is all. You two both have so much history and so does everyone else in the nether-bloody-weird and here I am sitting in the middle of it all with nothing more than thirty-odd years of life and a bonus year of death to work with. I genuinely find it all fascinating." Neither of them looked convinced, but Nik took pity on me.

"I'd wager most humans can't remember exactly where they've lived or visited over the course of their lives," he said, "so you can imagine how muddled the memories get when you've got centuries of them to work through. I could barely tell you the cities I've lived in, and I've only been around two centuries. Imagine how difficult it is for Eadric, here."

"Now you're dragging *me* into it," said Eadric. "For what it's worth," he went on, looking at me, "I don't consider anywhere other than Liverpool to be home, these last few centuries. I've owned properties in the city since I first arrived—one of the few benefits of the feudal system was that I got in early, as modern business parlance would have it. I made my money before equal rights and pay were so much as a twinkle in the eyes of the modern political system."

"And what a fair and equal system it is," I said sarcastically.

Eadric grinned. "You'd better get this city under control," he said, "or we'll be back in that feudal system quick as you can say 'A'right, our kid, go 'ead'". His passable but appallingly clichéd attempt at a Scouse accent made me laugh. Then I stopped, because if Eadric was making jokes this terrible, he really was nervous.

"I can't do it alone," I said. "I don't even know what it is I'm supposed to be doing."

"You're supposed to be taking that final step into being in full control," said Eadric. "We," he gestured to Nik and himself, "will always be here to help," Nik waved his book absently in acknowledgement, "but the city needs someone to stand up for it. And to it."

"How do I do that?" I asked, but I already knew the answer. Nik looked up and grinned.

"It's time to start wearing that crown."

STONE TAPE THEORY

"I'm sorry," I said to the cat, "I forgot." It was two in the morning, and the nearest supermarkets were all closed. I might live in the centre of one of Britain's busiest cities, but it's weirdly quiet at night. Even the most traditional of corner shops—those bastions of late milk, ciggies and munchies—shut before midnight, and the bars and clubs gather into little pockets of activity that all seem strangely disconnected from each other. Harrington Street is quiet as the grave in the early hours—except when there's a hungry cat in residence and he's decided to make it everyone else's problem. I was pretty sure any passersby out on the street would be able to hear Grimm's loud, boiling hiss. And I was all out of cat food. I decided to blame Kitty for this oversight —she and Grimm are such a tight unit these days, she usually reminds me well in advance if supplies are running short. And Kitty was still living it up (death-ing it up?) with Jonny, down in Shrewsbury. "I'll see if there's anything in the cupboard." I felt the cat's eyes on me as I scooted tins around. I haven't had to eat—or rather, haven't been able to eat—since I died, so the use-by dates were long gone on most of it. With a shriek of triumph, I finally pulled out a small can of sardines. Holding it carefully so Grimm couldn't see last year's date on the label, I pulled the tab and dumped the contents into a dish. "Here you go," I said, "special treat." He looked up at me, his amber eyes narrowed suspiciously. "Eat it or don't," I said, dropping the can into the bin before he decided to check for himself. "See if I care." For a few long seconds, the cat just stared at me. I held his gaze, because whilst cats might be apex predators, they still can't quite manage the ring pulls on tin cans and certain felines of my acquaintance need to remember on which side their fishy bread is buttered. Finally, he let out an annoyed snort and put his head down to eat. I paced the living room for a while. It was obvious why I was feeling antsy—discovering time portals in one's immediate environs will do that to a girl—but I wasn't yet sure what I could do about it. But was clear even meditation wasn't going to work tonight.

I decided to go out for a walk and, without even thinking about it, found myself heading towards the river. The waterfront was all but deserted, with only the occasional car zipping along the Strand. Music played faintly in the distance. I walked slowly, my hand trailing along the heavy chain-link fence that separates distracted tourists from the cold water below. A young couple were sitting on the grass next to the Billy Fury statue, too wrapped up in each other to even notice me walking past. I wondered idly whether Alan would one day get a statue of his own, and if so, whether he'd dare attend the unveiling. I thought he probably would. The Albert Dock loomed above me to my left, reassuringly solid in the darkness, and the lights of the coastguard patrol boat bobbed around on the other side of the river. I sat down on the river path. A bit of fresh air would do me good—perhaps I'd get a break from the constant swirling in my head. So many people were either relying on me or suspicious of me, yet none of them had apparently got the memo that I didn't actually have a clue what I was doing. *Maybe that's a good thing*, I thought, sliding down the reassuringly heavy stone walls until I was sitting on the river path with my head resting back against the bricks. Sitting here next to the Mersey, meditation felt more achievable. I closed my eyes.

"Want to talk about it?" The voice was uncomfortably close to my ear, and under normal circumstances would have risked its owner getting a sharp smack on sheer principle. Luckily for him, my brain was too tired to register its complaint quickly enough. I settled for a weary sigh.

"Not really," I said, my eyes still determinedly shut. "It'll work out, eventually. Things always do."

"True enough," said Liam. I finally gave in and turned to look at him. "We're still here, aren't we?" he went on. "Despite it all." He gave me a lopsided smile and for a second I forgot that I hated him.

"Why *are* you here?" I asked.

"I thought you might need me," he said, "but that you probably wouldn't admit it. To yourself, let alone me." He shrugged. "So I decided to visit anyway."

"Isn't that a bit risky?" I asked. "I might have raised an army of supporters to defend myself against you, for all you know."

"Have you?"

I stared out at the dark river. "No," I said eventually. "But I might have."

"True. I should probably be more careful." Liam did not sound like someone who was worried for his personal safety. Which was annoying in itself.

"What if Ivo was here?"

"Is he?" said Liam.

I sighed. "No," I said, "Ivo's not here. Or if he is, I don't know anything about it."

"You'd know if he was," said Liam. "I don't think much can happen in this city without you knowing about it, Red. Not now."

"Apart from developing an impressive ability to travel through time?" I said, with a hollow laugh. "Cos I didn't have a clue that was going to happen."

"I did hear talk," said Liam. "That's why I thought I'd risk a visit. It doesn't mean any harm," he went on. "The city, I mean. It's finally waking up and doesn't quite know what to do with itself. It's just getting a bit overexcited, that's all. Things will settle."

"A bit overexcited?" I snorted. "That's one way of putting it. Most people would consider it all absolutely fucking batshit. You're not supposed to be able to walk through town in one century and end up in a completely different one by the time you get to the end of the street, Liam. What if it keeps happening? We'll have people bumping into their own grandparents before they were so much as a twinkle in their granddaddy's eye, and then where will we be? Back in the twenty-first century with a fucked up history timeline and a city populated by people with major therapy bills. What?" Liam was grinning at me.

"The city's coming back to life," he said. "Isn't it allowed to get a tiny bit excited?"

"There's a big difference between being excited and getting so hysterically overwrought that it risks blowing all of us right out of the water," I said. "And how can it come back to life when it was never *not* alive?"

"Oh, it's always had energy," Liam agreed, "but it hasn't always been a conscious thing. All the exciting and terrible and dramatic things that have happened in this city over so many centuries? Those have been far more to do with the people than the place. But now the soul of the city itself is waking up."

"Why?"

"Who knows?" Liam shrugged. "Maybe it's angry, maybe it's just scared. Or maybe," he grinned, "it's just excited about us all being back."

"When you say 'us'," I said slowly, "you don't mean humans. Do you?"

"Who's bothered about humans?" asked Liam, the tone of his voice making it clear that the question was rhetorical. "They're boring and fragile and mostly quite stupid." I raised an eyebrow at him sharply, which he ignored. "But us," he gestured to himself and then me, before making a wide arc with his hand that encompassed everything around us, "well. We're different. And the city remembers, Red. It remembers what humans did to it and what we've protected it from. This city has a very long memory."

"How can a city remember anything?" I knew the version of the city that spoke in my head had plenty of memories, but that was because it was made up of the endless amount of people who'd lived here over the centuries. I didn't think it was that city Liam was referring to.

"Want me to show you?" he asked. There was a gleam of excitement in his eyes—but it was an almost childish kind, like when a kid's got a new toy and is desperate to show it off.

"Show me what?" I asked. "And no smart-arse answers."

"As if I'd be so uncouth," said Liam, with the ghost of a wink. I fought down the memory of him lying naked on the bed in the Baltic Hotel and concentrated on whatever deviousness he was planning now. "I can show you what it sees, Red. Not everything—just some of its memories. The ones big enough to be stained into the bricks and soil that make up this fair city. The ones that grow into the time slips."

"If you take a sonic screwdriver out of your pocket," I said, "I'm yelling for the police."

Liam shook his head, laughing. "I think you could probably fight me off, Red," he said. "Screwdriver or not."

"What if you take me into a different time," I said, "and we get stuck? That bloke in the pipe died more than a century ago, but he still turned up here again last week. Doesn't that mean he's spent all this time in that tube?"

"Well, he's been dead for the vast majority of that time," Liam pointed out, "so it's kind of a moot point. It would have been different had he been one of us, of course," he shuddered, "because I cannot imagine being trapped like that for so long with full awareness of it. But he was dead. Permanently and terminally dead, not our version of it. So it doesn't really matter how long he's existed there, or even whether he's always been there or just popped up for a while before going back to the nineteen-forties. But no," he relented, "I don't think we'd get stuck. That's not what I'm proposing, anyway. Time travel's beyond me, which is rather disappointing. But I can show you the memories that are embedded deep in the stone."

"Like a recording?"

Liam nodded approvingly. "Yes," he said, "almost exactly like that. Some believe that stone absorbs energy in the same way photographic paper absorbs light. It leaves a record. Hold my hand, Red." He held his own hand out and for a moment I stared at it dumbly. "I swear on the crown I gifted you, I mean you no harm."

"Ever?"

Liam grinned. "For now," he said. "That's as much as I can offer." I took his hand, and nothing happened. We sat side by side, holding hands and gazing out across the Mersey. The coastguard boat was still on the water over towards Birkenhead, a faint mist softening its lights against the darkness of the water. As I watched, the mist thickened and spread, until I could barely see the iron railings just a few feet in front of me. I jerked my head to look around, and Liam squeezed my hand gently. "Patience, Red," he said. "Memories can be difficult to catch hold of. Try to let your head take itself into the city." I wasn't sure how I was supposed to do that, but dutifully leant back and waited. It might have been my mind settling or maybe I just got bored and my thoughts wandered, but shadows slowly began forming shapes in the mist. I could hear distant shouting behind us, as though a huge and noisy crowd was being muffled by the density of the atmosphere. A large grey ship slowly became visible in the centre of the Mersey. It lurked low and deadly in the water, glowing faintly around the edges. I could see it clearly, even through the darkness.

"That's a warship," I said in astonishment. "What's it doing here?" Even as I said it, a metaphorical lightbulb flashed above my head. "The general strike," I whispered. Most people these days—in Britain at least —know the phrase 'Bloody Sunday' in reference to the 1972 massacre of unarmed civilians by British soldiers in Derry, Northern Ireland. Fewer know of Liverpool's own, earlier, Bloody Sunday, back in August 1911. More than eighty-thousand people had gathered on St George's Plateau for a speech by trade unionist and pacifist, Tom Mann. The general transport strike had been paralysing Liverpool since June, but workers were united and convinced of their ability to create real and permanent change through the sheer force of people-power. The enthusiastic response to Mann's visit unsettled the police, who resorted to baton-charging the enormous crowd. The ensuing panic and injuries caused uproar in a city already notorious for standing up for itself. Over the subsequent days, passions—and tempers—rose to a boiling point. Two days after Mann addressed the crowd outside St George's Hall, soldiers fired into a crowd gathered on Vauxhall Road and killed two local men. The future British Prime Minister and supposed war hero Winston Churchill was, at that point, Home Secretary. His response to the ongoing trouble in Liverpool was to send the armoured cruiser HMS Antrim up the Mersey to sit at anchor in front of the docks, her guns pointing directly at the city. The strikers went back to work shortly afterwards regardless, having finally been offered better pay and working conditions. But the brazen and violent threat to those who dared defy the government had never been forgotten.

"Yes," said Liam quietly. "This is what the establishment does to cities who don't follow the rules." The noise of the invisible crowd grew, as though powered by fury at the sight of the ship watching them from a distance. "You're going to need to practise that diplomacy of yours, if you're not to take this place down in flames."

"They wouldn't dare," I whispered. "Not in the modern world."

"Do you really think they wouldn't?" Liam snorted. "They'd have gunboats back in this river tomorrow if they genuinely thought they might lose control. I'm sorry to be the one to remind you of this, Red, but you're not on the side of the humans anymore."

"I'm still human myself," I pointed out.

"No, you're not." Liam squeezed my hand again, and I fought the urge to pull away from him. I liked the 'fun in the pub' Liam, not this serious and political version. "You haven't been human since the day you woke up dead. Not in the way they are." He nodded towards the ship, which was now horribly real. Its guns pointed straight towards Pier Head, toward the noise of the crowd. "They're bullies, Red," he went on. "All out for themselves and don't care who knows it. That ship," he nodded at the grey ghost on the water, "is crewed by children who've been brainwashed into doing whatever their supposed betters tell them to do. Even if that involves firing on their own countrymen in peacetime. Peacetime," he repeated, the scorn audible in his voice. "Ha!"

"It's not the same now," I said doggedly. "People—humans—are different."

"Some are," said Liam, "I'll allow that. But those in charge are exactly the same as they've always been, and no better than they deserve." I turned towards him and he met my gaze. We were still holding hands, but I wasn't going to give him the satisfaction of being the first to let go.

"You told me yourself that you believe this country to be yours," I said. "The entire country, you said. Despite some of it being Ivo's or Eadric's. Or even mine, if we're going down that route." Which we clearly were, whether I liked it or not. "How can you sit here telling me how awful and oppressive the government is when all you want to do is take the lot for yourself?"

"Are you calling me a hypocrite, Red?" Liam's eyes crinkled in amusement. "You, the supposed human who's already proved more than capable of killing people who get in her way?"

"That's different," I frowned. "I had no option."

"I've heard that excuse before," said Liam. "Even used it myself, once or twice. There's always a choice, Red." He finally let go of my hand and I snatched it back into my lap. When I turned back to the river, the warship was gone, replaced by the little rescue buzzing along in the misty darkness. "For what it's worth," Liam went on, tilting his head to gaze at me carefully, "I think it made the right choice. The city, I mean. You suit it."

"Suit what?" I pulled my legs up and hugged them, my chin resting on my knees as I looked out at the water. I wasn't in the mood to be patronised. "Suit losing what's left of my tiny fucking mind whilst this city spins entirely out of control? Because that's what it feels like right now."

"You get used to it," Liam said. "Eventually."

"You once told me you remember everything that's ever happened to you," I said. "Did you really mean it?" Liam nodded. "Absolutely everything?"

"Yes," he said. "And as I said back then, it's tiring. Even when you've been doing it for nigh on a thousand years, as I have. Perhaps more so."

"I had to shut mine away," I said. "My memories, I mean. There was just...too much. So I shut it all away in a mental box and locked that shit up good and tight. That's why it took me a few seconds to remember about the workers' strike." I leaned my head back against the wall and turned to look at the thousand-year-old king sitting beside me. "I just threw everything that wasn't immediately relevant into the furthest recesses of my mind and closed the door on it. Does that make me a coward?" Liam's eyes creased at the corners as he smiled at me. It was a kind smile, I thought.

"No," he said, "I don't think you're a coward, Red. A coward would have taken Eadric Silverton's offer of an escape to the country when he offered it, that first few days after you died. But you didn't." He squinted thoughtfully at me. "Why is that, I wonder?"

"Why didn't I run away?" Liam nodded. "Because running away doesn't solve the problems," I said. "It leaves them lurking in the background, just waiting to reappear and trip you up at a later date. I learned that when I ran away from Shrewsbury at the first opportunity."

"Because of your brother?" Liam's voice was curious.

"Yeah," I said. "I thought if I stayed away from home, I could pretend Cally never died. What actually happened was that I had to pretend he'd never existed, and that's not the same thing at all. So all that pain and angst just lay in wait, and jumped out at me when I was dead myself and couldn't get away from my own thoughts."

"What did you do then?"

I thought about being pinned to the wall in the damp Anfield catacomb whilst the woman who'd later become mermaid chow forced me into having visions of my dead brother, standing right in front of me and telling me why everything that had gone wrong was all my fault. And how I'd made my peace with him. "I got the fuck over myself," I said finally. "Feeling sorry for myself now doesn't change the fact my brother died over twenty years ago. I don't have time to work through everything that's ever happened in my life," I went on, "so I closed the lid on it all. But those are things that aren't really relevant anymore, so it doesn't matter. If I ran away from Liverpool, I'd be running away from my own fate."

"I thought you didn't believe in fate?" asked Liam.

"I thought you were determined you were the 'One And True King'," I did the air-quotes for emphasis, "and anyone who got in your way was automatically your enemy?"

"Oh," he said calmly, "I still believe that. But you're safe, Red. You're not going to get in my way."

I narrowed my eyes. "Then you don't know me as well as you think you do," I said. "I'm not going to let you just walk in and take over, as if the past however many centuries haven't even happened."

"I've told you before," said Liam, "I don't want you to bow down to me. I want you to join me. As a true equal. Between us, we could rule everything."

"But I don't *want* to rule." I wasn't sure whether I was upset, or just thoroughly pissed off. "I keep telling you this and you keep ignoring it. I. Don't. Want. To. Rule. Is that clear enough for you?"

"In general," he asked, "or just with me?"

I actually had to think about that for a moment. "I don't want to rule with you," I said eventually. "Sorry about that. I know I'm going to have no option but to take over this territory," a little voice at the back of my head squeaked at that even being a sentence out of my own mouth, "because Eadric wants me too. And so, apparently, does the city. But I don't want the rest of it."

"I'm surprised Silverton isn't pushing you towards taking up my offer," said Liam. I looked at him to check he was joking, but he appeared to be absolutely serious. "He must be worn out by now."

"I have absolutely no idea what you're talking about," I said. "Although I guess that's nothing new."

"Haven't you ever wondered why he's still here?" Liam asked. He smiled, and there was an edge of cruelty to the turn of his lips that I'd never seen before. "He never did learn to choose a side and stick with it."

"What's that supposed to mean?"

"You might want to read up on your local legends, Red," said Liam. He got to his feet and held out a hand to pull me up. We stood facing each other on the dark river path, the city's history back in the past where it belonged. "Especially now you're part of them." With that, he turned and sauntered off in the direction of Otterspool. I opened my mouth to speak, but nothing came out. I couldn't think of anything else to do, so I took the easiest option. I went home.

I let myself in the flat and locked the door behind me before hanging the keys on a hook inside the cupboard. Izzy had lectured me about my habit of dumping them on the windowsill, pointing out I was 'basically *inviting* burglars to play pick'n'mix with your belongings.' Heading into the living room, I looked around. Everything was the same as it had always been—a ramshackle collection of vintage (for which read 'cheap secondhand') furniture, draped with blankets and throws that I'd collected from relatives and charity shops over the years. Most of the surfaces were hidden under bric-à-brac, which I thought was cute and bohemian, but Izzy had declared—more than once—to be nothing more than 'random tat'. The floorboards had been bare since the unfortunate incident with Maria Silverton, on account of how the remains of disintegrated revenant are difficult to get out of carpets. Maybe I should redecorate. After all, I'd been here a good while now, and could be fairly confident I wouldn't be leaving any time soon. There was an old notebook on the coffee table, from the last time Izzy had ordered a Chinese takeaway. I'd kept looking at the list for a good few days afterwards, so envious of her ability to eat that I felt like weeping. It was the little things about being human I missed most. Late night snacks. Curling up in bed knowing you'll definitely fall asleep at some point and maybe dream exciting things. With a sigh, I picked up the notebook and turned to a fresh page. I'd rough out some ideas for new decor, that would make me feel better.

There were usually random pens all over my flat, but of course the minute I actually needed one, they'd gone into hiding. As I walked into my bedroom to see if I'd maybe left one on my bedside table, I stopped in my tracks and stared at the crown that hangs off the mirror on my dressing table. I'd only worn it once, when I'd had to confront the vampires of Edge Hill and needed something to give me, how can I put it, a little *gravitas*. The power it channelled into me had been as terrifying as it was exhilarating, and I'd kept it stashed safely unworn in my bedroom ever since. I liked having it around; it was confirmation that this newly paranormal life really was happening. The alternative was that I was just going quietly mad in the corner of some remote and highly secure psychiatric unit. Right now, the crown was glowing. I'd seen it do the same thing before and suspected it was caused by higher-than-normal weirdness in the local area, but that didn't stop it being creepy as fuck. Nobody needs a magical weathervane in their bedroom. Not that my bedroom had seen much in the way of magical action for a long while, unless you count Grimm racing round it after the occasional mouse. Stepping cautiously forward, I peered at the battered gold circle. It had long lost its stones, and the arches that would have originally curved over the top had been cut off at some point, leaving rough edges in their place. But there was still an eerie beauty about it. This was the oldest surviving crown in British history, after all. I'd actually checked once, not long after it had come into my possession. The current official record holder is the Bohemian Crown, which started life as the property of Anne of Bohemia, wife of King Richard II of England. The polar opposite of the crown I held in my hands, Anne's headpiece is ornate and heavily encrusted with precious gems, enamelling and pearls. It's on display in Munich to this day, and is—supposedly—the oldest surviving example of a crown worn by British royalty. *Ha*, I thought, *if only they knew.*

They can't ever know, said the city. I scowled, still gazing at the crown on my mirror.

Haven't you learned not to take me literally yet?

We can never be sure what you truly intend and what you merely exaggerate.

Shut up, Sigmund. It shut up. I stood still, gazing at the ancient crown. The glow came from within the metal, as though it was radiating light. Despite its battered appearance, it was quite the most beautiful thing I'd ever set eyes on. It was just unfortunate that no historian or museum curator had the faintest idea it still existed. Maybe Eadric was right, and I needed to just suck it up and literally wear the crown. I should probably try it on again, just to make sure it still fitted.

"Stop that right this minute," said a female voice behind me. "He meant it metaphorically, as you know very well." The voice was firm and authoritative and sounded very much like its owner would have made an excellent headteacher, had she only liked children a little bit more. I froze, my arm outstretched and fingers millimetres from the crown's beckoning surface.

"If I turn round and find something awful," I said slowly, dropping my hand, "there's going to be trouble. You'd better not be a zombie. Or an ogre. Or a bloody wraith." I'd had a close call with a wraith a few months earlier and was still bearing a finely balanced grudge.

"Oh, go on with yourself," said the voice. "Just turn yourself round and face me, you silly child. I don't have all day."

"Night," I said, turning round. "You mean you don't have all night.

It's not daytime for hours yet." I grinned at the woman sitting on my bed. "Hi, Gran."

~

Ivy O'Reilly was born in County Cork, not long after Michael Collins had been assassinated for his involvement in the Irish peace treaty ('peace' clearly being a relative term). Her parents decided it might be a good time to seek their fortune on the other side of the water, so they packed up Ivy and her sister and transplanted the entire family to Shropshire. Kitty was only four years old at the time and too young to really understand the change in scenery, but from the little I knew of the story, six-year-old Ivy was another matter. She was Irish, she'd tell anyone who'd listen, and she would be staying Irish, thank you very much. She'd long grown into an English accent and mannerisms by the time I was aware of her presence in my life, but from the day her feet touched English soil, Ivy had been angry with the world. And she made it everyone else's problem. Which is probably why her sister left home as soon as she could. "Where's that sister of mine?" asked Gran, as if reading my mind. "Off out gallivanting, no doubt."

"She is, yes." I gazed at my grandmother sitting primly on the edge of my bed, as though it was the most normal thing in the world. Jesusonamotherfuckingjetski, Kitty was going to lose her tiny mind when she came home to find her older sister in residence. "She's an adult, Gran," I went on, "she can gallivant all she likes."

"Hmph," sniffed Gran.

"Why are you here?"

"That's not very polite now, is it?" said Gran. She adjusted her neat tweed skirt so that it fell evenly over her knees. "If it helps," she shrugged at me, "I don't like it any more than you do."

A sudden thought struck me. "Hang on," I said, "how do you know about Kitty?" Gran looked politely blank. "You already knew Kitty lived here." Another blank look. "Where did you come from?"

"Oh," she said, "I was everywhere, Lilith. It turns out there is indeed existence after death," she shrugged. "Who'd have guessed?"

"Yeah," I said, "it came as a surprise to me an' all. So, is grandad with you?"

Gran frowned. "No," she said, "I've never seen him. Nor Cally, before you ask. In fact," she sat back slightly and looked around her, "I'm thinking it's just the women from the family who keep going, somehow. Are you sure there's only you and Kitty so far?" Now, that was a theory I'd never considered.

"Yes," I said slowly. "Who else were you expecting?"

"Oh," said Gran, "all of them, I should think."

"All of who?"

"Well," she tilted her head and gazed at me thoughtfully. "The O'Reillys, I'd think. We go back a long way, Lilith." Hearing her say my name again reminded me of something Mum had told me a few months earlier.

"You chose my name," I said. "Mum told me. You suggested Lilith, and when Mum asked why, you said 'it's the right name for that girl.'"

"I did indeed," said Gran, a hint of pride in her voice. "And I was right."

"Why, though?" I asked. "Why this name?"

"You know the story of Lilith?" I nodded and she smiled. She was far less stern when she smiled. She had pretty eyes and dimples that people rarely saw. "Of course you do," she said. "Well, your mum and dad were talking about names, and they were all absolutely ridiculous, if you don't mind me saying so. I looked down at you—you'd have only been a few days old then, a tiny wee dot of a thing—and you looked straight at me with those big green eyes of yours. Which was strange in itself, because most babies are born with blue eyes. The name just popped into my head from nowhere," she shrugged. "But I knew it was right."

"Okay, so I know this is going to sound ridiculous," I said, "but Mum thinks I might have some connection to the original Lilith." Gran looked amused. "Is that true?"

"Who knows?" She smiled. "Like most women in history, she was probably a combination of different people and different stories, all pulled together as a warning to other women."

"What sort of warning?"

"Mostly warning them not to step out of line, I'd say." Gran stood up and walked towards me. For one surprised moment I thought she might be about to hug me—which would have been unusual in itself—but she stepped past to where the crown hung on the mirror. "This," she indicated the crown, "is your permission slip, Lilith O'Reilly. It allows you to step as far out of line as you please. And there isn't a man on this earth who would dare stop you."

"Apart from Liam," I said.

"That man," said Gran, "has ideas above his station. I've been watching him circling, thinking he's got the upper hand. You mark my words, Lilith O'Reilly," she turned and, up close, I could see it really was Gran, as solid and present as anyone still living, "the only thing you have to worry about is not getting carried away with your own possibilities."

"And you're here to make sure that doesn't happen, I assume?" Gran had always been dead against anyone getting ideas above their station. '*Ooh, he thinks he's the big I am*' she'd say of anyone who appeared to have anything approaching a healthy level of self-esteem. It didn't make any kind of grammatical sense, but we all knew exactly what she meant.

"Just see me as the voice of reason," she said, giving me an unexpected wink. "And it's about time reason made an entrance round these parts."

THE OLD MAN'S CURSE

"Well she can't bloody well stay here!" Kitty had started shrieking the minute she'd arrived back at the flat and found her older sister in residence, and as yet was showing no signs of stopping. Gran was sitting in the battered armchair with her legs crossed neatly at the ankles and her hands folded in her lap. Her white hair curled the way it had always done, cut short and neat around her ears and the nape of her neck. I was pretty sure the outfit she was wearing—the same tweed skirt paired with a cream blouse and brown jumper she'd been wearing when she first materialised—was the one she'd had on the last time I'd seen her alive, back when I was a kid. Her shoes were neat black courts, of the style the Queen used to wear. Same generation, I guess.

"Kitty," I said for what felt like the hundredth time, "there's nothing I can do about it. She's my gran and she's here and we are polite to our guests."

"Yes," said Kitty, "but only guests who aren't interfering old bats with nothing better to do with their time than make my life a misery."

"You're dead," I pointed out. "You don't have a life to make miserable."

"That is irrelevant and you know it!" Kitty made a good attempt at storming out into the kitchen, but as she wasn't very solid at the best of times, she just sort of drifted away.

I looked over at Gran. "You're going to have to learn to be nice to her," I said, "if you're going to stay here."

"Who said I was staying?" said Gran. "I might have better things to do with my time."

"Have you?" I asked. "Got better things to do, I mean." Grimm was sitting on the sofa opposite Gran, watching her intently. His gaze hadn't left her since she'd headed out of my bedroom to 'see what sort of state you're living in' and come face-to-whiskers with a disgruntled cat blocking the way. Every now and then he made a quiet yowling noise, deep down in his throat. I was pretty sure Grimm had judged Gran already and found her sorely lacking.

"Not just yet," admitted Gran. "Need to get my bearings first." Her expression softened slightly. "I'm not here to make life awkward, Lilith," she said. "I'm here to help."

"Fat lot of good that old witch will be," said Kitty from the kitchen. "Her idea of helping is to make sure everyone lives in the bloody Dark Ages."

"Oh, do grow up," said Gran testily. "We're both dead, Kitty. Dead and gone and mostly forgotten. But we're still here and we still have a chance to make things right. So let's give that a go, shall we?" It was the most reasonable thing I'd ever heard Gran say out loud. In my experience, she just gave orders and people followed them. She'd had an outwardly happy marriage with Grandad though and it had never seemed forced, so perhaps there'd always been a nicer side to her underneath all the starchiness.

Not that Kitty seemed in any hurry to find out. "Why should I?" said Kitty petulantly. She appeared in the kitchen doorway, glaring across at her sister. "You were a judgmental little cow when we were alive, Ivy Rose, and I very much doubt being dead will have had a positive impact. Give it five minutes and you'd be lecturing Death himself on the best route across the black sand."

Gran rolled her eyes. "I have no interest in judging you, Katherine," she said, "nor anyone else." The faint glow that hovers around Kitty when she's stressed flared briefly at the use of her full name. "You were here with Lilith before me, and I'm not planning a lengthy stay." I tried not to let my relief show. "But I've clearly been put here for a reason, and as yet I don't know what that reason is."

"You really don't have any idea why you're here?"

Gran looked at me, her beady blue-green eyes glinting slightly in the reflection of the weak morning sun coming through the window. I could hear clear signs of life from the street outside now. It was my morning to open up Flora's, but I was worried that if I left the two sisters alone in the flat together, I might be hearing explosions by the time I'd so much as got the coffee machine warmed up. "Have you decided what you're going to do about that crown?" she asked, nodding towards the open door to my bedroom. "Because I'm thinking I must be here for you, in some way. And the only thing that isn't decided yet is your future."

"We all tread infinite different paths," said Kitty, the eternal flower child. "There's no set way to get anywhere, we just have to enjoy the ride." Gran snorted, an inelegant noise that didn't match her appearance.

"Oh, get on with you and your hippy nonsense," she said. "You always were a bit of a wet lettuce."

"That's enough," I said firmly. Gran opened her mouth to speak, but I beat her to it. "I don't give a monkey's sodding chuff that you're my grandmother," I said, "so you can pack the bitching in right now. We're all dead, Gran. Departed, deceased, dropped right off the bloody perch. So it's about time you learned to be nicer to your family." Gran stared at me in shocked silence. "Kitty lives here," I said. "Haunts here. Whatever. She's here and we've got on just fine so far, so you're not going to start stomping all over us in your neat little shoes and upset our lives. Do you hear me?" There was silence for a long moment, broken only by the sound of Grimm swishing his tail angrily against the sofa cushions. Just as I was beginning to wish I hadn't opened my mouth, Gran's face broke into a grin. It was so unexpected that I just stared silently at her.

"Well," said Gran, still grinning from ear to ear, "thank heavens for that. It's about time you started standing up for yourself, Lilith O'Reilly."

~

"Can I have a word?"

"Of course," said Eadric, getting up from his desk. He didn't seem surprised to see me, which was unnerving. "Want to go sit with Bella?"

"No," I shook my head. "I'd rather stay in here. But it has to be just the two of us."

"Nik's gone to the library," he said, "again. He informs me they've found a map he thinks you might find interesting. Personally," he gestured at me to sit in one of the overstuffed armchairs, "I think he's taken a shine to the new librarian." He sat in the other chair and gazed levelly across at me. "Want to tell me what's bothering you?"

"What happens if I take over?" I blurted. "To you, I mean. What would happen to you if I were to take over everything."

Eadric smiled. "You've been talking to Normandy," he said. "I did think it was only a matter of time."

"He turned up," I said. "I didn't invite him."

"No one invites him," said Eadric. "Not if they value both their property and their life. I think," he looked at me with an expression verging on amusement, "he's genuinely fond of you."

"Doesn't stop him being a dickhead," I said. "He's a power-hungry idiot with a very high opinion of himself."

"One thing Normandy isn't," said Eadric, "is an idiot. Although I can't disagree with the rest of your statement."

"So what happens?" I asked. "If I take over, I mean."

"Is this a serious question," said Eadric, "or a purely theoretical one?"

"Theoretical," I said. "For now, anyway. You know I don't want to take over. Not in the way Liam means, anyway. But I'm not sure I'll always have a choice in the matter."

"I suspect you're correct," said Eadric. "And it's a sensible question to ask, under the circumstances." He had a crooked smile on his face as he looked at me. "Do you believe in curses, Lilith?"

I frowned. "Like old-fashioned fairytale curses? Stay away from tall towers and enormous wolves, that sort of thing?" It wasn't lost on me that I was currently sitting at the top of a very high tower, but at least I was pretty sure the Silvertons weren't lupine in nature.

"Yes," said Eadric. "That sort of thing."

"I'd like to say no," I said, "but I suspect you're about to prove me wrong."

Eadric laughed. "Well, maybe curse isn't the right word," he said. "You might call it an obligation. Regardless, I'm not here of my own choice. And it's been that way for a very long time. You see, Lilith," he settled himself more comfortably into the chair, "I was once a traitor. And now I'm paying the price."

"Is this to do with Liam?" I asked. "When you were both alive?" He nodded. "I know the stories, Eadric," I said. "How you fought against him, but his armies were too strong, and you were forced into collaborating." His mouth twisted slightly. "But that's the thing," I went on, "you were forced. You didn't choose to side with Liam over your own people, you had no option."

"That's not how the people saw it," said Eadric. "And it's hardly as though I was squeaky clean before that, either. I once set fire to your own home town, did you know that?"

"Yes," I said, "I did. 1069, and all that. Didn't like to mention it, but as you've brought it up, yeah. That was a bit rude. If you don't mind me saying, like."

"I've apologised to your mother," he said, "if it helps."

"What did she have to say about it?" I couldn't get my head around the idea of an ancient immortal apologising to a spry, modern Englishwoman for burning down her home town almost a thousand years earlier. Mum's face must have been a picture.

"She was very gracious," said Eadric, "as always. Offered to give me a tour, should I ever decide to visit. Apparently, she thinks I'd appreciate how they rebuilt it."

"I guess that depends how much you like Tudor architecture," I said faintly. "Although you'd be impressed by the castle, I think. Bit sturdier these days."

"It would certainly be even harder to set fire to," agreed Eadric. "So, yes. I fought against Normandy. And then, when it became clear we would never win, I fought alongside him. Against my former allies. Which is the very definition of a traitor, no?"

"What's all this got to do with curses?" I said. "Or destiny, or whatever the fuck it is."

"Aah," said Eadric, "such a way with words." He smiled, and I wondered if he had any awareness of just how beautiful he was. These days I wouldn't have liked to bet on whether humans were created by evolution, gods, or aliens from a distant galaxy, but whoever or whatever was responsible for Eadric had certainly gone all-out with aesthetics alongside his sharp intellect. The cold January light that was forcing its way through the mottled old windows lit his chestnut hair at the edges, giving him a halo. "I'm not here for the same reasons as the rest of you," he said finally. "I'm a revenant, but I didn't come to it naturally as you and Nik did. Or Ivo, or Normandy. It was forced upon me by a higher power."

"Yeah," I said, "you've lost me now, love. Back up and start again slowly."

Eadric crossed his long, elegant legs and steepled his fingers in front of him, studying them for a moment before speaking again. "It's my punishment, Lilith. This immortal life." He looked me in the eye. "I betrayed my people and, as punishment, I cannot return to my love."

"Golda?" I knew Eadric had a first wife, long before he fell for the faked charms of the super-fucking-evil Maria. But he'd never told me the circumstances of her loss, and I'd never asked. To my shame, I'd barely given her a thought, even after the discovery that Maria had occasionally tormented him with visions of her. Golda, the one person he'd ever truly loved.

"Yes," he nodded. "I betrayed her as well. Not intentionally—and not even particularly cruelly—but she saw it as such. And because of that, she left me."

"What did you do?"

"Golda wasn't of this earth," he said softly. "But I needed her to be, in order to keep her with me. She agreed to stay, on one condition—if she ever went away, I was never to question her when she returned."

"That sounds a bit suss," I said. "She could have been having it away with the local squire or something, for all you knew. Why shouldn't you ask where she'd been?"

"Golda wasn't tempted by that sort of thing," Eadric said, his eyes crinkling into a faint smile. "But she had sisters, and her bond with them was stronger than it ever was to me. I should have accepted it—after all, why shouldn't a woman be devoted to her siblings? But her attachment to them took her attention from me, and I didn't like it." He gazed vacantly into the middle distance. "Mapp wrote a story about it once. It's quite tragically beautiful."

"So, you fell out with your wife because she spent time with her sisters?" Eadric nodded. "Bit caveman of you, don't you think?"

"Yes," he said, "I do think. But hindsight is a wonderful thing, Lilith. In reality, by the time I'd finished railing at Golda about what I perceived to be a lack of devotion, she was gone." He sat silently for a moment. "And she took our son with her."

"Whoa," I said, "you've got a son?" Eadric nodded. "Where is he now?"

"I've never been able to find him," he shrugged, "despite centuries spent trying. He could be in a completely different reality, for all I know."

"Oh no," I said. "No, no *no*. Don't you *dare* tell me there are parallel universes alongside all this stupid bloody quantum bollocks."

"I've just told you about my lost wife and child," said Eadric, one eyebrow raised, "and you're worrying about quantum?"

"Sorry," I said sheepishly. "I get carried away sometimes. Tell me about your son."

"There's nothing to tell," he said flatly, and I knew I'd ruined the moment. Well done, me.

"So, why are you trapped here?" I asked, hoping a change of subject would help.

"I'm proof of just how capricious the fates can be," he said. "I turned my back on my fellow countrymen and the land was lost. As retribution, I cannot die until those same lands are united in the nether-world. It has never been possible to reunite the territories, because no one was ever going to give way. Now you're here, Normandy believes he can do it—with your help. And if he does," a brief pause, "I will cease to exist." I stared at him for a long moment, my brain frantically attempting to make sense of what he'd just told me.

"So, if Liam gets his way and takes over the entire country," I said slowly, "you'll die?"

Eadric nodded. "Although I'm not sure dying is the right description," he said. "It's far more likely that I'll just...disappear. Not that the minor details really matter. I'll be gone, one way or another."

"You're going to have to help me out here," I said, "cos right now I'm even more confused than usual. You say you're forced to stay here against your will?" Eadric nodded. "So you want to die? You want Liam to take over? I thought the whole point of everything was for Liam to *not* be allowed to take over?" I slumped back in the armchair. "Fucking hell," I said, "just when I think there's no way things can get any more complicated, they go and get massively more complicated."

"When you've been around as long as I have," said Eadric, "you've had an awful lot of time in which to complicate things."

"So I see," I said faintly. "So, which is it? Do you want to die or not?"

"Yes and no," he said.

"That is not helpful," I snapped. "I'm trying to be sympathetic here and all *'oh I'm so sorry about your wife and don't worry about betraying your kinsmen it's all water under the bridge now'* and all you're doing in return is giving me a bloody headache and making me worry I'm going to be left to deal with Liam bloody O'Conner with no one to help other than Nik and Mapp. Both of whom, I'd like to point out, are more likely to run shrieking for smelling salts than be of any practical help."

"You underestimate both of them," said Eadric. I waited, but he didn't elaborate. "In answer to your previous question," he went on, "yes. I want to die. Because that's the only chance I have of being reunited with Golda. Perhaps there really is some form of heaven, even for those of us who are not truly of this earth. If she's there, I might get the chance to make amends. Or maybe not—but at least I can try. And if there isn't anything after...this," he gestured around us at the world in general, "I won't know about it anyway. So there isn't much of a downside from my personal point of view. But," he saw me opening my mouth to speak and raised an elegant hand to stop me, "I have responsibilities here. I let my people down when I was alive, and I will not repeat that mistake now I'm dead."

"So," I said, "what's the plan?"

"I think," said Eadric, "that's actually up to you." He tilted his head and gazed thoughtfully at me, his beautiful eyes tired but crinkled with kindness at the corners. "You could carry on with things as they are," he went on, "ricocheting from one drama to the next and constantly fire-fighting the chaos. Or," he frowned, "you could make the decision to take over."

"But I don't wa—" Eadric put a hand up to stop me.

"This has gone way past what you personally want, Lilith," he said. "We have been careering around this city like idiots for almost a year now, ever since you arrived on the scene. Before you say anything," he'd clearly seen my expression, "I am well aware that you didn't choose any of this. But you're here and the city clearly wants you. And, frankly, I think we could all do with a rest."

"I like my life," I said. "Or my death. Whatever you want to call it. I like my flat and I like being involved with Flora's."

"No one's going to stop you doing any of that," said Eadric. "You've made it abundantly clear that you prefer the," he was clearly struggling to find the right word, "*basic* life," he went on, "rather than the luxury version."

"I already told you," I said, "I'm not moving to Albert Dock."

"No," he agreed, "you're not. I'm going to offer the apartment to Isobel."

I gaped at him. "You're giving it to Izzy?"

"I'm a businessman," he said, "so no, I'm not *giving* it to her. I am, however, going to offer her a very long lease at a very reasonable price. Peppercorn rent, as they used to call it. It's wasteful leaving it empty, and with Isobel out of her current accommodation, I'd be able to start a proper refurbishment. Those steps need a good pressure-wash, for a start." The steps up to the front door of Izzy's building are way too convenient as a late-night toilet stop for drinkers making their way to and from Mathew Street. On the odd occasion I went over there, I was very careful not to step in any puddles.

"But," I started, "that's not—"

"Fair?" asked Eadric. I scowled at him. "Are you forgetting, Lilith, that I have offered you the very same apartment on many occasions? And not just because I am a generous man. It would be far more suitable—not to mention secure—for someone in your position. And yet you practically sneered every time it was mentioned."

"It just seems so..." I struggled for the right word, "ostentatious. You know? Like, those places are bought by footballers and models and there's hardly ever anyone even *in* them, because the owners spend half the year in Dubai or whatever. I thought I'd feel out of place," I trailed off, "and a bit stupid."

"Well," said Eadric brightly, "you can get over it by visiting Isobel after she moves in. Won't that be nice?" *Nice for Izzy*, I thought uncharitably. Most of the reason I stayed in the Harrington Street flat was because it kept things as normal as possible. Izzy had been living in her shabby little place on Button Street for so long now, it hadn't even occurred to me she might ever want to move. "Don't look so grumpy," Eadric said. "I've got a maintenance team and decorators on the books. Decide on some new decor for that ancient hovel of yours, and I'll send them over to do the work." He grinned. "They're paid well in return for ignoring any weirdness. You'll be okay."

"Do I have to put in a display case for the crown?" Two could play at being a smart-arse.

"Does it need one?"

"Probably not," I said. "I think it likes being in my bedroom."

"Normandy might have put an enchanted stone into it," said Eadric with a twinkle. "You might want to drape it with a cover when you're getting dressed." I jerked upright in horror before remembering the crown didn't have any stones left, and settled for glaring instead. "Things will be okay, Lilith," Eadric said. "But you really are going to have to take over. Properly."

"I don't want you to go!" I couldn't prevent a wailing tone seeping into my voice. "I'm, well..." I stumbled over the words, "...I'd miss you. That's all."

"And I would miss you in return," said Eadric. "But I'm not planning to leave you just yet." He stood up and walked over to the unlit fireplace, turning to lean back against it as he spoke. "I am happy to stay here," he gestured around the room, "for the time being. I will continue with the formal and legal management of this territory until the day comes when you decide you are capable of doing it for yourself. But," he went on, "you are not free of responsibilities. This city is becoming dangerously out of control, and that *is* your responsibility. It knows you're here and it feels the power rising, but as yet there's nothing to contain that power, nor guide it in the right direction. That's your responsibility, Lilith—care and guidance of the soul of the city itself."

"So nothing too major, then," I said sarcastically.

Eadric laughed. "I think you'll find the city can actually look after itself fairly well," he said. "But it needs someone at the helm. Someone looking out for its best interests. And its best interests are not letting it run away with itself to the point others are forced to become involved."

"Who would become involved?" I asked. "Liam wants me as well as the city, and I haven't heard from Ivo in months."

"Lilith," said Eadric, "if this current uncertainty is allowed to carry on, it won't be the netherworld itself that's the problem. The humans are beginning to notice something isn't quite right."

"If you're talking about David," I said, "I've got him under control." David Mansoor worked in the pharmacy on Castle Street and had been the first person to realise I was no longer quite alive. That was back when I'd only just sailed off the fire escape to meet my eternal fate as a permanently irritated immortal. It was also David's fault I'd had a near-terminal meeting with a very mardy vampire, but I try not to hold it against him. I'd assumed at the time that his meddling in undead affairs had led to 'death by vampire', but what I didn't know back then was that it had been Aiden who took over as the new chief bat. And as Aiden likes to do things in a civilised fashion wherever possible, David had merely been given a lecture on not messing with the underworld and then sent home. Presumably to change into clean underpants. He's back working in the pharmacy now—David, not Aiden, although Aiden would be pretty good at blood-letting—and I sometimes amuse myself by standing outside and staring in through the window. I hang around for just long enough to make him healthily nervous, then wander off, usually chortling like an evil gremlin. A girl has to get her fun where she can in this world.

"Who?" said Eadric. "Oh, you mean that boy from the pharmacy." David had to be in his late thirties at least, but then I guess anyone less than three hundred years old counted as young in Eadric's world. "No," he went on, "not him. You forget that we exist in what is still an all-too-human world, Lilith. If we're to stay integrated, then we have to fit in— as well as we can, anyway. Most areas manage it, their towns and cities populated by so few supernatural creatures that they go unnoticed by all but the most observant. Others are so densely populated with all kinds of life and death that oddness goes unremarked. One could be more openly 'other' in London than they might be in Chester, for example."

"So, what's the problem?" I asked. "We're in a city that has a hugely transient population. We're pretty much ninety-per-cent students, for god's sake. Weirdness is the norm round here."

"Liverpool is a small city," said Eadric patiently, "with a big heart. And that heart can get overexcited and overwhelmed, in very short order. The trick is to ensure it doesn't ruin things for itself in the process."

"And I'm the one who needs to calm it down? The zombie on the spot, as it were?" He nodded. "Then you've got more confidence in me than I have in myself," I said. "Why on earth should it listen to me? I'm not even *from* here, Eadric!"

"Which means it isn't so invested in you," he said. "You're pretty much perfect."

"Right, so you're telling me I'm a good one to try cos the city doesn't care too much what happens to me?"

"I didn't put it quite like that," he said. "But yes. Sort of. You're not of its soil, Lilith. You're meeting it as an outsider. In the same way it has itself been an outsider for so long."

"And if I do my best," I said slowly, "you'll stay?" Eadric nodded.

"Yes," he said. "I'll stay. For now."

"You're on," I said. "You'd better start teaching me about quantum."

UNEXPECTED VISITORS

I was walking back to Harrington Street when my phone rang. I hardly ever got phone calls and when I did, it was rarely for a good reason. Wondering what the fuck might have happened now, I dug around in my bag until I found it underneath a pair of knickers. There was no good reason for me having spare pants in my bag—chance would be a fine thing—but that didn't mean anything. I cultivate what I like to call a 'floordrobe', throwing clothes into and across the room at random. I'd once found a single filthy sock in my bag in the middle of a meeting with my bank manager, back when I was putting together my business plan for Flora's. It was probably more surprising I didn't have rats living in it.

The number flashing on the screen didn't calm my nerves any. "Hi mum," I said, wedging the phone under my chin so I could speak as I rearranged the bag over my shoulder. "What's up?" The rogue knickers were actually hanging out of the top of the bag, and I shoved them away hurriedly.

"How's things with you?" said Mum. She sounded cagey.

"Look," I said, "if something awful's happened please just come out with it, because I'm so weighed down with absolute bollocks right now that I cannot be arsed to beat around the bush."

"Aah," said Mum, a note of relief in her voice. "Gran's with you, then?"

I stopped in my tracks. "How did you—hang on," I tucked myself into the doorway of an empty shop and held the phone properly to my ear. "How do you know about Gran?" Realisation dawned. "She's been to see you, hasn't she?" Mum can see ghosts, but I only found that out after I'd died and she turned out to be a bit more knowledgeable about it all than I'd maybe have liked. These days Kitty pops in on her for a cuppa when she's down in Shrewsbury, although she can only do it when Dad's out of the house. Dad doesn't hold with that 'stupid spooky stuff'. I'm pretty sure he knows Mum's a bit different in some way, but chooses to pretend it isn't happening.

"Yup," said Mum, "and frightened the bloody life out of me. Your dad was only in the other room! He's out getting the car valeted," she carried on, "which is why I'm calling now. What's your gran had to say for herself?"

"What did she tell you?" I asked. I try not to involve my parents in my undead adventures. They're more breakable than I am, for one thing.

"Nothing much," said Mum, "just popped up next to me when I was filling the dishwasher. I had my head inside the bloody thing trying to fix that rail that keeps sticking." Mum's arguments with the dishwasher are legendary and I have no idea why she doesn't just replace it. I think she likes the sparring. "Stood up so fast I cracked my head on the sodding thing." Mum also doesn't swear much, as a general rule. Gran's appearance must have really put the wind up her. "She just said that she was here to see you, Lil. I told her you were in Liverpool and she gave one of her big huffs." I knew exactly what Gran's huffing sounded like. It made the recipient feel like the biggest heel on earth, often without having a clue what they'd supposedly done wrong. "But before I could tell her to pack it in, she disappeared again."

"When was this?" I asked.

"Yesterday," said Mum. "I'd have rung sooner, but your dad came home. And then it was date night, so I didn't get chance." I loved the fact that my parents still insisted on having what they called 'date night', despite having been together for decades.

"Yeah," I said, "Gran's here. Large as life and mardy as ever." A woman walked past with a small, scruffy dog on a leash. It stopped to sniff at me so I bent down to stroke it, but it backed off, snarling. Waving away the owner's mortified apologies, I tucked myself more tightly into the doorway. "She says she's here to help me," I went on, "but all she's doing so far is winding Kitty up."

"I know how Kitty feels," said Mum. "She was only here a few minutes, but it was long enough to remind me everything I do is apparently wrong and she's never going to not be disappointed in me."

"She doesn't mean to," I said. "It's just her way."

"Honestly Lil," she said, "it's amazing how that woman can get so much across in just a few resigned sighs." She laughed. "I should be used to it by now, of course. But I thought it was done with after she'd died. I'm not sure I fancy having her popping in and out for the rest of my life."

"You might not even escape when you finally drop off your perch," I said, and explained Gran's theory about O'Reilly women.

"Christ," said Mum, "it doesn't bear thinking about. Although it'd be nice to know I'd always have you around, Lil."

"Same," I said, the word choking slightly in my throat. "At least I know there's a chance I'll have you and Kitty for company for the rest of time. Maybe we can become some kind of undead Charlie's Angels." *Charlie's Angels* had always been one of my mum's favourite television programmes, and the advent of streaming services had enabled her to re-watch it in its entirety, many times over. Before I grew too big for messing around with my parents, Mum and I would occasionally pretend to be Angels, leaping around the kitchen brandishing imaginary pistols.

"Bagsy Sabrina," said Mum, and we both laughed. "Seriously though," she went on, "I do find it comforting to know you're all still around. I couldn't have coped with losing both of you, Lil."

"I know," I said quietly. "I'm pleased, too. Most of the time, anyway."

"That bad?" asked Mum.

I sighed. "Not really," I said. "It's better than the alternative. But it is very bloody weird round here at the minute, Mum. The rest of them seem to think I'm going to be able to just take control and sort everything out, but I'm not sure."

"Then you need to learn to be sure," said Mum firmly. "No one's going to hold your hand with this, Lil. And you don't need them to, anyway. You're more capable than you think."

"Thanks," I said, utterly unconvinced. "Anyway," I decided to change the subject, "I'd better go see what Gran's been up to while I was out. For all I know, the building could have been reduced to rubble by now."

"I wouldn't like to bet against it," agreed Mum. "But don't forget that it's *your* house they're in, Lil. Your house and your cafe. And your city, come to that. Gran and Kitty might have been around longer than you have, but they don't know the place like you do."

"I'm pretty sure I don't know this city myself anymore," I said, remembering what I'd said to Eadric. "I'm not even from here, don't forget."

"Nonsense," said Mum briskly, "you'll be fine. Anyone who knows you knows you've only got that city's best interests at heart. You might not have been born local, but you love the place as much as anyone. People can see that, Lil."

"I'm terrified I'm going to fuck things up and destroy everything," I admitted. "Possibly literally."

"Ha!" said Mum. "As if that city's going to let you bring it down. It'll be all you can do to keep it from taking off into the clouds, I'd imagine."

"Yup," I said. "If I can just stop it destroying itself, that'll be a start."

"Good girl," said Mum. "Now go sort your Gran out. And tell her from me that if she pulls that sudden appearance trick on me again, I'll exorcise her myself."

∾

"Where's Gran?" I asked Kitty as I walked into the living room. She was watching kids' television and must have found a channel showing old programmes, because it was currently playing *Trumpton*. It was way before my time, but I recognised it because the band Half Man Half

Biscuit once wrote a song about it, which had always been one of Dad's favourites. He'd found me some clips of the original show when I was a kid, but I definitely preferred the musical version.

"No idea," said Kitty, without turning to look at me.

"Ooh look," I said, "your pants are on fire!" Kitty jumped and panicked for a second before registering the sarcasm and glowering silently. Grimm padded into the room past my legs and hopped onto her lap, turning to gaze coolly at me. I sighed and flopped down into the armchair opposite them. "Want to tell me what happened?"

"Not really," said Kitty, then immediately launched into her story. "She's a horrible old witch and you know it," she snapped. "Turning up here and casting aspersions like that, how dare she?" Grimm settled down on her lap, but didn't take his eyes off me. I swear, that cat gets creepier by the day.

"She isn't staying," I said. "Or at least, I don't think she was planning to. I assume you've got rid of her already?"

"Yes, I bloody well have," snapped Kitty. "I'm sorry, Lil," she looked anything but sorry, "I know you wanted to find out why she was here. But I can tell you now, it won't have been for any good reason. She's poisonous and always has been."

"Okay," I said, getting up again.

"Where are you going?" asked Kitty fretfully. "I'm sorry, okay? I know I'm an unwanted guest myself and I try to keep out of your way, but I really can't cope with that woman being around, not after all this time." I could actually see ghostly tears pricking at the corners of her eyes. "I'm sorry," she repeated.

"It's okay," I said, "honestly. I know you struggle with her." Kitty hunched her shoulders and looked genuinely apologetic. "I'm just going for a shower," I went on. "Maybe a good scrub will clear my head." Not that I held out much hope of that. Nothing short of tipping bleach into my ears was going to work right now.

I decided on a bath rather than a shower. Maybe I could practise the 'remembering not to gasp underwater' thing, just in case I ever ended up in the Mersey again. I've seen some of the things they dredge out of that river and I'd rather not have them living in my lungs, undead or not. When the water was as deep and as hot as my outdated boiler could manage, I stripped off and slid carefully under the surface. I managed to get my head right down onto the base of the tub by sticking my legs up out of the water and pushing up against the taps with my feet. Opening my eyes, I gazed up at the cloudy surface with its layer of bubbles. I'd pay for it later—even immortal eyeballs grumble when soap gets in them—but for now, everything was peaceful. Which was, of course, the point at which a shadow moved across the top of the water. Someone was in the bathroom. I shot up, but not before something caught hold of my left foot and gave it a shake. I burst out of the water, coughing and spluttering. I'd put so much bubble bath in that the enamel was slippery and as I scrabbled onto my knees, I lost my balance and fell face first back into the water. I finally got myself wedged between the sides of the bath and resurfaced, snorting water out of my nose as I did so. "Elegant as usual," said a voice.

"For fuck's *sake*, Gran!" My grandmother perched on the loo, watching me with her eyebrows fractionally raised. Thankfully, the loo seat was down and her skirt was tucked carefully over her knees as usual. "What the fuck are you doing in here?" I grabbed for something to cover myself, but as the only thing to hand was a flannel, it wasn't very successful.

"I don't know why you're being so dramatic," said Gran calmly. "It's not as though I've never seen a naked human body before." I'd like to think I gave her my patented Hard Stare, but it probably came across more like a confused guppy with its mouth silently opening and closing. "I've got one myself, you know."

"For crying out loud," I said. "Give me a minute, will you?" I wriggled round until I was sitting sideways in the bath, knees up to my chest to cover what I could of my nakedness and hair dripping over my face like a tangle of orange seaweed. "What," I repeated, "are you doing in here?"

"My sister," said Gran, nodding towards the door, "made it clear that I am not welcome. No," she put a hand up to stop me speaking, "she's right, Lilith. I really am a terrible old woman and it's no wonder people dislike me."

"No one dislikes you, Gran," I said. It didn't sound convincing, even to me. "You and Kitty are just very different people, is all." My backside was wedged awkwardly against the bottom of the bath and I tried to wriggle into a more comfortable position, but only succeeded in spilling water over onto the floor. "Fucking *hell*," I muttered. "Hang on." I pulled the plug, then yanked the shower curtain across and clambered upright behind it. Then I shoved a hand out into the bathroom. "Pass me the towel?" I said to Gran. She dutifully handed it over and I managed to wrap it round myself with only one corner trailing into the draining water. Pulling the curtain back, I stepped out of the bath and perched on the edge. "You are what you are," I said to Gran, "and so is Kitty. It's just that what you are is absolute polar opposites."

Gran gave a sniff, but it was marginally less aggressive than usual. "Well," she said, "I realised why I'm here, and I thought I ought to tell you before I left. Whatever my dearest sister thinks."

"Your sister," I said, "just wants to be allowed to make the most of her unexpected extra life. Maybe you should consider doing the same."

"I'm not sure that just hanging around being dead is a very polite way of spending the time, Lilith." Another small sniff.

"We're *dead*, Gran!" I could have shaken the bloody woman, she was being so obtuse. "Nothing matters anymore!"

"Manners always matter, Lilith," she said. But I could see a tiny smile beginning to creep into the corner of her mouth. "Do you want to know why I'm here or not?"

"Yes," I said, "of course I do. But you're going to have to wait til I've got some clothes on. I feel," I screwed my face up, "disadvantaged."

"I'll meet you in the bedroom," said Gran, and promptly disappeared.

"Were you talking to someone in the bathroom?" Kitty asked suspiciously. Grimm was still on her lap and they were still watching TV, but the programme had switched from *Trumpton* to *Camberwick Green*. They're almost identical programmes, but the characters are distinctive. Windy Miller was cycling across the screen, and I was pretty sure he was from Camberwick. Kids' television is one of those things that my newly photographic memory likes to bring up at any opportunity. It's mostly harmless, so I don't attempt to shut it away like I do with other memories. And I used to really like those programmes. Dad tried to get me into *Mr Benn*, but I always thought the shopkeeper looked a bit creepy.

"Myself," I said. "I'm the only person I can get any bloody sense out of, these days." Kitty clearly wasn't fooled, but sensibly decided not to pursue it. She turned silently back to the screen. I stalked through to my bedroom and was thoroughly unsurprised to find Gran standing in the corner, next to the dressing table. "You'll have to wait while I get dressed," I said. "I'm getting fed up with people turning up wanting conversations when I barely get any peace and quiet as it is." Gran raised an amused eyebrow but said nothing. I pulled on a pair of jogging bottoms and a baggy sweatshirt, and wedged slippers onto my feet. Then I found one of the microfibre turbans I keep buying in the hope that drying my hair naturally will stop it being quite so frizzy, and fixed it round my head. "That'll have to do," I said. I sat back against the pillows on the bed and looked over at Gran. "Come on then," I said, "out with it. Why do you think you're here?" Gran had just opened her mouth to speak, when there was an unearthly yowling noise from outside.

I was up and out of the kitchen door before anyone could say 'animal instinct'. Rachel was in the corner of the car park, staring at something on the ground in front of her. She had her hands on her bony hips, and I could hear her hissing despite being several storeys up. Alan was with her and he was clearly trying to hold something down on the floor. "What the fuck are you doing?" I yelled. They both looked up at the sound of my voice, and the creature they'd trapped saw the opportunity for escape. I leaped down the fire escape as fast as I've ever managed it and caught the animal by its back leg. It fell and automatically rolled into a ball, taking me with it for the ride. I clung on hard as we bounced across the rough ground together, feeling thick fur beneath my hands. I briefly wondered just how many teeth this thing was going to turn out to have when we finally came to a stop. The creature twisted as we rolled, and managed to use me as a shield when we finally hit the brick wall. If I'd been human I'd have had all the breath knocked out of me, and almost certainly a few teeth. As it was, I just made a loud huffing noise and gripped tightly onto its fur in the hope of preventing another escape attempt. I'd have managed, too, had Grimm not chosen that moment to claw my face off. He landed on me like a furious raccoon, slashing with his claws and pulling his mouth back into a snarl that showed every last one of his tiny but razor-sharp teeth. "You hold on to it, then!" I yelled, and kicked out as hard as I could. Both the cat and his unidentified companion shot across the car park, hitting the underneath of the fire escape hard enough to wedge the bigger of the two into the bars. I got up slowly, dusting brick dust and city grime off my clothes and pulling the ridiculous turban off my head. "Oh, you want my help *now*," I snarked at Grimm, who'd backed off and was making a low keening sound under his breath, as his gaze flicked from me to the unknown animal and back again. "You hurt?" I asked him. He shook his head. Yes, I know he's a cat, but if Grimm shakes his head in answer to a question, I'm happy to take that as his final answer. "Who's your friend?" I asked him.

"Danger," hissed Rachel from behind me. "Danger-danger!" I turned to look across to where Rachel and Alan were standing together and watching me nervously. She was pulling at the sleeves of her over-sized sweater and shuffling from foot to foot. Alan, on the other hand, looked as smooth as ever. Wearing a dark grey suit that was narrow cut in a retro style complete with black velvet lapels, he looked like he should be in a Beatles tribute band. *It's no wonder people never question his strange appearance*, I thought to myself. *They probably all just assume he's part of someone else's film crew.*

"No one asked either of you to lay down the law out here," I said. "So why did you?" Rachel looked genuinely terrified, but Alan was made of sterner stuff.

"You look after us, Lil," he said in his sing-song voice, "so we look after you. This...thing," he gestured towards the fire escape, where Grimm sat huddled next to the strange creature, "is dangerous, girl."

"How do you know?" I asked. They both looked entirely blank. "How do you know it's dangerous?" I repeated, walking slowly towards what I could now see was, indeed, a cat. A really, *really* big cat. It had scrunched up tight in an attempt to make itself look small, but I reckoned it would be as tall as me if it stretched out. "Seriously?" I said to Grimm, who gazed balefully back at me. "You've got a pet were-cat now?" The larger animal was shuddering. "Is it injured?" I asked, and Grimm gave a slow shake of his head. "I think," I said slowly, "you'd better take it inside."

"No-no-no," started Rachel behind me. I turned to see her flapping her hands around helplessly. "Not-no-bad-danger," she pleaded.

"You lost your mind, girl?" Alan gaped at me in astonishment. "You can't take that...that *thing* indoors! What if it attacks you in the night?"

"Alan," I said, my voice calmer than I actually felt, "are you trying to tell me what to do?" He opened his mouth to say yes—I literally saw the word forming on his lips—then thought better of it.

"You're the boss," he said finally. "Course you are. We're just worried about you, is all. That thing—"

"I can invite whatever and whomever I please into my own home," I said, cutting him off. "Inside, Grimm," I said to the cat. "Both of you." His oversized friend got to its feet and started padding slowly up the metal staircase. It glanced at me as it made its way nervously past, and I noticed its unusual eyes. Grimm stayed behind for a moment, presumably to make sure Alan wasn't going to try anything, then slunk off after it. "Now, if we're done out here, I think it's time everyone went home." No one moved. "Go home, Rachel," I said sharply. "And you," this was to Alan, who was looking seriously antsy and clearly fighting the urge to go all macho and attempt to take over the situation. "Bedtime for grumpy immortals. Shoo!" Alan shook his head sadly at me. Rachel skulked past me and headed up to her flat, Alan close on her heels. I was about to ask him what the fuck he thought he was doing, then remembered they were both adults and I wasn't their mum. I watched the vampire and the ghost head inside together and waited until the door was firmly closed behind them. Then I gazed up into the night sky. "What the fuck," I said to the stars twinkling above my head, "am I doing with my life?" The stars didn't bother replying.

"You took your time," said Gran, as I shut the bedroom door firmly behind me and flopped onto the bed. She was sitting in the little chair that stands next to the dressing table. It's ancient and rickety and I only own it because Mapp hadn't been able to sell it and needed the space, but couldn't bear to trash it. If I'd tried sitting on it I was pretty sure it would have collapsed, but then I guess ghosts don't weigh much.

"Do you think you'd be heavier if you got more solid?" I asked.

"What on earth are you talking about?" Gran frowned.

"You're sitting on that chair," I said.

"How very observant of you," she sniffed. So I explained the fragility vs ghost-weight thing. "I'd imagine we're always lighter than the living," Gran said. "We're not carrying the weight of the world on our shoulders, for one thing."

"That's metaphorical though," I pointed out. "It doesn't actually weigh anything."

"Tell that to the poor and downtrodden," said Gran. "I reckon they'd disagree with you well enough. Anyway, what have you been doing that's taken you so long?"

"There is a giant cat asleep in my living room," I said truthfully.

"I know there is, you silly girl," said Gran. "That ridiculous animal of Kitty's."

"Not Grimm," I said, trying to hide my irritation at her assumption that Grimm belonged to Kitty. Although to be honest, I suspected it was more that Kitty belonged to Grimm. "Another cat. A much bigger one. Human sized."

"Don't be silly," she said. "Cats don't grow that big."

"Wanna bet?" I said. "And it's got human eyes." Gran looked thoughtful for a moment. And then, to my surprise, something like a twinkle appeared in her eyes.

"Can I see it?" she asked. "You'll have to get that sister of mine out of the way, I think."

"You have to promise me you won't start another fight," I said. "I love you both, and I don't want to have to keep getting in the middle of your spats."

"And I love you both in return," said Gran, "surprising as that might seem. Not that Katherine would believe that."

"Well, she's never going to believe it if you insist on calling her Katherine," I sighed. "Promise you won't hurt the cat?"

"Lilith," Gran looked me in the eye and she was as real as she'd ever been, "I'm not a monster. I might have seemed like one on occasion, I'll grant you that. But I grew up in different times. I didn't have the same life that Kather—Kitty—had." Her gaze softened slightly. "My life was filled with injustice and trodden-down rage, and I'm afraid I perhaps took that out on other people at times. But I know a few things that maybe even you don't, not yet at least." She smiled. "So I'd like to see this cat, if that's alright with you." I'd never heard Gran speak about anything personal before. I wasn't even sure I'd ever heard her use such long sentences. There's generally no need, when you're mostly just telling people off. It took me a minute to reassemble my thoughts.

"Yes," I said eventually, "of course you can. Wait there," I got up off the bed. "I'll go prime Kitty."

"Good luck," said Gran, as I shut the door on her.

"Why's she come back?" Kitty hissed. She had been sitting in the armchair when I went back into the room, gazing at where the big cat lay asleep under a blanket on the sofa with only the top of his head visible. Grimm was curled up in the hollow of its back, facing outwards and clearly on guard. "And more to the point, why did you let her in?"

"That's enough," I said, not bothering to remind Kitty I'd yet to find a way of preventing ghosts walking into the flat if they wanted to. "This is *my* home, and I can have anyone I please in it. Including my own grandmother." For a second I thought she was going to argue, but she settled for scowling silently. "Gran just wants to see Grimm's friend, is all. Come in, Gran," I said to the bedroom door, "it's not going to get any safer."

"Why?" demanded Kitty as soon as Gran appeared. She actually used the door rather than just walking through it, which is unusual for a ghost. Clearly, being dead hadn't affected Gran's ingrained belief in good manners. "Why do you have to go sticking your stupid old beak in, Ivy? What are you planning to do with him?" She nodded towards the sleeping cat. "Have him put down for not living up to your high standards?"

"SHUT UP." The voice came out before I had chance to stop it. Not only did Kitty shut up as requested, the slumbering feline also bolted upright and immediately attempted to scrabble backwards off the sofa. Grimm stood in front of it, hissing at each of us in turn. There was so much going on that it took me a few seconds to register the cat was now noticeably more human-shaped. It was also noticeably more naked, its dark fur nowhere to be seen. Perched on the back of my sofa was a wiry-looking white man, with a shock of black hair and bright green eyes. I'd have estimated him to be in his mid-twenties at most, with the bony-but-muscled physique of someone well used to physical work. And he wasn't wearing any clothes. He realised this just as I did, and grabbed a cushion from the sofa to protect his dignity. It didn't entirely work, but at least I could look him in the eye now. "Oops," I said. "I'd apologise, but none of you deserve it. Hi," I gave the cat-man in the corner an awkward little wave. "Got a name?" He looked absolutely petrified. I found myself hoping nerves didn't affect his digestion, because right now he had his bare arse on my upholstery.

"We're all friends here," said Kitty brightly, getting up and stepping towards him. In response, he leaped off the sofa and bounced right past my ghostly aunt, settling on the chair she'd just vacated. Grimm made a sharp yowling noise, and the man's head snapped round to look at him. They locked eyes for a few seconds, before the man gave in and slumped down into the chair.

"Now, young man," said Gran, "what's happening here, then?" Kitty looked like she was about to say something snippy again, but I grabbed her arm and shook my head at her. She stayed silent, but it was begrudging. "Let's start with the basics," said Gran, in the face of Cat Man's silence. "Are you a man who turns into a cat, or a cat who turns into a man?"

"Ooh," I said, "good question! I hadn't thought of it like that before. What?" Everyone in the room—Cat Man, Grimm, Gran and Kitty—was staring at me. "Well, it *is* a bloody good question," I said sulkily.

"Could I have a towel or something?" asked the man. His voice was soft and quiet, with a faint Irish accent. "Only I'm feeling a bit exposed, here." I grabbed the blanket he'd been sleeping under and threw it across to him. "Thanks," he said, wrapping it round himself, "I thought I was after being arrested for indecency for a minute there." Gran coughed, and he turned to look at her. "Oh," he said, "sorry. I guess I'm a man who turns into a cat? At least," he looked around at us all and then back down at himself, "this is the version of me I'm most used to."

"Do you have a name?" asked Gran.

The man thought for a moment. "They call me Finn," he said eventually. "Those that know me, anyway."

"Well, Finn," said Gran, "I am very pleased to meet you." He looked relieved, but unconvinced. Gran turned to me with a smile. "I haven't seen one of these for a very long time," she said. "Finn here," she gestured towards the confused-looking young man, "is a pooka. At least, I think that's how you say it."

"What's a pooka?" asked Kitty, intrigued despite herself.

"If I remember rightly," said Gran, "pookas are a form of goblin. Clearly the handsome kind." She actually winked at him, and for a second I thought I'd once again dropped into a parallel universe. One in which my entire family was clearly even more insane than they were in this version. "Irish, I'm thinking."

"The accent's kind of a giveaway there," I said drily. "So you're telling me that, as well as a creepy cat, a ghostly aunt, and a majorly weird undead grandmother, I now also have an Irish goblin in my house?"

"A pooka," said Gran. "Like I said. They're called pookas."

"And how do you know about pookas?" I asked. Gran wouldn't have been my first option if I'd been out looking for an expert on Irish folklore. She had the bloodline, fair enough. But as far as I knew, it had been well and truly tamped down by years of practical cynicism.

"I met one once," she said, "years ago. Nice little thing he was. Ran away, though. Disappeared in the middle of the night and no one had a clue where he might have got to. I think it was because his owner wasn't interested in him anymore."

"They have owners?" I eyed the very human-looking man on the sofa. "That doesn't sound very ethical."

"Maybe owner isn't the right word," said Gran. "Guardian, maybe? Anyway, this pooka had been living in a human household after being found injured in the wild, and they all got on grand. But eventually the owner wanted to make a life of his own, and the pooka clearly wasn't invited. I think it just got upset and ran away." I felt my throat tightening with sadness for a mythological creature I'd never even met.

"Who was its owner?" I asked. If it was anyone I knew, I was going to be having sharp words with them. I just needed to sort out the current pooka situation first.

"That's the thing, Lil," said Gran. "You know him. It was your father."

~

"You're telling me that Dad—the one person in this family who insists he has no interest in spooky stuff—used to have a pet *goblin*?" I'd been pacing the kitchen for a good twenty minutes, utterly unable to get my head around what Gran had told me. Finn-the-pooka had been reassured no one was going to dump him in the Mersey and was persuaded to put on an old pair of shorts and a Bob Marley t-shirt I'd found at the back of my wardrobe. He'd then gone back to sleep on the sofa, with Grimm sitting guard by his side. I had no idea what I was supposed to do with him in the long-term, but that was the least of my concerns right now.

"They're not really goblins," said Gran. "At least, not in the way you're thinking. More like shapeshifters, I'd say." She was looking remarkably calm for a woman who'd spent her entire life dismissing anything out of the ordinary, only to find herself reappearing in Liverpool years after her death, in the company of her dead sister, her undead granddaughter and an overgrown bloody were-cat. "Mischievous little beggars, generally. Your Finn," she nodded towards the living room, "is one of the better behaved." She sniffed. "Which is how it should be."

"He's not *my* Finn," I said. "He's nobody's anything, and he is going to have to find somewhere else to stay pretty sharpish." I looked around my flat, which now contained at least three more paranormal creatures than I am strictly happy to share my space with.

"That'll be easier said than done," said Gran, "if my memory's correct. And it usually is, even now I'm dead and gone."

"Not gone enough," muttered Kitty from where she stood in the corner of the kitchen. Gran just rolled her eyes.

"What do you mean, easier said than done?" I asked, a sneaking suspicion already crawling its way up my spine.

"Oh, he'll think he belongs to you, now," said Gran airily. "You protected him, see. And I can't imagine that cat of yours is going to take kindly to you evicting him."

"It's not up to Grimm who gets to stay here," I said. Both Gran and Kitty gave me pitying looks, which I chose to ignore. "Anyway, back to Dad. How do you know about his..." I thought carefully about the words I was about to utter, not sure it made sense even now, "pet pooka?"

"Small world," said Gran, "isn't it? I knew his family, way before he started courting your mother." The way she said 'courting' made it sound grubby, somehow. But then Gran used to turn the tv channel over if anyone on the soaps so much as kissed, tutting as she did so. "There'd always been talk. He came from a strange family, your dad."

"What do you mean, strange?" I asked. "Stranger than ours?"

"Well, we didn't know how strange our side was back then," said Gran, "did we? And your dad's lot, well—they weren't strange like we are now, I don't think. Just...old fashioned. Most people know the superstition about not doing any laundry on New Year's Day," I shrugged, it being a new one on me, "but Geoff's mum wouldn't even hang it out overnight, whatever the time of year. It'd go out at first light and be back indoors by dusk, dry or not. Said it was asking for trouble, leaving it out."

"What sort of trouble?"

"I asked her that myself," said Gran. "Overheard her telling a woman from one of the new houses that she needed to get her sheets in off the line. Still dripping, they were. The poor girl just sort of mumbled and shot back into the house quick as possible, but Irene stood there for ages, looking at the sheets and clearly fretting. I went over to her in the end, all jolly and normal," I couldn't imagine anyone less outwardly jolly than Gran when she'd been alive, but didn't say anything, "and asked her what was up. 'Ooh,' she said, 'there'll be sprites into everything if she leaves those out.' Anyway, I chivvied her along with talk of the new bus services they were bringing in, and she didn't mention it again." Gran paused, a faraway look in her eyes. "Of course," she went on, "the woman with the sheets had terrible luck, after that. Husband left her and all sorts."

"I reckon it's more likely he left because they just didn't get on anymore," I said, "not because she left the sheets out overnight. Can we get onto the stuff about Dad now, please?"

"I already told you, Lil," said Gran. "They were a strange family. He told your mum they'd had a pet cat when he was a young lad. A black tomcat called Lorcan. She mentioned it to me one day, when they'd not long started going out. I remembered that cat myself, though. It was huge—big as your Finn, there. And they had a lad who'd be staying at the house sometimes, but suddenly he'd be away a while and no one ever mentioned it. I asked Irene about him one day. Just casual, like. 'How's that handsome big cat of yours, Irene?' I said. I was quite envious, you know—we had no end of trouble with rats and mice eating the veggies out in the garden, but Irene and Paddy never had any problem and I'd always assumed it was cos of the cat. Anyway, Irene decided to confide in me," Gran puffed up proudly, "and said she'd tell me a secret, but I wasn't to tell another living soul about it."

"And?" I'd stopped pacing for fear of wearing out the lino. And also, because the constant back and forth was making me feel sick. "What was the secret?"

"Lorcan was a pooka," said Gran, as though it was the most obvious thing in the world. "I asked what a pooka was when it was at home, and Irene said he was a sprite himself, but a good one. Looked out for Geoff and the other kids. Kept the rats down as well."

"And you believed her?"

"Of course I didn't," snorted Gran. "What a ridiculous story. But then I had to call round their house a week or so later, just to drop off the local community newsletter." Gran was always one of those people who was professionally interested in her neighbours, and probably drove them mad as a result. "I was just walking up their garden path when I heard a noise over in their orchard. I thought maybe the local kids were scrumping, and that wouldn't do. So I went over to check."

"To be a nosy old witch, more like," said Kitty from the corner.

"I went to check," repeated Gran, "and suddenly this enormous...*thing* dropped out of the tree in front of me. I frightened it as much as it frightened me, I can tell you that for nothing. Just stood there I did, staring at this enormous black cat. Bigger than any dog I'd ever seen, that's for sure. Then it ran off into the bushes and I went back to doing my rounds and never questioned Irene's pooka ever again."

"Didn't you tell anyone about it?" I asked. I couldn't imagine Gran being able to keep something like that quiet. She'd have been over at the local council demanding they get the animal warden out right this minute.

"No I did not," said Gran. "Promised, didn't I? And I'd known it was Lorcan, soon as I saw the face. I'd recognise those eyes anywhere."

"You're telling us now," said Kitty. "So much for keeping secrets."

"Well, none of you are living," said Gran, "are you? So I've stuck to my side of the bargain, thank you very much. Where are you off to, Lil?" I'd grabbed my bag and was hunting in the kitchen drawer for Basil's keys.

"I'm off for a long overdue chat with my father," I said. "You two are to be on your best behaviour, you hear? And keep an eye on that bloody were-cat."

A Boy And His Cat

"Whoa, love," said Dad. He looked shaken, as well he might. "What do you mean, 'why didn't I tell you'?" By the time I'd calmed down enough to think straight, I was already on the motorway and heading towards Chester. And by the time I got to Wrexham I was regretting having taken Basil and wishing I'd asked Eadric for a loan of his lovely fast Alfa. But that would have meant explaining my reason for an emergency visit to the 'shire, and I wasn't ready for that. So I settled into Basil's mid-speed chugging and concentrated on getting my thoughts in order. Dad had always dismissed anything remotely paranormal, to the point of walking out of the room if Mum was watching *Most Haunted*. Mum's interest had been explained by the discovery she'd been seeing ghosts all her life, even if it only happened occasionally. And I'd put Dad's dislike of it all down to being suspicious of anything that wasn't explainable by science. His own favourite programme was *The Sky At Night*—he said it was because planets were solid and real, and put things into perspective. But now I was having to consider the possibility that his nervousness around the more creeptastic side of life was actually down to him being as spooky as the rest of us and just not wanting to let on.

"Why didn't you tell anyone about the pooka?" I repeated. Mum was staring at me in astonishment. I'd been too wound up to explain anything to her in advance and had settled for sending a brief text as I started the car, telling her I was on my way and that Dad wasn't allowed to leave the house before I got there. She'd tried ringing me back as I came out of the Kingsway tunnel onto the Wirral side, but I'd ignored the call—and not just because it's bloody difficult to keep a VW Beetle straight whilst also fiddling with its stupid speakers. When I finally got to their house, she'd clearly heard the car's engine and was waiting on the doorstep, only to step back against the wall in astonishment when I'd walked straight past her to find Dad sitting at the kitchen table.

"What do you mean?" said Dad, but he was looking shifty.

"What's going on?" asked Mum. "This isn't like you, Lil."

"He," I pointed at Dad, "knows more than he's letting on. He's been having everyone for a total fool for years."

"That's a bit harsh, love," said Dad, not quite meeting my gaze.

"Are you okay, Lil?" said Mum. "Shall I give Isobel a quick ring?"

"I am absolutely fine, Mum," I said, "apart from being bloody dead." Her eyes widened in shock, and she whipped round to look at Dad, presumably expecting immediate intense drama. What she actually got was Dad giving a big sigh and shrugging.

"Aah well," he said. "Probably better to have it all out in the open, anyway."

"You knew?" Mum was staring at him incredulously. "All this time," she nodded towards me, "you knew?"

"Yep," said Dad, sitting back in his chair. "Knew the minute she walked through the door that time."

"You knew I was dead," I said, "and it didn't occur to you to say anything? What the *fuck*, Dad?"

"Oi," said Dad, "we'll have less of that language, thank you."

"I don't think you're in a position to tell anyone what to do right now, Geoff." Mum took a step forward, but changed her mind and stopped. "You're telling me you knew that our daughter—our *daughter*, Geoff—was dead, but you didn't think to say anything?"

"What was I supposed to do," said Dad indignantly, "just accept it? Stand there in front of my daughter who was clearly dead but still walking around and say what? 'Hi Lil, hope death isn't proving too complicated'?"

"Well I just asked her straight out," said Mum. "Maybe you could have tried that."

"But you didn't mention it to me, Helen," said Dad. "Did you?" Mum stayed silent. "Why was that, then?"

It didn't take her long to rally. "Because you'd dismissed my ghosts and whatnot as 'that silly witchy stuff' for years, Geoff," she said. "And I know you never meant it nastily, but it hurt. It *hurt*, Geoff! I could see people who shouldn't be there, and they were as real to me as the nose on my bloody face, but all you could do was mock. So no," she went on, "I wasn't inclined to tell you Lil's secrets. For bloody good reason." They both looked on the verge of angry tears, which was unsettling. Seeing your parents' getting upset is up there with accidentally calling your teacher 'mum' on the list of Most Uncomfortable Situations Ever.

"Shall I put the kettle on?" They both turned to look at me blankly, as though they'd forgotten I was even in the room. "Let's all sit down with a cuppa," I ploughed on, "and talk this through." For once, Mum actually did as she was told, taking the seat opposite Dad. From there she just stared silently at him, while he looked increasingly uncomfortable. I made as much fuss and noise as possible as I filled the kettle and got mugs and teabags out of the cupboard. Anything to fill the awkward silence. "Here we go," I said finally, passing each of them a mug and putting my own down on the table. I took the seat at the end, not wanting to look like I was siding with either of them. "So," I started, "anyone else think it's about time we had a family confession session?"

"Quite the snappy title," said Dad, with the ghost of a wink.

"It isn't funny, Geoff," snapped Mum. I'd never seen her properly angry with Dad before, and I didn't like it. "Do you have any idea how much I'd have appreciated a bit of support over the last few months? Can you imagine how difficult it's been for me to cope with knowing Lil's dead, let alone not being able to talk to anyone about it?"

"Can you imagine," said Dad quietly, "how difficult it's been for me? Knowing she's dead, but not being able to talk to you about it?" I could see tears pricking at the corners of his eyes and felt absolutely fucking awful. Maybe it would have been better to get him on his own.

But I'd jumped in feet first as usual, and now the whole thing was turning into a horrible drama. "I'd kept my family's secrets all my life, Helen," he went on, twisting a teaspoon between his fingers. "If I'd let on I knew what was going on, you'd realise I'd been lying to you all this time." The spoon dropped with a clatter onto the table. "And I couldn't bear the thought of that. So I took the coward's way out and just pretended none of it was happening."

"What," said Mum slowly, "is a pooka?" So I told her about Finn, who was presumably still snoring on my sofa back at the flat. And about Gran surprising the pooka in Dad's family's orchard, and how Irene had made her promise not to tell anyone.

"Please don't tell me your mother's back," said Dad wearily.

"Don't you start on my mother," snapped Mum. "She's the least of our bloody worries right now, Geoff."

"Actually," I interrupted, "she's mostly Kitty's worry."

"Your Kitty's never reappeared?" Dad looked at Mum in astonishment. "After all this time?"

"She was with me when I visited," I told him. "That first time after I'd died."

"Can I ask what happened?" said Dad. "To you, I mean. It wasn't," he hesitated, "anything awful?"

"I'm not sure there's much that's more awful than actually dying, Dad," I said. "But no, it was nothing more traumatic than me falling off the stairs outside my flat." The details could wait til later, I decided. Dad looked relieved.

"Well, that's something," he said. "I've had all kinds of horrible theories going through my mind, ever since I realised."

"And yet I didn't have a clue," said Mum. "How long have we been together, Geoff?"

"Fucking decades, Helen," he said, smiling slightly at her shock. "But never long enough." She subsided slightly. "For what it's worth," he went on, "I did it for your sake. Ignoring Lil being dead, I mean. I had no idea whether or not you'd realised, but honestly thought you'd have said something if you'd had an inkling anything was wrong. And I was worried it might set you off, you know?" He looked helplessly from Mum to me, then back again. "After Cally..." he trailed off.

"So you thought it was better to pretend you hadn't noticed and at least you'd still have one child around," I said. Dad nodded. "Hang on," something occurred to me, "you didn't see Kitty? When I came here, and Mum realised what had happened?"

He shook his head. "Nope," he said, "never noticed a thing. Although that's not really surprising, given the shock I'd had seeing you come through the door looking absolutely normal but clearly dead."

"How do I look 'clearly dead'?" I asked. "No one else ever seems to notice anything."

"Got the family sight, haven't I," said Dad with an apologetic shrug. "But I've never seen ghosts. So, like the fool I am, I assumed no one else saw them either, and those who said they did were kidding themselves. I'm sorry, Helen," he slid a hand across the table towards Mum, "I should have told you. I was scared."

Mum looked at his hand, but didn't take it. "What were you scared of?" she asked. "My abilities, or your own?"

"Neither," said Dad. "I was scared because I'd spent years hiding my family's weirdness from people. And especially from you, because what you thought of me mattered. It really mattered, Helen." He looked at her almost pleadingly. "I loved you and I wanted to be with you forever, but you were from a polite, upstanding family and I was from—well," he gave a quiet little laugh, "I was from what sometimes felt like a group of absolute lunatics. I loved them and I definitely wasn't ashamed of them," he looked at both of us in turn, a determined expression on his face, "but they perhaps weren't quite right. Not for a lovely girl like you."

Mum finally relented, her hand reaching across to hold his. "I wouldn't have minded," she said softly. "I'd have liked to have met your, what was it?" She looked at me. "Puck?"

"Pooka," I said. "Lorcan was Dad's pet. Wasn't he?" I raised an eyebrow at my father.

"Yes," he said, "Although it was more that Lorcan had decided I was his to protect. Big bastard, so he was." He grinned. "Bloody hell Lil, but that cat was huge."

"Hang on," said Mum, "it was a cat? Why all this drama over bloody cats?"

"Oh," said Dad, "Lorcan wasn't your average cat. As Lil clearly already knows." I raised an eyebrow. "He spent some of his time as a cat, sure. But other times he was a kid. Bit older than me, mind. But we had fun together. And he looked out for me. No bully ever came back for a second go after Lorcan had given them a visit."

"Were-cats, Mum." She looked at me. "Were-cats," I repeated. "Bloody great big shape-shifting cats, size of your average adult human."

"Not all of them are that big," Dad interrupted, "some are smaller. Those don't usually survive very long, though."

"Why?" asked Mum. "I'd have thought a massive cat would be pretty good at defending itself. Giant claws and teeth must be pretty savage."

"Teeth and claws aren't much defence against guns," said Dad. "Any pooka foolish enough to get too close to humanity usually ends up being shot by a panicked farmer. Or if it's a member of the public who's spotted it, the government send someone official over to dart it with tranquilliser and take it off for tests."

"What sort of tests?" I asked. "And how do you know?"

"The sort of tests," said Dad, "that people—cats—don't come back from. That's how I know. The sort that involves science labs and scalpels, I reckon."

"But that's unethical," I said, "surely?" I didn't have much experience with dangerous wild animals—unless you include the less civilised members of Joe Williamson's underground gang of spooktastic weirdos —but I was pretty sure the vast majority were considered protected species. Dad gave me a strange look when I said so.

"They're only protected if people know they're around and need protecting," he said. "Given that the government refuses to so much as acknowledge their existence, I'm not convinced they're going to stick to international welfare standards when they do get hold of one."

"What happened to Lorcan?" I asked. "Gran said he ran away."

"Aah then," Dad looked uncomfortable, "I think it might have been my fault."

"Yeah, she said that as well."

"Of course she did," he sighed. "She's right, though. I told him to go away, but he didn't want to. And I needed him gone, so I told him I didn't like him anymore. Didn't want him interfering with my human life, sort of thing. I shouldn't have done it." His voice was quiet.

"Why did you want him to leave?" I asked. Dad sighed, and took Mum's hand again.

"I'd met your mum by then," he said, "and knew I was going to ask her to marry me." His thumb absently rubbed against Mum's wedding ring as he spoke. "As I said before," he went on, "I thought it was just my own family who were a bit odd. I certainly couldn't imagine telling your Mum here that we'd be needing to buy a house with a bit of extra space for my enormous, shape-shifting cat. That sort of talk gets you nothing more than psychiatric appointments and prescription for controlled medications."

"You sent him away because of me?" Mum had tears in her eyes. "Oh, bloody hell, Geoff," she said, "you needn't have done that. I'd have married you even if you'd had an entire wildlife park needing space in the back garden."

"Aye, well it's too late to think about the whys and wherefores now," said Dad. "Lorcan ran off, and knowing the speed that lad could move I reckon he'd have been three counties away by morning. It was a long time ago, Helen," he went on. "I'd imagine he's dead by now."

"What makes you think that?" I asked.

"Because he's never come back," said Dad sadly. "I took him for granted, Lil. I'd been told there was an unbreakable bond between a pooka and its human, so I guess I thought I could send him away, but he'd eventually reappear. Like those dogs you see in movies, you know?" He looked at both of us in turn. "The family moved two hundred miles away and the dog escapes and makes for its original home, sort of thing. But I overestimated my own importance," he went on. "Didn't realise that by sending him away like that, I was breaking Lorcan's trust—and our bond—completely. He'll never come back."

"Promise you won't hide anything like this again," I said to Dad as I opened Basil's driver's door and dumped my bag and sweater inside. Mum stood next to him, a look of floundering comprehension still on her face. I suspected there was going to be a lot of talking and tears in my family home for a while. But as I caught her eye to give her a reassuring smile, Mum caught hold of Dad's hand and held it. His expression didn't change, but relief was clear in his eyes.

"I promise," said Dad. "Anyway," he smiled weakly, "there's not many families who can say they're not worried about their daughter walking the streets alone at night."

"Oh," I said, "there's still danger on the streets of Liverpool. It's just that these days, the danger is mostly me."

I pulled Basil into the car park next to Flora's and turned off the radio. I'd fully expected the music to be replaced by the sounds of unholy screaming and shouting from the flats above, but was met by nothing more than the mumbling background noise of a city at night. Getting out of the car, I looked across to where Billy was sitting in his usual place. "No one's dead," he said, nodding up towards my living room window. "Or at least, no one who wasn't dead already."

"It's a start," I grinned, walking over to him. "How's tricks?" I sat down next to him on the pavement, putting off the moment I'd have to go back inside and face my dysfunctional family. He turned to look at me, a look of amusement on his face. His eyes were creased and twinkling, and his ruffled hair looked styled, rather than messy. Billy's learned from Kitty how to change his appearance and these days looks more like an edgy pavement artist instead of the rough sleeper he actually is. Or rather, the *ghost* of a rough sleeper. As solid as he might seem, it's all an illusion. Billy's no more real than Kitty, and can appear and disappear just like she does. I actually find it really disconcerting, but who am I to spoil their fun?

"Better for seeing you," Billy said. "You're the only sane one around here, I'm thinking."

"Christ, you must have a very low bar for what counts as sane," I said. "I spend most of my time struggling not to lose my unholy shit with people."

"How was your trip to the old town?" he asked.

"You heard about that, then?" He nodded. Billy might be long dead, but he's always got one ear to the local grapevine. Considering how much the vampires like a good gossip, it would probably be more surprising if Billy hadn't known about my recent adventures. I'd only recently had to have sharp words with Aiden about why it wouldn't be a good idea for two of the younger members of his clan to take the regular spot they'd been offered by *Liverpool Live* radio. He'd argued their case, saying it would do them good to integrate and anyway it was only a late-night music show that hardly anyone would even listen to. I'd countered with my conviction that it would only be a couple of weeks before their between-songs banter turned into chat about the best ways into the secret parts of the Williamson Tunnels and why they thought they ought to be allowed to hold parties in the unused bits of the Western Approaches military bunker. I sighed. "I've got to get the city under control," I said eventually.

"I'm not sure this city will ever allow anyone to control it," said Billy.

"Exactly." I leaned my head back against the wall and stared up at the night sky, arms folded defensively around myself. "I want what's best for it, which is something. But that doesn't mean it believes me. And it certainly doesn't mean it'll listen to me."

"I think," said Billy slowly, "this city is more like a wild horse." I turned to look at him curiously. "It's going to go its own way whatever happens," he went on, "but if you're confident enough to ride out the bucking, it'll probably head in the direction you're after. Eventually."

"I never had you down as the horsey type," I said.

Billy grinned. "Lots of horses round my way when I was a kid," he said. "Learned to get on them when I was still a wee baby, and by the time I was five or six I could be reasonably sure I wouldn't get thrown straight back off. Been run away with enough times to know how to deal with it," he went on. "No point tugging on the bridle, however strong you are. Once a horse has a mind to run, a bit of metal in its mouth isn't going to stop it, however much it hurts. Better to crouch low and see it through. Point the beast in the safest direction you can find and just let it run. Sooner or later, it'll get tired and start slowing down, which is when you quietly take control again. Give it a wee tug on one rein," Billy mimed twitching his fingers delicately, for all the world as though he was riding a high-class dressage horse, "and it'll start turning in a circle. Before you know it, you're back home safe and everyone thinks you're braver than a bloke wearing a red shirt to a bullfight."

"You think I should just let it run?"

"Gods no," Billy laughed. "That'd be a recipe for disaster in anyone's book. I'm thinking more that you should maybe learn to hang on and guide it in the right direction." I was about to say something about how I wasn't convinced I'd bounce if I fell off a city racing at full gallop, when Gran appeared in front of us.

"Fucking hell Gran," I spluttered, "can you not warn me before you pull that trick?"

"You need to wash that mouth of yours out with carbolic, young lady," said Gran, without malice. "Good evening, William," she nodded at Billy, "I hope you're well?"

"I, erm..." Billy mumbled, lost for words. "M'okay, thanks for asking."

"Good, good," said Gran, "glad to see it. Now, Lilith," she turned to me, "I need to be off."

"Kitty hasn't been rude again, has she?" I got to my feet. "I'll go tell her to pack it in. Come back inside, Gran, it'll be fine."

Gran smiled at me. "I know when I'm getting in the way," she said. "And Katherine's right—this is her life now, not mine. For what it's worth," she nodded down to where Billy still sat against the wall, blinking up at her like a rabbit in headlights, "I like the company you keep. Mostly." She scrunched her face in a brief expression of distaste, but I had no idea who she was referring to. "Anyway, I've got things to do. You're not the only O'Reilly who needs visiting, you know."

"Who else is there?" I asked.

"I remember there being talk of a cousin over on the Wirral," she said, "back in the fifties. She fell off a cliff into the sea and everyone assumed she was lost. But the milkman called a few days later thinking to pick up the bottles that had been left on the doorstep all week, and she came out to ask him why he'd stopped delivering. Nearly gave the poor chap heart failure, so she did."

"Whoa," I said, "you mean we've got more undead relatives?"

Gran caught hold of my hand. Her own hand felt solid, but tingled in the same way Kitty's used to, before she became more or less solid. "I reckon most people have them," she said, "it's just that they can't see them. Whereas we," she squeezed my arm gently, "can see *everything*. I'd been thinking it was a curse," she went on, "but now I'm wondering if it's not a blessing after all."

"It's been nice to see you," I said weakly. "Don't leave it so long next time."

"There won't be a next time," said Gran flatly, "if you don't sort this city out. It's the living you want to be watching out for, Lilith. Not the dead. Anyway," she squeezed my hand surprisingly hard, "I must be off." With that, she disappeared into thin air. I looked down to where Billy was sitting with a confused expression on his face.

"William?" I gave him a quizzical look. "Seriously?"

"Never met her before in my life," said Billy. "On my honour."

"Hmmm," I said. I felt something in my hand, and opened it to reveal a ring that had definitely not been there before. It was made up of a thin band of gold, with four purple stones set in a row. I knew they were amethysts and that the ring itself was very old, because I'd first seen this ring when I was very young. I could still remember sitting at the table in Gran's kitchen and noticing the glint of the ring as she ladled porridge out into bowls for me and Cally. Cally liked porridge because he was still young enough to be in a highchair and he could throw spoonfuls of sticky oats right across the table if he put enough effort in. We rarely stayed with our grandparents, mostly because Gran definitely did not appreciate small children throwing porridge in her kitchen. I thought Mum and Dad might have been away at a friend's wedding, but it was a long time ago and the memories were foggy. Which was weird in itself, because my undead brain was pretty good at memories, even if the worst of them had been locked away for safekeeping. In fact, when I came to think about it, I didn't have clear memories of anything to do with Gran, at least not from back when I was alive. But I remembered the ring. It had seemed an unlikely choice of jewellery for a woman who considered wearing eyeliner second only to red shoes on her list of things that marked the wearer out as a wrong 'un. She didn't even wear the gold band from her wedding to Grandad, leaving it in a little ceramic dish on the dresser in her bedroom. I'd once asked why she didn't wear it, and she'd said she didn't need gold to make her feel married, and anyway it got soap stuck behind it when she washed her hands. Gran always used coal tar soap, and for years the smell would make me think of her washing her hands in that little kitchen. The amethyst ring was anything but plain and must have collected soap and grime much more easily than a wedding band would, yet I never saw her without it. And now I was gazing down at it, the stones glinting dully back up at me, colourless under the streetlights.

You might as well put it on, said the city in my head. *We have clearly reached the 'magical amulet' stage of this particular fairytale*.

There's nothing magic about it, I said, twisting the ring around to look inside. *It's got a standard hallmark inside it*.

Anything can be magical if circumstances are right, it replied. *Rings, crowns...even you*.

This is not a fairytale, I told it firmly. *This is twenty-first century Liverpool. Some people need to start remembering that*.

Says the dead girl with the were-cat sleeping on her sofa.

Billy loudly cleared his throat. "I don't like to interrupt," he said, "but is there any meaning behind that thing?" He nodded at the ring in my hand.

"Nope," I said honestly, "not that I know of." Without thinking, I went to put the ring on the ring finger of my right hand, but stopped before it was actually on.

"Maybe it's just supposed to be a memento," said Billy. "In case she never visits again." His voice sounded hopeful.

"Yeah, you're probably right," I said. "And I'd hate to lose it." I pushed the ring down over my knuckle and ignored the feeling of static that ran through my hand and up my back. I gave myself a literal shake and turned to Billy. "Well," I said, "I haven't turned into a pumpkin so far. Now I need to go sort out a litter tray for my new tenant." With that, I turned and headed up the stairs, leaving Billy staring after me.

❧

I was pulling blankets for Finn out of the storage crate under my bed when my phone pinged. Picking it up, I read the message. *You know where I am if you need back-up x*

Scowling, I sat on the bed to compose my response. *'That's very kind of you'*, I typed, *'but I don't need back-up from someone who'd just as quickly stab me in said back.'*

Absolutely not, came the immediate reply. *I'd just stab you in the front if I needed to. There's no hidden motives with me, Red. Not like the others.*

I sighed, and thought for a minute before typing. I pressed send on *'Fuck off, Ivo x'* and shoved the phone safely underneath my pillow. And then I went back to making up a bed for a giant cat.

ALL ABOUT EVE

"So anyway, I'm going to need lessons in the care and feeding of giant bloody cats, if either of you fancy helping a girl out." I was halfway into Eadric's office and already talking before I realised he had company. Two women were seated opposite him at his desk. The one nearest to me was white and older than me, with expensively tinted ash blonde hair. She was wearing a neatly tailored grey skirt suit and sensible black mid-heeled shoes. The woman on the other side of blondie was dark-skinned and impossible to put an age to. She had closely cropped black hair, eyes that tilted up slightly at the outer corners, and the sort of angular features that put me in mind of an Egyptian cat. Her green trouser suit was topped with a purple jacket worthy of Mapp's fashionable envy, and her crossed legs showed off a pair of silver ankle boots. The women were the most unlikely pairing this side of Cher and Tom Cruise, and I was immediately suspicious.

"Lilith," said Eadric politely, getting up from his seat, "this is Donna," he indicated the blonde, "and Eve." They both nodded. "You haven't met yet." Donna held her hand out for me to shake, but didn't get up.

"Donna Karnstein," she said. "And no, we haven't met." She had that generically polite accent that implied she probably grew up in the

Midlands, but went to work in London years ago and put all that northern nonsense behind her. I begrudgingly leaned forward to shake her hand.

"Lilith O'Reilly," I said. "Should I be pleased to meet you?" Donna laughed. I was pretty sure she was aiming for a friendly, all-girls-together tinkle, but it sounded pretty fake to me.

"I know who you are, Lilith," she said. Never a good start. "Whether you will be pleased to meet me depends on what happens in the future."

I frowned at Eadric. Clearly he knew something I didn't, and that always sets me on edge. "Donna's from London," he said. "Civil service. Isn't that right, Donna?"

"You could call it that," she said. There was a faint smile on her face that I didn't like one tiny bit.

"Which department?" I asked.

Donna swivelled her chair to look directly at me. "I'm with the Department of Miscellaneous Affairs," she said. "You won't have heard of us."

"Uh huh," I replied, not giving her the satisfaction of asking. "Do you need me for anything?" I asked Eadric. "Only I've got a cafe to run."

"I heard you mostly leave that to your friend these days," said Donna. "Isobel Jones, isn't it?"

"How do you know that?" I asked.

"We know a lot of things, Lilith," said Donna. "Your mother Helen has just started a part-time PhD and your father took early retirement a couple of years ago. I'm sorry to hear about your brother. You live on Harrington Street with your cat, and your great-aunt is your," she coughed slightly, "lodger."

"I don't know who you really are," I said sharply, "but my family are nothing to do with you. And my brother died a very long time ago, so your platitudes are a bit late. Wait," I'd belatedly caught up with what she'd said, "you said my aunt lives with me?"

"Your great-aunt," Donna corrected. "Katherine O'Reilly, late of this parish, etc etc. Have I got that right?"

"Donna knows about us," Eadric interrupted before I could reply. "She's always known about us."

"Well," said Donna, "I personally have only known about you for the past five years or so. But the department has been aware of your existence for a long time. A *very* long time."

"Are you trying to sound intimidating?" I asked her. "Because it isn't going to work. And why," I turned to Eadric, "haven't you told me about this already?"

"I didn't think it mattered," said Eadric. "Not just yet, anyway."

"But then you, aah, brought yourself to our attention," said Donna. "And of course, we have a duty to investigate such things."

"What duty?" I demanded. "And what things?"

"It's fine," Eadric tried and failed to sound soothing, "Donna's department has made occasional visits since they were first established. You just haven't been around long enough to meet them."

"Newcomers are...rare," said Donna. "We like to establish the facts before we allow you to carry on."

"'Allow'?" I asked. "What's that supposed to mean?"

"Lilith," said Eadric in a warning tone, "this is neither the time nor the place. Donna isn't here to threaten you. Are you, Donna?"

"Of course not," said Donna with a smile. Liar. "We're just checking in, nothing more. My job is to ensure the safe coexistence of humanity with—" I could *hear* her struggling not to say, 'you people', "—with your kind." Which didn't sound any better.

"Was it that idiot Mansoor who told you about me?" I asked. If it was, I'd be down Castle Street and glaring through that pharmacy window every opportunity I got.

"Who?" asked Donna. She was either very good at blank expressions, or she really didn't know.

"Doesn't matter," I said. "Okay so you're here, you've checked in and as you can see, everything's just fine and dandy. Don't let me keep you." I stepped backwards slightly to indicate that the door was open for Donna's departure; she just needed to make her exit.

"It's not that simple," she said, not moving from her seat.

"I thought that might be the case," I sighed. Faint noises from the next room suggested that Nik was determinedly staying out of the way, and I couldn't blame him. I'd rather not be stuck in a room with this cow, either.

"Why don't you sit down, and we can chat."

"Why don't you chat, and I'll stand?" We gazed at each other for a few long seconds, neither willing to give an inch. In the end Eadric made a show of getting up with a loud cough, and fetched a chair from the other side of the room.

"Here," he said, putting the chair down next to me. "Just sit for a minute and we'll clear the air." I narrowed my eyes at him, but for once in my life decided that discretion probably was the better part of valour. Thank god I hadn't gone into detail about my newest furry lodger as I walked in. Somehow, I didn't think Donna would be very impressed. "I hadn't mentioned the department before," Eadric said to me, "because as I said, we rarely have direct contact." He sat back down at his desk and looked over to where I was scuffing my sneakers on his polished wooden floor. He was definitely fighting the urge to ask me to stop. I held his gaze and kept scuffing. "Donna is merely here to check that everything's okay. There's nothing to worry about."

"Who said I was worried?" I asked. "I haven't done anything illegal and neither have you. Have you?" I shot him a look.

"No," he sighed, "I haven't done anything illegal. But we have an... agreement," he went on, "with London. We don't give them anything to worry about, and in return, they leave us alone."

"So, why is she here?" I jerked my head at Donna, who was looking way too smug for my liking. Eve, on the other hand, appeared to be struggling to keep a straight face.

"Because you've given us things to worry about," said Donna.

"Like what?" I was indignant at both her interference and her general tone. I didn't know this woman from sodding Adam, yet suddenly I had to be careful not to upset her with my mere existence.

"Like your mere existence," she said, as though reading my mind. I shot her a poisonous look, but she seemed impervious. *Smarmy, stuck-up cow*, I thought to myself.

She thinks she's in charge, said the city. **You're going to be told off and made to feel small and she'll go back to London feeling thoroughly pleased with herself.**

Well, fuck that shit, I replied silently. *We're not having this.*

This is why we like you, Lilith—you think like us. But don't rise to the bait. She's just trying to annoy you.

Why?

To see what you're really made of. She's not sure the stories are really true, but she wants to get a result, nevertheless. She's ambitious.

What result is she after?

We suspect she merely wants to prove she has power, it said. **She's possibly trying to prove it to herself, as much as anyone else.**

I stayed silent for a little while longer, refusing to ask Donna what she'd meant by her comment. Amazingly, Eadric did nothing. I'd expected him to make small talk in order to break the awkward silence, but he merely sat quietly, his eyes flicking from one of us to the other and back again. I could have sworn he was suppressing a smile. Just as Donna looked discomforted enough to think about speaking, I beat her to it. "Can I ask what your role is in all this?" I asked Eve, who grinned at me as though she'd been waiting for this moment.

"I'm here as Donna's mentor," she said. "I've been around longer and am better acquainted with the...*unusual* side of life, shall we say." She nodded towards Donna, who clearly didn't like the suggestion she wasn't in charge and had a poisonous look in her eyes. "Of course," she went on, "Donna is far more specialised than I." Donna simmered down a fraction. "She works only for this department, whereas I bear responsibility for overseeing several areas of the government's more," Eve fished for the right word, "esoteric portfolio." Looking into her calm hazel eyes, I noticed a silver glint to them. I wondered just how old Eve really was.

"Perhaps one of you would like to explain to me just what the current situation is," I said, "and how it relates to me. If at all." Eve nodded to Donna, indicating she'd leave it to her.

"As you know," said Donna, her narrow eyes not leaving mine, "there are certain elements within society of which the general public are not aware. Our job is to ensure that these," she hesitated, "*elements* do not impinge on normal life."

"Uh huh," I tilted my head and held her gaze, "you've already made that clear. So, what do you want from me?"

"A guarantee that this city will not misbehave," said Donna, and looked genuinely shocked when I started laughing. Eve just sat quietly behind her, an amused smile on her face.

"You want me to promise that Liverpool will behave itself? *Liverpool?*" I snorted in amusement. "The fact you even think it's possible to tell this city what to do just shows how little you know, Donna. When's the last time you came here?" Donna hesitated.

"This is Donna's first visit," said Eve smoothly, "but I'm sure it won't be her last. She'll love the place once she gets used to it." She gave me the ghost of a wink. I decided I liked Eve.

"I haven't had reason to visit until now," said Donna, clearly determined to reassert her authority. "But we can no longer ignore the potential risks to the wider population."

"What risks?" I asked. Donna looked blank. "Tell me the specific risks this city creates, Donna. Just one will do." I sat back in my chair and gazed at her levelly. "I've got all the time in the world, believe me."

"We cannot be sure that you are not a danger to others," said Donna, recovering herself. "Some believe we should require you to undergo assessment in order to confirm your abilities." My blood ran cold. Or at least it would have, if it moved fast enough.

"And what sort of assessment would that be?" I asked carefully. "The kind where you keep people locked up and run tests on them?" Donna's eyes flickered, and I knew I'd hit a nerve. Eve was carefully expressionless next to her. "Because I don't think that's a good idea."

"That's not what Donna means," said Eadric hurriedly. "No one from the department means to harm you, Lilith. Or anyone else."

"Well, that's good to hear," I said, not taking my eyes off Donna. "It wouldn't do for a government to threaten its own people, now would it?"

"No one gets threatened at all if they're not a risk," said Donna defiantly. "It's our job to make sure of that."

"And it's my job to make sure you don't harm any of *my* people," I said.

"Your people?" said Donna. "We were under the impression that Mr Silverton had overall responsibility for this area." I looked at Eadric, who was desperately trying to convey the danger of putting myself in the firing line via the medium of panicked eyebrow twitches.

"We both are," I said firmly. "Everyone needs a rising star as backup, don't you think?" I looked at the two women. "And I'm sure Eve's very pleased with you so far."

By now, Eve was visibly struggling not to laugh. She took a deep breath and looked at me. "I have no concerns about local management at this time, Lilith," she said. "This is merely a courtesy visit. We'd been advised there was what you might call," she coughed politely, "a new kid in town, and thought it prudent to introduce ourselves. I'm sure you and Donna will get along just fine." From the scowl on Donna's face, I suspected the feeling wasn't shared across the entire department. I got to my feet.

"Has Eadric ever shown you the view from up here?" I asked Donna. She looked confused for a second, then shook her head. "Well, that's very remiss of him," I said, eyeballing the eldest Silverton as I spoke. "Come on," I said to Donna, "let's go out onto the balcony. Just the two of us." I walked off towards the French windows without waiting for a reply. As I swung them dramatically open, a metallic glint caught my eye from where the feature window had recently been repaired. The glass had been made to look exactly the same as the rest of the old glazing, but the metalwork was distinctly and obviously new. I wondered if Donna Karnstein knew the damage had been caused by me throwing William the Conqueror through the very same window just a few months earlier. Did she even know he was still around? I was going to be having words with Eadric after I'd got through this. I was sick of being wrong-footed by people whose existence I'd previously been unaware of. "Come on out," I said to Donna, who was standing up but looking nervous about following me. Eve stayed in her seat, watching me with interest. "I'm not going to push you off, for heaven's sake." I let out a purposely strangled-sounding laugh. "As if I'd do anything to hurt someone of your importance. No," she was picking up her handbag, "you can leave your bag in here. Wouldn't want it to blow away." Donna reluctantly handed her bag to Eve.

"I can assure you," said Eadric, "Lilith is perfectly safe company. And the views really are tremendous." Unable to think of anything to say that wouldn't betray her nerves, Donna had no option but to walk across the room and out past me onto the balcony. It was a cold day with a distinctly frosty nip in the air, but the upside was that the sun was peeking weakly out from behind pale grey clouds. The surface of the Mersey glinted as I gazed across it, and I thought how satisfying it would be to simply throw Donna sodding Karnstein to the mercy of the feral mermaids that live in its depths.

"I'll close the doors," I said to Eadric and Eve, already shutting them as I spoke, "wouldn't want to let the draught in." Eve just smiled, and to my amazement, Eadric grinned at me. Actually *grinned*. Just as the doors were closing, Nik stuck his head nervously around a doorframe on the other side of the room and gave me a thumbs-up. *They're scared*, I thought to myself in astonishment. *Two immortal men, actually nervous about being in the same room as people from the sodding government.*

It's time someone stood up for this city.

I'd have thought it was perfectly capable of sticking up for itself.

It can't deal directly with those in power. It needs a— The version of the city that was talking to me—the one made up of people rather than the actual spirit of the place—appeared to be struggling to find the right word. **An...advocate**, it finished. **Someone human, but with the city's best interests at heart.**

Some would argue I'm not human, I pointed out.

You look human, said the city. **That's all the real humans generally care about.**

That was a whole other can of bigoted worms, but now wasn't the time to think about it. I turned and found Donna standing in front of me with her arms folded. She was about my height and maybe ten years older, although it was difficult to tell. Donna clearly kept to a good skin-cleansing routine. She leaned back against the balustrade, presumably to make it clear she wasn't nervous. There was a determined expression on her face. "What's this all about?" she asked sharply. I matched her pose, leaning back against the windows with my own arms folded to make it clear two could play at that game, and I held the advantage.

"I just prefer chatting out in the open," I said. "That way, no one has to worry that things might be secretly recorded." The brief flash in her eyes told me I'd been correct in my suspicion she was recording the meeting, probably on a phone tucked into her sensibly capacious tote bag. "Tell me," I said slowly, not taking my eyes off her, "what would you do if I *didn't* behave as you'd like?"

"In what way?" said Donna defensively.

"What would happen if I didn't keep a lid on things here in Liverpool?" Donna frowned slightly. "What if I just let it run free? How are you going to stop us, Donna?"

"It's not down to me to stop you," she said. "We have people for that." I raised an eyebrow, but didn't say anything. "We just need to know you've got it under control," she went on. "That's all."

"Oh," I said lightly, "I've got it under control. We're not interested in you, Donna." She looked confused. "We don't care what you do in London," I went on, "and we don't care what you think of us. What we care about, Donna," I took a step forward, and she visibly flinched, "is that you leave us alone. Because if you don't," I stepped towards her again, this time close enough to feel the warmth of her breath in the air, "I will do my own research, Donna Karnstein. I will find out about *your* family, same as you've done with mine. I might even visit them. Or perhaps," I tilted my head to gaze at her carefully, "I'll send some of my friends to visit you in London. Wouldn't that be nice, Donna?" Donna had a look on her face that suggested she did not think that would be very nice, actually. But she hadn't got to the lofty heights of the secretly spooky civil service by being scared off easily.

"Are you threatening me, Lilith O'Reilly?" she said.

I grinned at her. A full-beam, properly unhinged grin. "As if I'd do that," I said. "What a thing to accuse me of. I think it's probably best if you left, Donna. It's a long way down," I nodded towards the edge of the balcony and Donna's eyes twitched involuntarily, "and I'm sure you'd prefer to use the lift." I stood to one side and opened the balcony door. Donna looked like she wanted to say something, but was being overpowered by the animal instinct for survival. As she brushed past me through the door, I caught hold of her arm. She froze to the spot, glaring at me in defiance.

"You can't treat me like this," she hissed. "I will be reporting back about you."

"Donna," I spoke quietly, but gripped her elbow *just* tightly enough to cause her discomfort, "it was you who came here and made thinly veiled threats. Imagine having the brass neck to come here—Liverpool, of all places—and tell me I need to bow down to the government. You're picking on the wrong city, Donna Karnstein. I don't know how they," I jerked my head towards where Eadric and Eve were sitting in the office armchairs watching the show, Nik now also in the room with them, "dealt with your department, but I'm different. You stay out of my business, and I'll stay out of yours. But," I squeezed hard enough to make her wince, "if you ever threaten me or this city ever again," I smiled at her again, "I will make sure every supernatural creature of my acquaintance pays you a visit. For the rest of your life. Do we understand each other?"

She glowered at me. "If you don't keep this city under control," she said eventually, "there will be consequences."

I sighed. "What do I need to do in order to ensure you and I never have to meet again?" I asked.

Donna gazed levelly at me. She had some gold-plated bollocks, I'd give her that much. "You shut the time slips," she said. "And you stop meddling. You stop this entire *city* meddling, Lilith. It's clear you and I will never be friends," no shit, Sherlock, "but I do not wish you any harm." Lying again. The tiny twitch in the corners of her eyes suggested she'd very much like to make sure I was crossed off her to-do list forever. "However," she pulled her arm out of my grip and made a point of looking me up and down, "there can be no more disturbances of a paranormal nature. If there is, be in no doubt that London will take steps to stop you. *Permanent* steps." She shook herself down, pushed past me and stepped back into the relative safety of Eadric's office.

"Lovely to meet you," I said loudly, as Eve got up and handed Donna her bag. "Please don't come again." Nik was already holding open the door to the elevator that led down into the public side of the main building. To my surprise, Eve walked across to where I stood, holding out her hand. I took it, but rather than giving me a handshake as expected, she just held it. She was taller than me, the silver boots making her well over six feet.

"It's been a pleasure meeting you, Lilith," she said in a low voice. Then, to my astonishment, she bent to kiss my hand. It was only the lightest brush of her lips, but it felt like an electric shock. "Hopefully we'll meet again sometime." She dropped my hand and smiled. "Come along, Donna," she said, turning away and leaving me staring in astonishment after her, "let's not keep these lovely people any longer. I'm sure you've got notes to write up." Donna opened and closed her mouth soundlessly as Eve walked past her to the elevator, then settled for merely giving me a sour look and turning to follow her boss. We all stood in silence as the doors closed, waiting for the muffled clank of the mechanism that would deliver them safely back down to the ground floor. "Should one of us have gone with them? Just to make sure they leave?" I asked eventually.

"Their driver's waiting out front," said Eadric, going back to his desk. "They won't hang around."

Nik made a whistling noise. "That was weird," he said, "even by our standards. You've clearly still got it, Lil." I stared blankly at his raised hand for a second, before realising he was attempting a high-five. I slapped his hand gently in return and flopped down into one of the armchairs.

"So, what's the tea on Mizz Starchy-Knickers?" I asked Eadric. "And more to the point, why didn't you tell me about her and her friends?"

"Lilith," he said, "they haven't sent anyone to check on us for nearly a decade. No one was purposely keeping anything from you. It had genuinely slipped my mind."

"Humph," I said. "Is this another of those '*it was all fine, but now that woman's walking around dead and we don't like it*' things?" There'd been a lot of those, this past year. April would mark the first anniversary of my exit from this mortal coil, yet I was still here. And still winding people up by my mere existence.

"Pretty much," said Eadric, unable to suppress a smile. "You have that effect on people."

"What's Eve's role in all of this?"

"Eve has been around for a very long time," said Eadric, "and never seems to change. I sometimes think she finds entertainment in those who know their own mind. She's certainly different."

"She's certainly cute," I said. "Reckon she's single?" Eadric raised an eyebrow. "Keep your friends close and your enemies closer, and all that," I shrugged. "The pillow talk might be interesting, at least."

"Lilith," said Eadric wearily, "I'd really rather you didn't seduce anyone from the government. However cute they may be."

"As if Lil could seduce anyone without somehow turning it into a ridiculous drama," said Nik. I scowled and he grinned unrepentantly. "That's my job. So, what exactly did you say to Donna?" He perched on the arm of the other chair. It wobbled slightly underneath the lopsided weight, but he still managed to dangle one leg dramatically over the side. "Did you threaten to feed her to the birds?"

"As if I'd do something like that," I said. "Anyway, she'd give them indigestion. I merely explained that I'm quite fond of this place and I'd much prefer it if she left us alone."

"She isn't going to leave us alone," said Eadric. "The government won't allow it."

"Then," I said, "the government are going to have to face me themselves."

"However rebellious you might be," said Eadric, "We need to get things under control. Because if we don't, London will be the least of our worries."

"Are France still behaving themselves?" asked Nik from the armchair. "They're usually pretty tolerant, but I'm not entirely sure Normandy's reappearance won't kick start something over there. Eventually."

"France will be fine," said Eadric. My gaze flicked from one to the other and my eyebrows were somewhere up in my hairline, but both men appeared utterly oblivious to my consternation. "It's the areas closer to home that are likely to cause problems." He looked at me. "Has Normandy told you anything about his plans?"

"Liam hasn't talked to me about anything remotely interesting," I lied. "And if he had, I'm not sure I'd tell you anyway. Not now the buck is clearly stopping with me." I thought Eadric would take offence, but a broad smile spread across his beautiful face.

"Well done," he said. "That's more like it. Now," he sat back in his chair and raised an eyebrow, "want to tell us about these cats?"

THE PAST IS A
DANGEROUS PLACE

"Eadric says you're to keep the cats under control," I said as I let myself in through the kitchen door, "or he'll be taking them off for neutering."

"I'm thinking that's a contravention of my basic human rights," said Finn. He was standing next to the kettle, clearly waiting for it to boil. A mug sat on the worktop in front of him, and he reached into the cupboard to pull out another. "Cuppa?" he said, waving the second mug at me. "Your Kitty says she hasn't quite got the hang of it yet, shame to be boiling it for just the one."

"Erm," I faltered, "I usually have espresso. From the machine. Don't worry," I said, seeing Finn's confusion, "I'll do it myself in a minute."

"He's a lovely helpful chap," called Kitty from the living room, "isn't he?" I walked into the room and found her in her usual position on the sofa, with Grimm on her lap.

"This flat," I said, "is supposed to be a single-person occupancy." Kitty looked up at me blankly. "Right now it contains one person, one ghost, one cat and..." I scrabbled for the right words and failed, "*something* that is possibly a cat but also a human. And also might just be a figment of my clearly overstressed imagination."

"Nah," said Finn, coming into the room with his cup of tea. He took milk, I noticed. "I'm just a bloke." He gave it some thought. "A bloke who sometimes turns into a cat."

"Oh," I said, "because that's *completely* normal, isn't it?" I looked at all three of them and they all gazed back at me. "I'm getting in the shower," I said. "And no one is to disturb me. Is that clear?" Finn shrugged, and Grimm just blinked owlishly.

"That's a good idea," said Kitty brightly, "a good scrub will do you good. Wash the stress away." I rolled my eyes so hard it should have been audible from Wapping, and headed into the bathroom.

I turned on the shower and went to find clean clothes while the water heated up. My bath towel was draped across the dressing table and, as I pulled it off, it snagged the crown. I caught it before it hit the floor and stood for a moment, gazing down at the plain gold circlet sitting in my hands. *Such a nondescript little thing*, I thought, *but so many people have died for it*. Once, this crown had adorned the head of a young and doomed Anne Boleyn; now it sat hidden in plain sight in the bedroom of a grumpy Liverpool cafe owner. *You deserved better*, I murmured to it.

Did it really, though? The city interrupted my musings, and I replaced the crown on the dressing table with a sigh. **That's the crown itself putting thoughts into your head**, it went on. **That's why it's so dangerous**.

All the more reason it should stay with me, I said. *So I can keep an eye on it.*

Just don't get into the habit of wearing it, the city warned. **It won't end well**.

I need to get to the source of the time slips, I said. Silence. *Any idea where that might be?*

Nothing for a few seconds. Then, **It's dangerous to meddle with what you don't know.**

I've been forced to meddle with all sorts of things I don't know over the last few months, I pointed out. *No one's been too worried about my safety so far.*

This is different, said the city. **Time is beyond our reach for good reason. It needs to stay there.**

Time, I pointed out sharply, *is making a fucking mockery of me right now. Time needs to be given a damn good spanking and sent to bed without its tea.*

Time, came the measured response, **is the ultimate power. Time is what makes humans mortal. It's what makes humanity itself strive for change. Time is the ultimate judge, jury and executioner.**

Time is a pain in the bloody jacksy and it needs to start bloody well behaving itself. Now, are you going to tell me how to find the source, or not?

Not. I was genuinely taken aback. I'd been expecting an argument, but not a flat-out refusal. I'd got so used to sharing my skull with a grumpy ancient spirit that I'd grown to quite enjoy the bickering—so long as I got my way in the end.

Oh, get a bloody grip, I said. *I'm a big girl, I can look after myself. I can't even be killed, for heaven's sake!*

This is nothing to do with you, it said. **This is about the future of...everything.**

If you're worried I'll suddenly become my own grandmother or something, I said, *then it's you who doesn't understand time. I'm pretty sure that if I did happen to do something that might impact on the future, time itself would chuck me back out into the present. It won't let me do anything that might change things.*

How do you know that?

It's just a theory, I admitted, *but I'm pretty confident.*

That's not enough.

Are you going to help me?

No.

Look, I went on, *I know you want what's best for everyone—*

Not everyone, it said, **just the city.**

Whatever. You want what's best and you're trying to keep the city safe. That's good. But if I don't stop these bloody time slips, I grabbed my towel and headed into the bathroom, *we risk losing everything.*

We will not bow to authority.

Not even if it wants what's best for you?

Authority never wants what's best for this city, it said. **It wants what's best for itself.**

Usually, I persisted. *But Eve's different, I think.*
Eve's interested in you, we think.

Har-bloody-har. Anyway, I decided to change the subject, *I'm getting in the shower. You've got until I'm back out of it to come up with a better plan, or I'm off time-travelling.*

The silence was deafening.

I spent as long as I could in the shower, but the city didn't reappear with any useful advice. "Fuck it," I said out loud. "I'll sort it out on my own, then." I knew what I was going to do. It was risky, and I needed backup. I rifled through the drawers in my bedroom, searching for the most anonymous-looking clothes I could find. The best I could do was a shapeless grey jumper, over the top of a darker grey skirt and leggings. The leggings had a monochrome leopard print on them, but it couldn't be helped. I pulled on thick socks and my DMs, laced them tightly, then tied my hair up out of the way. I could have done with hiding it under a hat, but haven't yet found even the stretchiest of beanies big enough to fit over my mop. "I'm nipping out," I said to Kitty, as I walked back into the living room. She was sitting on the sofa with Grimm on her lap as usual. Slightly less usual was the enormous cat curled up at her feet. They appeared to be watching old episodes of *Blind Date*. I only recognised it because Izzy had once done an appalling impression of Cilla Black's over-the-top Scouse accent whilst drunk in the pub, and she'd had to explain it to me via YouTube clips. I stepped gingerly past them into the middle of the room and gazed down. "Finn?" The cat stretched slightly and blinked up at me.

"Someone let a firework off outside," said Kitty, "and it frightened him into changing. Didn't it, baby?" She leaned down and stroked Finn's head, and he purred in response.

"I bet that was an interesting sight," I said drily.

Kitty laughed merrily. "It was actually fascinating," she said, "you should have seen it, Lil! One minute he was sitting here like a normal person, then there was an *explosion* of fur! I blinked a bit, and he was sitting here like this."

"What's happened to his clothes?"

Kitty looked nonplussed. "What do you mean?" she said. "Cats don't wear clothes, silly."

"The clothes he was wearing before he changed," I said patiently. "I always wondered what happened to the clothes. You know, like in the movies when people transform into werewolves and suddenly they're like, this naked wolf, but the minute they go back to a human form they're fully dressed again."

"That's because movies aren't real," Kitty said patiently, "you know that. Our Finn's real, though," she bent to scratch the cat's ear, and the purring got louder, "aren't you? Yes, you are!"

"Just mind which bit of him you're scratching," I said. "It could be embarrassing if he changes right in the middle of it. And," I held up a warning finger to the cat, who gazed back at me with his enormous eyes, "no licking your arse in the living room. Understand?" Finn gave a visible shrug, before settling back down on the carpet.

"Where are you off to?" asked Kitty.

"Nowhere exciting," I said, hoping it turned out to be accurate, "just need to sort a couple of things out." I shrugged as casually as possible. "City stuff. You know."

"Have fun!" said Kitty, already turning back to the television. Neither of the cats so much as looked at me. Wondering for the billionth time this year what the fuck I'd done in a previous life to deserve such levels of madness in this one, I headed outside.

As I'd hoped, Billy was still in his doorway. "Hey Red," he said, "what's up?"

"I'm off to talk to the city," I said. "About politics."

Billy frowned. "Can't you just speak to it here, like you usually do?"

"Not the normal city," I said, "not the one I usually speak to. I need to speak to the *actual* city. The deep down, right-to-the-ancient-bones-of-it city. Whatever it is that really gives Liverpool its power."

Billy nodded. "It'll have a lot to say, I'm thinking." He didn't seem remotely surprised by my plans. "How are you planning to find it?" I told him, and he nodded. "Yeah," he said slowly, "that might actually work."

"And I need someone with me," I said. "Just in case I don't come back."

"You think it's a possibility?"

"I think it might be dangerous," I said. "On a really deep-down, metaphysical level." And it was Billy's unrealness that made him the safest option as a companion. If I took Missy or even Mapp into a potentially dangerous situation, they'd be at risk of physical damage. Okay, so revenants are pretty sturdy and there's not much can actually permanently kill us. But where I was going had potential to be more dangerous than I cared to admit, even to myself. So it was far better to take someone who couldn't accidentally get their head lopped off. Or at least could disappear themselves before the blade hit its target.

"Aah well," Billy grinned, "isn't everything a risk? When it comes right down to the metaphysics," he said, "you're the walking dead and I'm a ghost. There's surely a limit to how dangerous things can be."

"I just hope you're right," I said. "You in?"

Bill shrugged. "Why not?" he said. "It's about time someone took proper charge around here."

"You sure this is the right place?" Billy looked around him, sounding unconvinced. We were standing at the edge of Derby Square, with our backs to Castle Street. We'd only seen one person since we left Harrington Street, the damp weather helping to keep people indoors. Or at least in the pubs, where it was cosier—I was pretty sure that Mathew Street would be as busy as usual, had we taken a stroll down there instead.

"I hope so," I said, gazing over the empty square. "Hold my hand," I took his, and he squeezed my fingers gently, "and concentrate."

"On what?" Billy sounded nervous, and I hoped it hadn't been a bad choice to ask him to keep me company.

"The city," I said, stepping slightly closer to him, so my arm pressed up against his. "On what used to be here, before all this. Before the high-rise buildings and the pavements and the streetlights. Before Victoria sat over there," I nodded towards the monument to a long-dead queen, "peering out at us like a disapproving nanna." Billy snorted quietly. "When all this was just...Liverpool," I said. "The birthplace of a city and a people that nowhere else can match. Think about what's at the heart of this place, Billy." He didn't say anything, just squeezed my hand again. When I glanced sideways, he had his eyes closed. I did the same, and tried to follow my own instructions. I thought about the layout of the original seven streets of Liverpool, and how the one we were standing on had been named, quite literally, for the castle that lay at the end of it. The castle that originally sat much higher than the modern square, looking out over the newborn town and the river beyond. I felt a breeze running through my hair and down my neck, and had to force myself not to open my eyes. "Keep your eyes closed," I said to Billy. "You'll see in a minute." He squeezed my hand again in response. The breeze grew colder, and I shivered despite myself. I knew it wasn't real. Or did I? Logic said it couldn't be real, but then logic would say I couldn't exist either. Logic would be firmly of the belief that I should have died when I fell off the fire escape that night, and the fact I hadn't didn't mean anything other than perhaps having an unusually strong physical build. But at the same time, I knew logic meant nothing anymore. Revenants weren't logical, and neither were ghosts who could pass as human to even the most suspicious of cynics. Logic said I couldn't move time around any more than I could move the planets, but logic didn't know how determined I could be when it was needed. Logic could, quite frankly, go shove. I opened my eyes and saw what I'd done. "Look, Billy," I said, nudging him. I watched as his eyes opened, blinking in disbelief at what he saw in front of him. "Isn't it amazing?" I said, turning to follow his gaze. Right in front of us, looming like a particularly well-made set piece from an old Hammer horror movie, stood Liverpool Castle.

Built in the early thirteenth-century on the orders of William de Ferrers, Earl of Derby, Liverpool Castle sat on a man-made promontory high in the centre of the town. The Liverpool Castle that exists to this day, forty miles down the road in Rivington, is actually a folly that was built to look like the ruins of the original, as they were left after the Civil War. The castle that stood in front of us now was definitely the real deal. Lurching up above our heads were the crenellated towers that backed up the gatehouse, their battlements reaching for the clouds above. The track to the entrance in front of us went over a wooden bridge across a moat, which was deep but appeared to be empty. "What the holy—" began Billy, stepping backwards away from the monolith in front.

"If anywhere's the heart of this city," I said, "I reckon this is it." I started forward, then stopped when I realised Billy wasn't with me. Turning, I found him staring at both me and the castle in fascinated horror. What was even stranger was that I could still see modern-day Castle Street behind him. It was fuzzy and out of focus, but definitely still there. The faint outline of the Town Hall was visible at the other end and, as I watched, a lorry turned in from Dale Street in front of it. But there was nothing alive in the time slip other than me and Billy, and we didn't really count. The change in era occurred somewhere just behind Billy, near the entrance to lower Harrington Street. I wondered if that was a coincidence. Maybe there was just a maximum radius that the time slips could stretch. Billy was standing in the middle of a track worn into the rough ground, but only a few feet behind him, it morphed into the tarmac and white lines of a modern-day city street. I watched in fascination as a lone taxi came towards us, hit the boundary of the time slip and disappeared into thin air.

"You don't have to come with me if you don't want to," I said, really hoping he wouldn't take the get-out option. "I can do it on my own."

"Aah," said Billy, "I can't be having that, Red. Seems to me that if you're going to do this, you ought to have company." He walked forward to join me, and I turned so we were both facing the castle. "Door's open," said Billy with a grin, nodding towards the stone entrance arch. "Let's go visit our ancestors."

It was the open door that made me think something wasn't quite right. Not that there's *anything* particularly right about being able to walk through time, you understand—it was just that I'd assumed it would include the inhabitants as well as the city itself. But not many people get the chance to literally walk through history, so ignoring my misgivings, I stepped forward. The wooden bridge had the chains attached to make it a drawbridge, but it didn't look as though they were used very much. The whole place had a weirdly unfinished air about it, as though it had been built to designs drawn up by someone who knew what a castle should look like, but hadn't actually seen one. It was asymmetrical, the gate house and two towers marking three corners of the castle's square footprint, the fourth nothing more than plain stone walling. The moat was indeed empty, and I could see the tool marks on the sides from when it had been dug out of the bedrock. The bridge was sturdy, and didn't look as though it had been used very much. Billy and I walked across it to the open portcullis and stepped through into the outer keep. From here, the castle seemed even more massive than before. It towered above us at least three storeys high, with wooden platforms fixed around the walls way above head height. The immense doors that filled the next arched stone entrance were tightly closed, but a smaller access door had been left helpfully open. "I don't think anyone's here," I said, looking across at Billy. He was staring up around us with an awestruck expression on his face.

"The lights are on but nobody's home," he said, nodding to a lit torch that was flickering on the wall to the side of the door.

"Don't you think that's weird?" I asked him. "That it's just...waiting for us, somehow?"

"How do you mean?" He'd gone ahead and was about to step through the doorway, but stopped to look back at me. "You think it's dangerous?"

"I know it's dangerous," I said. "We're travelling through bloody time, Billy! It can't be anything *but* dangerous. There's something else, though."

"A massive fire-breathing dragon, just waiting to chomp us up for its scran?" asked Billy. He had a grin on his face.

"I'm not sure you're taking this seriously," I said.

"Red," he said, "this is the biggest adventure I've had in decades. And that's speaking as someone who's had to rescue your boyfriend from the top of the Radio City tower."

"Liam is not my boyfriend," I snapped. "How many bloody times do I have to tell people that?"

"Aye," said Billy, "and neither is Ivo, so you keep telling anyone who'll listen. And that," he pointed upwards, "is half a pound of raw pork that you see flying past the battlements." I'd actually lifted my gaze to look before registering what he'd said.

"I think this is a memory," I said, deciding to ignore him. "The city's remembering."

"Seems real enough to me," said Billy, knocking the stone walls for emphasis. "And look," he nodded back the way we'd come, "the street's disappeared." He was right. The view back out through the castle gates should have been of the weirdly dissolving Castle Street, but now there was nothing but a worn track heading down towards the town. On the left of the track was a small row of houses, but to the right there was nothing but empty land, divided up into what looked suspiciously like the sort of strip-farming sections we'd learned about in GCSE history . "Might as well crack on, I reckon," said Billy. "Nothing to go back for."

The stone entrance arch was deep, and lit with more torches fixed high on the walls. We walked under a second portcullis—also conveniently and suspiciously raised—and into the open courtyard of the castle proper. It was actually a relatively small castle once you were inside its impressive walls, and clearly built to be functional as much as defensive. One corner of the yard had a low fence around what looked like a stable, although when I checked, there was nothing inside it. Straw lay across the floor and there was a filled water barrel in the corner, but no animals. Next to the pen was a well, and I wondered at just how deep they'd had to dig in order to get water up through it. Billy was wandering along the far wall, peering into various low wooden structures that looked like storage of some kind. "Empty," he said, "whole lot of 'em. It's like everyone just...disappeared."

"Like I said, it's not real." Or rather, it *was* real—but the reality that the city itself remembered. "The soul of the city is deeper than people," I said, walking over to him. "It just remembers what's been done to it over the years."

"In that case," said Billy, "I'm doubting it much liked having that moat gouged out of its flanks. What's in here?" He pushed open a heavy oak door that was set into the inner wall. I followed him through, and we found ourselves inside what was clearly the second, more private courtyard. This one was empty apart from a vague idea that there might have been plants in it at some point. If I unfocused my eyes, I thought I could see the faint edges of flower borders around the edges, but they disappeared as soon as I focused again. Definitely memories rather than reality. "Come on," said Billy, nodding towards the corner tower, "let's go inside. There's clearly no one here, we might as well have a look around." The door at the base of the tower was also, predictably, unlocked. It opened with a creak as Billy pushed at it, revealing the start of a set of spiral steps.

"This is like that time I went to Ludlow Castle with my parents," I said as we started up the staircase. "Just don't be getting dizzy and falling back down." A woman walking behind me and Mum that day had decided to follow us up the tallest tower, which was narrow and steep. Halfway up she'd announced she felt faint and sat down on the steps, causing a bottleneck of tourists for several minutes before her grand-daughter managed to wriggle her way up and escort her embarrassed nan back down to safety.

"What's the worst that could happen if we fell?" asked Billy. "We're already dead, remember."

"How could I forget?" I muttered, following him upwards. The stairs opened out onto a landing, before heading upwards again. There was an arrow slit in the wall to our left and torches again flamed on the walls, illuminating a small room behind an open door to the right. There was a large wooden four-poster bed in the centre, surrounded by drab velvet hangings. I was about to step into the room when the flag-stones began rumbling beneath my feet. Billy and I looked at each other with panicked expressions, and he peered out through the arrow slit.

"I think the castle's falling down," he said in a horrified voice. He was right. The walls were shuddering, their large stones coming loose in the mortar. The entire castle was disassembling itself, with us inside it.

"Up!" I yelled to Billy, but he was already running. I shot past, grab-bing his arm as I went. He struggled to keep up, but there was no way I was leaving him behind, not now. The walls were slowly tumbling in on themselves as if in cinematic slow-motion and the air was thick with dust. Spotting daylight ahead, I closed my eyes and ran as fast as I could —straight out into thin air.

For a few seconds, it felt as though we were hovering above the castle, watching it disintegrate beneath our feet. Then gravity kicked in and we fell together, landing hard in a tangle of limbs and rubble. I tensed, waiting for the huge stone boulders of the castle to come down on us, but it didn't happen. Instead, we appeared to have crashed into the ruins of a modern building, with bricks and splintered timber all around us. Broken walls suggested we were in what was once somebody's house, but was now nothing more than a crumbling skeleton, open to the sky. "You okay?" I asked, dragging myself to my feet. Billy had somehow ended up beneath me as we fell and had absorbed most of the impact.

"Depends what you mean by okay," he replied, sitting up and dusting himself down. "Good job I'm already dead, aye." He looked around. "Where are we?"

"Exactly where we were before," I said, "just in a different time." I pointed across to where the Victoria monument stood amidst the chaos, somehow undamaged despite the hellscape that now surrounded it. Even as I spoke, I heard the whining noise start high above us, and pulled Billy back down behind the pathetic cover offered by the ruined walls.

"Holy Mary, Mother of God," he muttered as we both clutched our heads in our hands and tried to make ourselves as small as possible, "we've landed right in the middle of the war."

WORLD WAR CATS

Liverpool was second only to London in the amount of damage it suffered during the Second World War. Everyone knew it would be a focal point for bombardment, given the port's strategic importance in the war effort, but what few expected was just how relentless the attacks would be. It's the reason St Luke's on the corner of Berry Street is now better known as the Bombed-Out Church, having lost most of its innards when an incendiary device dropped neatly through the roof of the nave on the night of May 6th, 1941. The May Blitz was the worst of all the raids on Liverpool. And I was pretty sure that was exactly where—or rather, when—we'd landed.

"I should be able to take us both back to reality," said Billy, as we sat against the wall watching dust clouds billowing down South Castle Street. I could just make out the poor doomed Custom House in the distance. "I don't understand."

"We're not really in the past," I said, as we huddled together, staring at the vacant gap in the middle where the massive Liverpool One shopping complex would sit in my own time. "Like I said before, this is a phantom reality. It's literally ghosts of the city's past. We're walking through its memories, not the real thing."

"That's mad talk," said Billy. "I'm a ghost, I can't be trapped by anything." As he said it, another enormous explosion ripped away what was left of the buildings behind us. A roaring blast of heat and debris had us both ducking our heads and closing our eyes. "This shouldn't be affecting me," said Billy again. "I'm not real, Red! I'm a walking memory, the echo of a person. You know that as well as I do. I should be able to just grab your hand and click my fingers and have us both back on Harrington Street in a blink."

"I think," I said slowly, "this is as much a memory as you are, so it's holding onto you. And I'm stuck here because I'm solid, and literally have to find a way to walk out through it. I think," I said again, the horrible realisation crystallising in my head even as I spoke, "we might both be stuck. And I'm not sure there's anything we can do about it."

"Why aren't there any people here," asked Billy, "if we're in the city's own memories?"

"This city is more than just people," I said. "It's alive and real and much bigger than the people who live in it. I think," there was another explosion a couple of streets away and I clutched Billy's arm, "it's only remembering itself. And what it's been through over the centuries. It's remembering the pain and fear and horror of the war, in the same way that it remembered the castle being built as a symbol of human ownership."

"Fuck me," said Billy, as yet another explosion rocked the ground beneath us, "if ever I saw anything that needed a bit of trauma therapy, it's this place. We've got to do something, Red," he went on. "I don't know about you, but I'm not prepared to die for good trapped inside someone else's nightmare."

"We have to move," I said. "I know that much. We need to keep walking until we manage to get into a different bit of its memory. A nicer one."

"I'm not sure this city's got many nice memories," said Billy sadly. "Not of its own, at any rate. It's been battered and bruised for centuries and all anyone does is keep accusing it of bringing troubles on itself." He leaned back against the wall and turned his head to look at me. His eyes shone brightly, and I realised with a start that he was trying not to cry. I hadn't even realised Billy *could* cry. "There's been nothing but sadness in all the time I've known it, Lil." It was the first time I'd ever heard Billy call me by my real name, and I looked at him in aston-ishment.

"Don't you dare go all soft on me now," I said, rallying myself enough to speak sharply. He looked at me blankly. "You've survived this last couple of centuries in one form or another," I went on, "and if I have anything to do with it, you'll survive a good few more. Do you hear me?" He didn't say anything, but the brimming tears were fading away. "We are both going to get out of here, and that's the end of it." I looked out towards where mounds of rubble had replaced the houses that had previously been there. "That's James Street," I said, nodding to our left. "We'll head towards the river."

"Wouldn't we be better going inland?" asked Billy. "Away from the docks, I mean. They're the bombers' main target." He still looked worried, but less immediately panicky and more like he might actually fight for survival instead of just giving up.

"You forget," I said, "the advantage of being from the future is that we know which buildings survived the war." I grinned at him. "Let's go visit Bella and Bertie."

We waited until I was as sure as I could be that the raid had ended, at least for now. I had no idea whether time was running at normal speed, nor even whether it was working chronologically. For all I knew, the city might just be sifting through its endless painful memories in random order. Knowing my luck, it'd get distracted, start thinking about the Civil War and drop us straight into the middle of a bloody siege. I stood up and looked around at the silent, empty mayhem. "Come on," I said to Billy, "we're not going to get a better chance." The sky was dark as we ran down James Street, fire illuminating spots where bombs had found their targets. Just as we turned onto the Strand, the distant rumble of planes began again, out to sea. "Run!" I yelled. Unable to go as fast as I'd have liked for fear of leaving Billy behind, the short time it took us to get down to the riverfront felt agonisingly slow.

"Do you think we'll be able to get inside?" asked Billy, when we finally reached the safety of the Liver Building's front entrance. I gazed out onto the river, empty but for the bombs missing their target and landing in the water as phantom explosions.

"We're not going inside," I said. "It's too dangerous."

"I'm reckoning it's more dangerous out here right now, Red," said Billy, flattening himself back against the filthy stone. "I haven't felt this fragile since Victoria was still on the throne."

I reached for his hand and gave it a squeeze. "I promise," I said, "the bombs aren't the biggest danger right now."

"That isn't as reassuring as you might think," said Billy.

"It's relative," I said. "The Liver Building survived the war, right? So as long as we stay here, I reckon we're as safe as it's going to get."

Billy didn't look convinced. "Why can't we go inside anyway?" he said. "You know your way around and we can, I don't know," he looked out at the water just as another bomb landed in it, sending the spray high into the air, "sit with Bella, or something. Reassure her a bit." He wasn't wrong in thinking the birds could have done with some familiar company—I could hear them shrieking from where we stood on what in my lifetime would become Canada Boulevard. Right now, it was nothing but a grey mess of dust and debris, with ships crowding the dockside beyond.

"What if Eadric's in there?" I looked up at the building towering above us like a huge stone sentry guarding its people. "There doesn't appear to be any logic to this shit so far."

"And?" Billy turned to look at me. "Surely that's a good thing? He might know how we can get back to our own time. Well," he thought about it, "your time. The time where I'm haunting the doorway opposite Flora's. I kind of miss that pavement, Red." He looked wan, even for a ghost.

"What if Eadric *is* in there," I said, "and him seeing us makes a loop in history, or something? This isn't like Daisy—she's probably as confused as we are right now. But Eadric's, well." I paused. "He's what ties all this together. At least, he is in my world. If I bump into him now, things might spiral and send us into a completely different reality."

"It might be a more peaceful reality," said Billy hopefully. "Surely it's worth a try?"

"We can't risk it."

"But," Billy's voice brightened, "you said yourself that history shuts you out if you do anything that risks changing the future." He held my gaze, his eyes bright. "If we make a point of finding Eadric Silverton, it might all shut down and we'll find ourselves back on Harrington Street."

"I don't think that's going to happen, Billy. Something's changed." I slumped back against the filthy stone. "It didn't shut me out when I met Daisy, so I really don't think it'll do it for Eadric. Things are going badly wrong," that was the understatement of several lifetimes, "and I can't risk making it even worse."

"Why? Look," he waved his hand towards the ghostly death and destruction still going on around us, "we can't stay here. And we don't even know where we need to be in order to get back through to the future! It might be somewhere underneath the rubble, for all we know. This might not be the world's biggest city, Red, but it's big enough for a time slip to hide in. Especially when it's stuck inside a city that appears to be having an existential breakdown."

"Breakdown or not," I said, "this city will get through. It always does." I crossed my fingers behind my back. "All of this was and always will be here. The only difference is that it's usually hidden in the background. See that boat over there?" I pointed towards where a barge laden with cargo sat moored at Manchester Dock, low in the water, as though trying to hide from the barrage. "One day, the Museum of Liverpool will be built there. And it'll have endless displays and artefacts, all about what we're seeing now." I didn't mention that I was fairly sure the dock we were looking at had been filled in well before the war, and the fact we could see it now was just more evidence of the city's currently unstable mental state. "This city is a survivor, Billy," I said, gripping his hand tightly. "Always has been, and always will be. Way past the time any of us are still wandering its streets." I wasn't entirely sure that was true, on account of me being immortal and all that. But it sounded powerful and encouraging, and I thought that might be exactly the sort of thing Billy needed to hear right now.

Before he could respond, an unearthly yowl sounded in the distance. We both turned just in time to see a large shape coming out of the gloom from the direction of where the Isle of Man ferry terminal would be, sometime in the future. What started as a vague shadow became more solid as it closed the distance between us. It seemed to be growing in size, and as it got closer I realised it was an animal of some kind, running on all fours. A flash of burning light from an explosion over what I thought might be poor old Derby Square again illuminated the giant cat that was barrelling towards us. This cat was a lot bigger than Finn, and close enough now for me to see its eyes, which glowed with yellow fury. It slowed to a gentle lope and came to a halt about fifty feet away, its horribly focused pupils not leaving me for a second. As I watched, it lowered itself slightly and for a second, I thought it might be giving up. Then its head dropped to the ground and its back arched and I realised it was preparing to pounce. "Up?" yelled Billy, but I was ahead of him and already scrabbling up the front of the Liver Building, levering myself up and over the first balcony before Billy had even got off the ground. I leaned over to see him trying and failing to get a grip on the smooth stone. Fucking hell, I was going to have to go back down and help him. The cat was wriggling in excited preparation for the hunt, its long, thick tail swishing ominously from side to side. Immortal or not, I didn't fancy getting on the wrong side of monster-sized claws. I swung myself off the balcony and hung suspended for a few seconds, debating my next move. *Fuck it*, I thought—*if I break something, it'll heal. Eventually.* With that, I dropped to the ground below. I'd made sure to bend my legs so I didn't shatter my ankles as I landed, and amazingly I found myself rolling backwards on the ground still, apparently, in one piece.

"Get on my back," I yelled. Billy gave me a disbelieving look, but fear took over and he hopped onto my back like an overgrown toddler. "Hold on," I yelled over my shoulder, already scrambling up the face of the building even as the cat took a flying leap at us, missing my foot by what felt like millimetres. Billy's arms gripped so tightly that if I'd been human, I'd have struggled to breathe. Although had I been human, I was pretty sure I wouldn't have been able to climb the sheer front of the Liver Building with a fully grown man on my back. Billy might have been a ghost, but right now he felt as real as could be. I concentrated on getting as high as possible as the wind whistled round my head and explosions flashed in my peripheral vision. It wasn't until we reached the base of Bella's dome that I thought we might just manage to survive. The bird was shrieking in fear and rage, her metal wings vibrating with fury as we watched the city being destroyed below us. Streaming spirals of light swirled above her head, matched in their terrified aerial ballet by those above Bertie, whose position on the inland side of the building meant he was being forced to watch the worst of the destruction. I put a hand on Bella's leg, and she jerked backwards before tilting her head down to look at me. I could see fragments of her original gilding, still visible around her big blank eyes. "It's okay, girl," I said, "we're here now. We're with you." She shuddered and quieted slightly, her screaming replaced by low, plaintive cries.

"Oh shit," said Billy beside me. I glanced down and saw that the cat had made it as far as the first balcony, but was now stuck there, craning its colossal head around to look up at us. It occurred to me to wonder just how long-lived the were-cats might be—for all I knew, it could be Finn's grandad down there, scrabbling angrily at the shuddering brickwork.

"It's okay," I reassured him. "I don't think it can get any higher."

"Not that, Red," said Billy. "Look over there." He nudged me and nodded to the right, where huge flames licked up from behind the Stanley Dock Tobacco Warehouse. That warehouse was, at the time, the biggest and highest storage facility in the world. So the fact we could see flames right over the top of it was terrifying, even given our high vantage point.

"It's Huskisson Dock," said Billy. "I was here when it happened."

"When what happened?" I asked. "Oh shit," I said before he could reply, realisation dawning. "The Malakand?" Billy nodded without turning his head, his eyes wide as he stared at the flames. The SS Malakand had been berthed in Huskisson Dock during the 1941 Blitz, its hold loaded with more than a thousand tons of munitions. Fire from an earlier blast had spread through the warehouses that sat close together along the dockside, and workers battled through the night to stop the flames from spreading to the ship and its lethal cargo. The Royal Navy sent a salvage vessel to assist, but as she arrived on the scene early the next morning, the Malakand finally blew. The ensuing explosion destroyed the dock completely, sending debris flying across the city out to a radius of nearly two miles. Four people were killed, and an unfortunate horse tethered nearby was sliced in two by a large piece of steel that was blown off the ship. Now we were sitting at the edge of the blast radius, perched precariously on top of one of the highest buildings in the city. And I wasn't entirely sure that being dead would save us if we were thrown off and crushed on the streets below. Billy was still showing a worrying inability to disappear himself in the usual way, and despite being immortal, I was definitely still made of flesh and bone. It's one thing being able to put your own limbs back together, but quite another to reassemble yourself after being pulverised under several tons of fallen masonry. But before I had time to suggest we drop down onto the roof area in order to take shelter behind Bella's tower, the ghost of the Malakand blew up in our faces.

The blast wave hit as hard as any real one could, sending me flying backwards off the dome. I somehow managed to grab hold of Bella's leg and hung on grimly as a wall of heat rolled over me, my eyes closed tightly against the roiling dust. The thudding explosions seemed endless, but it was almost certainly just a few minutes before I dared crack one eye open to face the damage. Ghostly flames danced across the docks, beautiful in their awfulness. I was grateful this was the phantom version we were stuck in, because at least we weren't being forced to witness death alongside the destruction. I let myself drop carefully down onto the roof below Bella's tower and looked around me. "Billy?" I called. Nothing for a few seconds, and I was just beginning to panic when I heard a voice from the other side of the building.

"Over here," he called. He was standing with his back to me at the base of Bertie's tower—he must have been blown right across and somehow wedged himself into the shelter of the inland dome. I stepped carefully over the bomb debris that littered the roof and made my way to where Billy stood gazing down at the road below. A man was standing in front of where a sports bar sits in my modern-day reality. "That's the first person we've seen," said Billy. "He's got to be one of us." The man was staring at the tangle of wood and metal that used to be the overhead railway but was now sprawled across the Strand, near its junction with James Street. He looked familiar, somehow, but I didn't recognise him for who he was until Billy called out to him. "Oi mate," he called, even as I was grabbing his arm to stop him, "friend or foe?" And then his face dropped in shock as he, too, realised who he was shouting at. Before I could gather my wits enough to do anything to stop it from happening, the man on the street looked up. It was Billy. Still a ghost and still walking the streets of Liverpool, even in the middle of a world war. The two men saw each other, equally horrified expressions spreading across their faces as they realised what had happened. And then, with a horrible sucking noise that sounded as though it came from the very fabric of reality, they both disappeared.

"Shit, shit, *shit!*" I paced the roof underneath Bertie's tower, bombs still exploding around me and both birds screeching as though anger alone might be enough to see off the enemy, if only they tried hard enough. Judging by the noise currently wafting over from behind the Tower Building on the other side of the road, their mother was also giving it full-throttle fury from her perch on top of Mersey Chambers. Billy had vanished right in front of my eyes, and it was my bloody fault. I'd been confident that I would be reasonably safe from messing up time, for the simple reason that I hadn't been in the city during the Second World War. Mostly because it was a long time before I'd even been born. But I'd assumed that Billy didn't matter, because he was already a ghost by the time of the Liverpool Blitz. And that was the problem, wasn't it? I hadn't thought he'd matter. "Fuck!" I added for extra emphasis, as I peered down onto the street below and spotted the were-cat, still prowling for a potential route up the building in order to snag itself a Lil-flavoured lunch. It let out a frustrated snarl as it looked up and spotted me, making a futile leap at one of the large stone windowsills. It snagged a hold with one paw for a few seconds, before dropping back down onto the street. As I watched, it stalked off round the corner of the building, presumably planning another attempt via the balconies on the building's front wall. "I need to go," I said to Bertie, who made a low throaty sound in response. I couldn't bring myself to look over at Bella. "I'll see you soon," I said, with more confidence than I felt. "I've got to get home and figure out how to save Billy." With one last glance to make sure the cat hadn't reappeared, I hopped the balustrade. It was easy enough to get down to the main lower roof—I just swung myself on and off each section of the tower, dropping down a floor at time. The lower half of the building was a different story. Built as an enormous rectangular block, the remaining floors between me and solid ground had nothing more than the occasional fake balcony jutting out from their smooth outer surface. I debated just leaping off and hoping for the best, but that relied on the cat not spotting me before I pulled myself together again (possibly literally). As though reading my mind, a yowl came from the other side of the building. Peeking over the edge, I saw a second cat prowling towards the first, its tail swishing aggressively. *Fuck me*, I thought, *this city is* literally *feral*. I wasn't going to get a better time to make my escape. The cat fight was, of course, brewing on Bella's side of the building, which would normally be the one place I could possibly get down without breaking my immortal neck. In desperation, I ran for the opposite corner, where the walls offset each other at right angles and create a recess. Clambering gingerly onto the edge of the once familiar building that now felt very tall indeed, I dropped my legs over and wedged my feet against the opposing bricks. Then I hung wedged there for a few seconds whilst I tried to figure out how to do the same with my hands. There was nothing else for it. I dropped first one hand and then the other, smacking them out so violently against the stonework that a crack appeared between the fingers of my right hand. Gravity was doing its best to force me downwards at high velocity, and I realised I was going to have to do it fast or not at all. And 'not at all' was no longer an option. The sound of a cat fight kicking off spurred me on—with any luck, I could make my escape while they were too distracted to eat me. Pushing outwards with all my strength, I somehow skittered my way down the building like one of those sticky bug toys kids get in their Christmas stocking. *'Throw her and see her stick to the wall! The amazing, scrambling Lilith!'* Gritting my teeth to stop myself screaming in pain as the stone took the skin off the palms of my hands, I made it down to street level far quicker than planned and once again rolled like a mis-aimed bowling ball along the filthy gutter. Something dark and fast flitted past in the entrance to Brunswick Street and I scrambled to my feet in the hope it might be Billy. Running across the rubble-strewn

Strand, I spotted the figure against as it turned onto Fenwick Street and stopped. I knew a vampire when I saw it, and today wasn't the day for meeting more characters from the past. Knowing my luck it would be Aiden, and we'd both get flung into a weird historical offshoot of time in which he was my only company. I'd probably be forced to bodge together a warning crucifix in order to ever escape his insistently polite chat.

"The vampires are hiding out up at Edge Hill." The voice was female, and so close to my ear that I let out an involuntary squeak. Spinning round, I came face to face with Eve. Dressed in the same clothes as she'd worn for her visit to Eadric's office, she was immaculately clean, even as she leaned casually against the filthy brick wall. "Aiden's predecessor just comes down occasionally to check on the birds."

"You're telling me that bundle of evil rags that attacked me up at Anfield cares about what happens to Bella and Bertie?" I snorted. "Pull the other one, it plays Jingle Bells."

"Evil is as evil does," said Eve with a smile. "But even evil knows what's really important."

"Where's Eadric?" I asked. There were a million other questions more important than knowing where the Silvertons had got to, but right now they'd all slipped my mind.

"In London," said Eve. "With Elizabeth. He'll be back in a few days. He never leaves the birds alone for long."

"Nik?"

"Staying with Elizabeth for the duration," she said. "London was his spiritual home for a long time—he doesn't want to leave it in its hour of need."

"Do they know you're here?"

"The Silvertons have no idea of my existence," she said. "Yet." She pushed herself upright and slid her hands into her trouser pockets. As she stood there like a beacon of bright colours in the midst of the muted grey carnage, she looked for all the world as though she was modelling for a magazine feature. It would be themed in an edgy modern style, and probably shot in a scrapyard. "Lilith?" Eve said, pulling me out of my daydream, "are you okay?"

I snorted. "I've been dodging bombs and running from giant killer cats," I said, "and I've lost my friend along the way. So no," I shrugged, "I am very much not okay. Anyway," I narrowed my eyes, "what are you doing here? And more to the point, why didn't time shut me out when I saw you? I know you in the future," I went on, "so surely time should be kicking up a stink about me bumping into you now?"

"Aah," said Eve, "but I already knew you'd be here. I've been aware of your existence for a long time, Lilith. This," she gestured at the two of us, "doesn't change anything I think or know in the future, so it won't change anything now." Both the city and the sky were still grey around us, but sunlight was trying to break through at the periphery. And although I could still see and hear the explosions, they were beginning to lose focus around the edges. Reality was forcing its way back in.

"You'd better not be a fucking witch," I said. "I've had enough trouble with them over the past year or so."

Eve laughed. "Then you've met the wrong witches," she said. "Most of them are very nice. But no, I'm not a witch. I'm far older than that."

"How do I get Billy back?" I blurted. "I've fucked up and lost him, and now I need to find him again. Can you help?"

Eve tilted her head slightly and appeared to be assessing me in some way. "I have every confidence that you can work it out for yourself, Lilith," she said finally. "You just need to press the reset button. And you need to do something about the cats, before the delightful Donna gets too involved. Talking of which," she looked past me towards the river, "this might be a good time to start running." A hiss that sounded dangerously close behind me backed up her suggestion. I risked a glance over my shoulder and saw the first cat padding slowly towards me along the Strand. It appeared to have a torn ear, and what definitely looked like blood on its front paws.

"But where will you—" I turned to look at Eve as I asked the question, but she'd disappeared. Shit. Tucking my head down and acting on instinct, I ran in the direction of Harrington Street. You don't turn to look when something's chasing you, because that's when you trip. The trick is to pretend your pursuer isn't there and just concentrate on getting to your destination. Now, I'm fast—I could beat most human athletes in a hundred metre sprint—but although immortality increases strength and stamina, you're still limited by your own body. Revenants have nothing stopping them doing anything and everything to the absolute bounds of their physical limitations, but they're still physical limitations. So, although I can run and climb faster than most, I can still only do it at a rate in keeping with the physique of a thirty-something woman of average height and weight. Cats, on the other hand, are built almost entirely for stealth and speed—and I was pretty sure this one was planning to have me for dinner. The soft, regular thud of heavy paws was getting closer, but the city—the modern, present-day city—was coming into view ahead. The ground beneath my feet began to feel more solid, and I sped up. Just as I was daring to think I might make it, the huge, crumbling wall of rubble appeared in front of me. Summoning all my undead strength, I made a running leap and might have vaulted it with an ease that would have impressed my primary school PE teacher had my foot not caught on a rogue brick sticking out at right angles. As I bounced down the other side, the were-cat's claws swiped frantically over the top. I assumed it would just leap after me, but instead it dropped back. I risked a scramble back up the mound and saw it patrolling its own side of the blockade below me, explosions still rocking the gloom on the waterfront behind. "Ha!" I yelled triumphantly. "*Ha!* You can't come over here, can you? No city-centre snack-stop for *you*, kitty cat!" There was a furious yowl, and the cat swiped a huge paw upwards, a claw catching at the side of my face. I screamed and dropped backwards onto the hard but reassuringly modern tarmac of Castle Street.

"What the fuck?" A pair of teenage girls were staring at me, one of them already filming the action on her phone. I got to my feet and brushed myself down, ignoring the stares from other pedestrians. It was daytime, and Castle Street was embarrassingly busy. A blaring horn reminded me I was in the middle of the road, and I scuttled to the pavement without looking at anyone. "You alright?" said one of the girls. "Did he push you out of the car?" asked the other. Her tone was sympathetic, but she hadn't stopped filming.

"What on earth are you talking about?" I asked them brightly, giving a big grin into the camera for extra effect. "Haven't you seen anyone parkouring before?" The girls looked confused. "Lost my footing," I shrugged, "good job the cars stopped."

"You came out of nowhere," said the first girl.

"Literally nowhere," said the second, still filming. "We saw you just appear in the middle of the road."

"Don't be daft," I said, already walking away, "we're not in a movie, love. This is the real world."

FACING THE MUSIC

"What do you mean, you've lost Billy?" I'd been hoping my adventures would turn out to have happened outside of normal time and I'd be able to skulk back indoors while it was still dark, but no such luck. Flora's was already open by the time I got back to Harrington Street and by the time I got up the fire escape to my kitchen door, Izzy and Missy were both hot on my heels on the stairs behind me. Missy cheated and launched herself past Izzy so she could be in the doorway waiting for me, and now she was as furious as I'd ever seen her. I'd walked in past her and trudged through to the living room, where I was now slumped on the sofa and trying to ignore the worried faces—both alive *and* dead—who surrounded me. The commotion had given Finn a fright, and he was currently hiding behind the chair opposite me in cat form, his swishing tail the only part of him that was currently visible.

"He needs to get in control of his nerves," I said, nodding towards the chair. "He's going to do himself an injury one of these days, changing that quick."

"Don't change the subject," said Missy, who was standing in front of me. "What did you do to Billy?"

"I didn't do anything to him," I said. "Time got in the way."

"But why did you take him with you?" she said. "Surely you must have known it was risky?" I looked around at the assembled group. Absolutely bloody everyone was here, it seemed. Everyone connected to Harrington Street, anyway. Izzy stood next to Missy, her expression one of both relief and worry. Kitty was on the chair with Grimm on her lap, one hand trailing down to pet Finn reassuringly. Even Rachel and Alan had come upstairs to see what was going on.

"Cooeeee!" came a voice at the kitchen door. "We heard there was drama occurring, and thought we'd better check it out. Just to be on the safe side, you understand." Mapp walked into the room, closely followed by a worried-looking Heggie. Although to be fair, Heggie looks worried most of the time, so it wasn't necessarily relevant. All I needed now was for Eadric and Nik to turn up. "Eadric says he'll speak to you later," said Mapp helpfully. "Nik just rolled his eyes a lot." Oh, this was just too fucking brilliant.

"I didn't do anything to hurt Billy!" I stood up sharply and Missy took a step back. She narrowed her eyes, just to make sure I understood I was still under suspicion. "I had to go back in time to try to fix something and thought Billy would be safe company. I didn't know he was going to meet himself on the bloody street."

"Billy...met Billy?" asked Missy. I nodded. "Shit."

"Yes," I agreed. "Shit. But I didn't know it was going to happen, for fuck's sake."

"What, if you don't mind me asking," said Izzy carefully, "the fuck? Why were you wandering around in the past in the first place?"

"Don't you have a cafe to run?" I deflected.

"Todd's down there." Oh well. It had been worth a try. "He says if anything's happened to Billy, he won't be happy."

"It wasn't my fault!" I paused. "Well, okay, it was my fault." I sat heavily back down on the sofa and sighed. "I thought I might be able to fix the time slips, okay?"

"Looks to me like you made them worse, girl," said Alan. I glared at him, and he shrugged. "Just sayin'."

"Well, don't," I said. "I know I fucked up and I don't need you lot lecturing me. I was in the past," I said, turning to Izzy, "because I thought I might be able to find the city itself. Talk some sense into it, that sort of thing."

"But isn't the city with you already?" asked Izzy. "Couldn't you have asked it from here?"

We told you not to mess with it.

"*Don't you fucking start!* I'm sorry," this was to Izzy, who was backing away from me, "that wasn't aimed at you. The city," I went on, "the one you're talking about, isn't the actual city. *Don't you dare!*" this was in response to the huffing I could hear in the back of my head. "The city," I started again, "has different personalities. The one that talks to me *but only when it fucking feels like it*," I squinted hard, trying to suppress the confused and tired tantrum that was clearly brewing, "is the spirit of the people, not the city itself. I thought that if I went back to a quieter time, I might be able to talk to the city proper. Y'know, calm it down a bit. Or something like that," I trailed off.

"And where did you actually end up?" asked Missy. I looked around the room at the row of expectant faces.

"Right in the middle of the Second World War." Every last one of them started talking, all at once. Both Missy and Izzy were shouting straight at me, whilst Kitty muttered worriedly down at the cats. Alan was clearly having to explain to Rachel what the Blitz actually was, whereas Mapp and Heggie were hugging each other and apparently crying. "Oh, for fuck's *sake*," I yelled, "will you all just SHUT UP!" Immediate silence. "Thank you. You might not realise this," I said, scowling at each of them in turn, "but I didn't actually intend to land in the middle of a fucking apocalypse. We were wandering around the castle—I'll explain that bit later—and everything was fine, but there was no one around. And before we could decide what to do next, everything went insane and suddenly we were in the middle of the bombing raids and—WILL YOU PLEASE STOP BLOODY WAILING?!" this was to Heggie and Mapp, who were getting thoroughly carried away with the emotional drama. "You hardly have anything to do with Billy," I said to them, "so you can cut that crap and start helping me figure out how to bloody well fix things."

"No need to be like that," sniffed Mapp. They did at least both stop snivelling. "Hang on," he said, "you were at the castle? The original one?" I nodded. "And you thought you might be able to find the source of the city there?"

"Uh huh," I said. "I thought maybe the city would talk to me. Y'know, as I'm supposedly Queen fucking Bee round these parts, not that anyone seems to appreciate that."

"To be fair," said Izzy, "we'd perhaps appreciate your royal regalness a bit more if you didn't keep starting massive fucking dramas. What?" she shrugged. "You know it's true."

"You try acting as therapist to one of the biggest cities in this entire bloody country," I said, "and see how you get on."

"Excuse me," said Missy, "are we all forgetting the current issue?" She looked round at us all. "I know Lil fucks up sometimes," she held a hand up to me, "no, don't interrupt, I'm trying to be nice here. I know Lil doesn't always get it right, but for whatever reason the city has chosen her, and we're stuck with it."

"Gee, thanks," I muttered.

"So, the problem right now," Missy continued, "is where Billy might be."

"*When* he might be," corrected Mapp.

"Well, I'd assume he's in 1941," I said, "in the middle of the Blitz. Because that's where—when—I lost him. Although I would like it established that I did not *lose* him, exactly. He just disappeared. Pooof," I clicked my fingers, "just like that."

"Because he saw himself," said Mapp.

"Yes," I said, "I already explained that bit."

"What century were you in when you went to the castle?" he asked.

"I dunno," I shrugged, "maybe the thirteenth? Fourteenth at a push, but no later. There were only two towers and the gatehouse," I explained. "The fourth tower wasn't added 'til the fourteen-hundreds. And the whole thing seemed," I thought for a second, "quite new? It was difficult to tell, on account of how there were no people around."

"So when you...walk through time," said Mapp slowly, as though he couldn't quite believe he was even saying it, "there's no human involvement? Just the surroundings?"

"Buildings and streets and fields," I nodded. "And the river, of course."

"Of course," said Mapp faintly. "And you think you're really travelling through time?"

"She needs a stripy scarf and a metal dog," said Izzy.

"K9 would struggle to get up these stairs," I pointed out.

"Maybe it's like with the Daleks," said Izzy thoughtfully. "He could learn to float."

"Are you two *completely* insane?" asked Missy. "No," she went on, "don't answer that. I'm not interested in imaginary robot dogs or whatever it is you're talking about. None of us are."

"I am," said Kitty from underneath the very large cat that had crawled out from his hiding place and was now curled up on her lap. "Me and Grimmy have been watching that series, haven't we, Grimmy?" Grimm gave her a slow blink from down by her feet. He didn't seem overly bothered that Finn had taken over Kitty's lap.

"That...cat...is unhygienic," said Missy, narrowing her eyes at Finn. "I'm sure of it. Anyway, I'm not interested in television. I'm interested in helping Lil sort out this mess."

"I'm interested in making sure Todd's okay," said Izzy, squeezing through the packed living room towards the door. "Let me know if you need any help. I'm sure I could stick a sink plunger on my forehead in an emergency." With that, she disappeared out of the kitchen door and I heard her feet tippy-tapping down the fire escape.

"I'm going to speak to Eadric," I said, getting up off the sofa. "Might as well face the music, it's got to happen at some point. Anyway," I remembered Eve's comments about the cats, "there's other stuff I need to tell him about as well. Make sure those cats stay out of trouble," I said to Kitty, "because I'm pretty sure we're being watched. And they," I indicated Little and Large sharing the chair with her, "are on the suspicious list." Grimm narrowed his eyes at me. "You're safe," I said to him, "for now. I'm not so sure about your friend here." Finn's eyes widened in fear, but Grimm gave me a casual eyebrow twitch that looked suspiciously as though it translated roughly as 'who cares, so long as I'm okay?'.

"We'll come with you," said Mapp. Heggie looked less than enthusiastic, but was nodding in agreement anyway.

"No, you won't," I said. "I'm not a toddler, I don't need constant supervision."

"I dunno about that," said Alan. "What?" Rachel had given him a shove. "That hurt, girl," he protested. She just glared at him in return.

"You're a ghost, Alan," I pointed out. "You can't get hurt."

"We can clearly get lost, though," he said. "Billy's lost, isn't he? I can't imagine what that must be like," he went on. "It sounds scary to me."

"Okay, that's enough thank you," I said sharply. "I feel shit enough as it is." Alan opened his mouth to say something, and then shut it as he caught Rachel's eye. "Thank you," I said to her. "It's nice to have one person on my side, at least."

"No-no-you-made-mistake," said Rachel, her words running together with her usual painful sibilance. "Just-not-rude-please."

"Oh well," I sighed, "just so long as you're all polite whilst shredding my stupid life choices. Not a bloody *word*." This was to Missy, who'd opened her mouth to speak. She closed it again and settled for glaring at me balefully. "You," I pointed at Alan, "are to go downstairs and stay with Rachel. And you two," I looked at Mapp and Heggie, "are adorable and helpful and I really appreciate the offer of support, but I need to see Eadric alone."

"Why?" Mapp had never been one to soften his words, and he clearly wasn't about to start now.

"Because I bloody well said so," I retorted. "Now if you don't mind," I was already heading for the door, before anyone could start arguing, "I'm off to sort out this bloody mess."

~

"And now I have to figure out how to get back and save him." I finished my tale of woe and looked across to where Eadric was sitting in the other armchair. Nik had been sent to his room whilst the grownups chatted, and had surprised me by being perfectly happy to do so.

"I'm not cut out for politics," he'd said as he headed out of the room. "I'd rather spend the afternoon under a blanket with this." He'd waved a copy of *The French Lieutenant's Woman* at me.

"I never understood how she ended up with Rossetti," I'd said, nodding at the book. "No one deserves to spend their life with that prick."

"I'll tell him you said that," Nik had grinned, disappearing through the door before I had chance to ask questions.

"What do you expect me to do about it?" asked Eadric.

"Erm, help me?" I said. "Yes, yes, I know, like you usually do. You're the elder statesman and I'm the young whippersnapper who has to learn to control their power, we both know how this goes."

"You misunderstand, Lilith," said Eadric. "There's nothing I can do about this. This one's on you."

"What?" I frowned at him. "Why are you being like this? Look," I said, "I know I probably shouldn't have gone back in the past without talking to someone about it first. Okay, yeah, I should definitely have spoken to you first. But I was *trying*, Eadric! Trying to do the right thing and take control and sort shit out, just like people keep telling me I should."

"When did anyone tell you to put your own friends in danger?"

A sharp pang of guilt stabbed me right in the back. "That's low," I said, glaring at him. "There's no need to make me feel bad, Eadric—I feel shit enough about it all already. Anyway," I'd just remembered what Eve had said, "it's not just Billy that's the problem right now."

"Of course, it isn't," said Eadric drily. "We can only dream of things being that simple." He sighed wearily. "What else is going wrong?"

"I've been warned about the cats," I said. "The authorities are onto them."

"Who told you that?"

"I can't tell you," I said, "because you don't know the person yet. I mean," I fumbled, "you do now, but you didn't then. I don't bloody know how to explain it," I shrugged, "but I can't tell you and I'd prefer it if you didn't try to guess. Things are messed up enough already."

Eadric gazed at me thoughtfully for a moment. "The cats are reappearing," he said eventually, "and that's drawing attention? Official attention that we could do without?"

"Correctamundo," I agreed. "And I think the attention will only come here," I added, "not to any of the other territories. I suspect Liam has contacts in high places even now, and will be conveniently ignored." *And probably has the power to make my life very difficult if he chooses to*, I thought to myself. I'd just have to hope that his desire to add my own power to his was enough to keep him from trying to fuck me over entirely. For now, at least.

"What about Laithlind?"

"Ivo doesn't trust anyone," I said. "Me least of all." Eadric raised an eyebrow, but didn't say anything. "Anyway," I shrugged, "he's further north. And far more rural, for the most part. No one from London will bother him. They get altitude sickness as soon as they get past Manchester."

"The cats are, I think, your responsibility," said Eadric. "Make that animal of yours their boss, or something. Pass the responsibility off onto someone else. It seems to work for human politics."

"You're telling me I should promote Grimm to Captain of Cats? Fuck me," I said, "as if he isn't cocky enough already."

"That's why he'll be good at the job," grinned Eadric. "And it's probably better if he's distracted," he said thoughtfully. "Who knows what trouble he might get into if he's not kept busy. Anyway," he went on, "what *do* you expect me to do about it? The Billy situation, I mean."

"Well," I said, slumping back down into the chair, "if I'm being completely honest—"

"That might be best, yes."

"If I'm being *completely* honest," I said again, "I was hoping you'd come up with something. Y'know," I gave him what I hoped was a winning smile, "you being the ancient and wise overlord, and all that."

"You flatter me," Eadric said. "But I can't help you. You might be able to walk through time, Lilith," he went on, "but I can't."

"Of course you can," I said. "You know! You just sort of...think about it, and suddenly you're there."

"The only thing I know right now," he said, "is that you're not listening to me. I cannot travel through time, Lilith." He looked straight at me, his hazel eyes tired. "I might be old and apparently wise, and I sit up here keeping things at least roughly on the straight and narrow, even though some help with it would be nice," he raised an eyebrow, "but there are still things I cannot do. Time travel is one of those things. In fact," he leaned back in his chair and gazed levelly at me, "I don't know anyone else who can time travel. It's just you." I remembered strange Jonathan walking sadly with me through old Toxteth and knew Eadric was wrong, but didn't say anything.

"Billy came with me though," I ploughed on, "so he must be able to do it as well."

"No," said Eadric, "that was all your doing. In the same way that Billy can hold on to someone who's solidly human and transport them to a different place, despite it being technically impossible, you can travel through time and take certain people with you."

"I'd assumed we'd get thrown out if anything was going to go wrong," I said. "Time not letting anyone become their own great-aunt, and all that. They covered this stuff in *Back To The Future*. Oh shit," the penny finally dropped, "he started disappearing, because he'd changed things and now, he wouldn't exist." Eadric looked blank. "In the film," I said. "Marty goes back in time and ends up messing with his own family history. The future starts changing even though it hasn't happened yet, and he begins to fade away. But I haven't had to stop my own mother developing a romantic interest in me," I went on, "so it shouldn't count."

"That sounds like an incredibly strange film," said Eadric, "that I'm not sure I'd ever want to watch."

"Not like that!" I looked at him in horror. "It's funny." He looked unconvinced. "Anyway," I said defensively, "it's a long time since I've seen it, and I might be getting bits wrong. But he definitely started fading as the future changed." Cold pinpricks made themselves felt up the back of my neck and I looked worriedly at Eadric. "You don't think that might have happened to Billy?"

"I have no idea what's happened to Billy," he said. "That's the truth. And neither do I know how to put things back to how they were."

"That's the thing, though," I said. "I don't *want* to put them back as they were! I need to change them. Things have to change in the past in order to keep the city safe in the future. I just have to not lose Billy along the way."

"You can't change the past, Lilith," said Eadric. "Take it from someone who knows."

"No, listen to me," I ploughed on. "We all make mistakes, and we have to learn to live with the consequences. But sometimes—just sometimes—people deserve a do-over. And Billy's one of them. Anyway," a thought occurred to me, "I wouldn't be changing the past, would I?" Eadric looked blank. "I'd be fixing the future. Putting it back to how it was before I jumped in feet first and started messing things up."

"Aah," said Nik, reappearing in the doorway, "we finally have acceptance of your own mistakes. It's the first stage in learning to deal with it, you know." He looked at Eadric. "Am I allowed back in yet, Dad? Only Bertie's cross about something and I need to go find out what."

"There isn't much else to talk about," said Eadric, ignoring my frown. He seemed defeated, somehow. "I'm sure Lilith will do whatever she deems best."

"Cheers," I said, getting up from my chair. "Thanks for the support. I'm going to talk to Bella. She's about the only person with any oomph around here." I stalked out before either of them could argue that Bella wasn't a person.

Whilst it's true that Bella can't actually speak, she definitely understands. And she's an excellent listener. I clambered up onto her dome and wedged myself between her giant feet, my back against one metal leg and my feet on the other. She creaked happily as I settled myself in, giving a little wiggle as though she was a mama bird brooding her young. "What am I going to do, Bell?" She tilted her head slightly to indicate that, whilst she obviously couldn't discuss the situation verbally, she would definitely be giving it some serious consideration. "I know I've been a brat about all this," I gestured vaguely at the city, "but it's not a bad life really, is it? Afterlife," I corrected myself. "But I'm still here and I've still got Izzy, and now I've got you as well." I patted her leg, and she gave a happy grumble. "So what we've established," I said, to myself as much as anyone, "is that I need to speak with the city itself, not its people. The *oldest* city. But where do I find it?" Bella creaked thoughtfully. "It's underneath," I said, "I think. Under all the buildings and the humans and the stupid modern world. No," this was in response to a worried rasp from above my head, "you're not part of the modern world. I couldn't do any of this without you, Bella." She settled again. "Or you," I called over to Bertie, who was making grumbling noises from the other side of the building. "No favouritism here." But I gave Bella's leg an extra pat, just the same.

BOSS LEVEL

'*Try not to feel too smug about it,*' I typed, '*but I need some advice.*' I sent the message and settled in for what I expected to be a reasonably long wait. Not long enough for me to give up and consider asking someone else, but enough to reassert a bit of dominance.

As it turned out, a reply flashed up in less than a minute. '*Ask me anything,*' it said. Now I was the one feeling smug. *Ha*, I thought, *still keen underneath the bluster.* I wrote a precis of what had happened to Billy, and ended by saying I'd appreciate any and all suggestions for ways to potentially fix things. '*What's in it for me?*' came the predictable response.

'*You get to do the right thing for once,*' I replied. '*Feel good about your-self for a change.*'

'*You're assuming I ever feel bad about the things I do,*' came the reply. Again, predictable. I ignored it, busying myself with tidying the dressing table and carefully not touching the crown. I was fine with having it in the room. I just didn't want it telling me what to do.

But you're going to take advice from the enemy? said the city. **He'll betray you, Lilith. He'll betray all of us.**

No, he won't, I said. *He can't afford to.*

That man is not trustworthy, it fretted.

Are any of them? I sighed. *The immortal ones, I mean. They're all after* something, *even if the levels of dastardly plan varies.*

And you think he can help?

Well, until someone else comes up with a better idea, I'm kind of stuck, I said. *Anyway, where have you been recently? It's usually difficult to get five minutes' peace, but I've barely heard from you lately.*

It was silent for a few seconds. Then, **Things are changing, Lilith. Something is, as you might say, in the air.**

Tell me something I don't already know, I sighed.

And you really think he can help?

A reply popped up on my phone, as I'd known it would. *'You win'*, it said, *'this time. You owe me a drink.'*

'What do I need to do?' I asked, ignoring the flirtation. So he told me —and it was exactly the same as the only plan I'd come up with myself so far. I groaned. Now I was indebted, and he hadn't even helped. *'You really think this'll work?'* I asked.

'I don't think you've got any other option,' came the reply. *'You have to reset things so they're on a different track.'*

'Okay,' I typed, *'but where?'*

'Liverpool is your city,' Liam replied, *'not mine. You'll have to figure that out for yourself. Oh, and be careful with the cats. People are talking.'* I didn't bother replying.

"I'm going out. I may be some time."

Kitty narrowed her eyes at me suspiciously. "No need to be quite so dramatic," she said, and I pulled a face. "Where are you off to at this time of night?"

"It's only," I checked my watch, "three o'clock. Practically morning for the undead amongst us. Which includes you, I might add. What are you watching?" Kitty pressed pause on the remote control. I wasn't sure whether to be impressed that a ghost could press buttons, or just relieved she'd stopped getting the cat to do it for her. Grimm was intimidating enough as it is, gods only knew what he'd be like if he learned how to use household appliances. I'd noticed the kitchen stunk of pilchards a few days earlier and had briefly wondered whether he'd figured out the microwave, but decided to just not think about it. "It's a comedy about a bookshop," she said. "The owner's really grumpy and horrible to the man who works for him, and there's a funny woman who has a shop next door selling tat. She reminds me a lot of you."

"Cheers," I said. "Just call me Fran, why don't you. Anyway," I sat down to pull on my boots, "I'm only nipping into town. I won't be long."

"You're already in town," Kitty pointed out. "Can't get much more town than here, Lil."

"Old town," I said, getting up to leave. "Original town. Proper town. From before all this," I waved my hands vaguely in the air, "was here."

"Is any of it even still here?" asked Kitty. She looked concerned. "I'm not sure you should go messing with the city itself, Lil. It might not want to be disturbed."

"It's already bloody disturbed," I said. "On all levels. And if I don't get things under control pretty soon, I'm going to be disturbed an' all." I thought about Donna Karnstein for a moment. And also about Eve, who was also disturbing, but in a very different way. "Also possibly arrested."

"Who would arrest you?" Kitty looked alarmed. "Have you done something wrong?"

"I haven't done anything except exist," I told her. "It's just that there's some people who'd perhaps prefer it if I didn't. Exist, I mean. Anyway, it's about time this city helped *me* out for a change. Don't wait up!" I was out of the flat and heading down the fire escape before she could reply.

～

I bounced off the staircase from the second storey and nearly flattened Missy in the process. "Bloody hell," she hissed, flat on her back on the pavement, "what are you doing?"

"I could ask you the same," I said, getting to my feet and dusting myself down. "How come you're down here at this time of night?"

"I decided to make sure you weren't thinking about doing something stupid," she said, sitting up on the pavement. "Looks like you were ahead of me."

There was no point lying. "I'm going back to save Billy," I said. "I can't just leave him there, wandering round in the wrong era."

"You don't even know exactly which era he's in," Missy pointed out, "so how are you planning to find him?" I took a deep breath. The night smelled of frosted grass and burning wood. Missy was wearing a knitted green jumper, and I realised the wood smell was coming from her. She and Al must have lit the fire in the house up on Priory Road. For a second I felt an almost paralysing yearning for a quiet house on the outskirts, with an open fire and friends for company. But the city was my home, and I needed to look after it. All of it.

"I'm going to stop him dying," I said.

Missy looked confused. "Like, at all?" she asked. "How are you going to do that? Oh my god, Lilith O'Reilly," her face took on an expression of genuine panic, "don't you dare tell me you've taken up necromancy."

"What the fuck are you on about?" I stared at Missy. "You think I'm going to raise the sodding dead?"

"Wouldn't be the weirdest thing you've done," she pointed out.

"Missy," I said slowly, "I'm not going to turn Billy into a zombie. I promise. Apart from anything else, I don't even know where his body is."

"Then how are you going to stop him dying?" she asked.

"Oh, he'll still die," I said, "but at the right age for it. Maybe at home in his bed with his wife next to him and his adult children standing around looking dutifully sad. Or," I shrugged, "maybe he'll still end up on the streets. I'm not a bloody clairvoyant, I don't know what will happen."

"You can't go messing with time, Lil." Missy looked genuinely shocked. "That's a step too far. Even by your standards."

"I can," I said, "and I will. Anyway," I started backing off, "I need to get going. Time waits for no woman, and all that."

Time doesn't wait for anyone, said the city. ***And it certainly isn't going to let you twist it for your own ends. It'll throw you out soon as look at you.***

We'll see about that. I forced myself to sound more confident than I felt. The city was right—if I got this wrong, time really would shut me out like a bouncer dealing with an annoying drunk. And I wasn't entirely sure it would bother checking it was dumping me back into the right era, either. But Billy was still in there somewhere, and I needed to know I'd at least done everything possible to save him.

Missy took a step towards me. "I'm coming with you," she said. "It's too dangerous on your own."

"Absolutely not," I said. "If I take you with me, then it's my responsibility if something happens to you. And there are people round here who would make my afterlife a never-ending hellscape if I let anything awful happen."

"When are you going back to?" Missy asked.

"Eighteen-hundreds," I said, "or thereabouts. Sometime before Billy —the real, alive Billy—was killed. I just need to divert him onto a slightly different path."

"You don't even know how to act in the nineteenth century," Missy said. "At least I've been through it once already. I've got *experience.*"

"And I've got a history degree," I pointed out. "With a focus on the Victorians. It'll be fine."

"Do you even know which streets were safe to walk down back then?" she asked.

"None of them," I said brightly. "Unless you know different?"

"Nope," Missy admitted, "that's about right. I just don't understand why you even want to do it," she went on. "What's Billy ever done to deserve this kind of personal risk?"

"He's been my friend," I said, "since the day I died." And he would have been my friend before that as well, if I hadn't been a stupid human who was nervous around homeless people for no real reason other than a lifetime's-worth of media opinion drip-feeding itself into my subconscious. "If I can help him, I will."

"He might already be dead and gone," said Missy.

"Nope," I said with certainty, "he's still around. He was already dead, don't forget. He can't die twice."

"I don't like this, Lil," she said unhappily. "I don't like this at all."

"Neither do I," I said. "Laters!" I turned and walked away before she could argue. As I walked down Castle Street, my phone pinged in my pocket. It was beginning to rain, so I found a sheltered doorway to hide in before taking it out.

'*Good luck with it*,' read the message. '*Call me when you need rescuing.*' Smiling despite myself, I tapped out a quick response.

'*Liam*,' I wrote, '*the day I have to rely on you to save me is the day we all need to start* really *worrying x.*' The message had been delivered before I registered the fact I'd automatically put a kiss at the end. Oh well, it'd give him something to think about.

The Church of Our Lady and St Nicholas sits on the corner of Chapel Street and the Strand, just over the road from Pier Head. The city's official Anglican parish church, there's been a place of worship on the site ever since the tiny chapel of St Mary del Quay was built in the mid thirteenth-century, not long after Liverpool received its charter from King John. St Nick's—aka 'the sailors' church'—replaced St Mary's in 1361 and saw its share of troubles from the start, being the site of mass plague burials that same year. The church continued to serve as a central point of worship for the city's burgeoning population well into the nineteenth-century, by which time members of the congregation were becoming concerned that it was unsafe through lack of maintenance. These worries were proven horrifyingly well-founded when, one Sunday in early 1810, the church's enormous spire suddenly collapsed down into the nave below. Twenty-five people were killed—at least twenty of them young girls from Moorfields Charity School, who had the misfortune to be heading into the church for morning worship when the disaster happened. The spire was rebuilt, but more than a century later, the Germans took out the body of the church itself. Given its awful history, you'd be forgiven for assuming St Nick's is a hotbed of paranormal activity, but I'd never found it anything other than perfectly peaceful. My personal theory was that the area was so sick of tragedy that it just kept itself to itself and stayed out of the way of any drama. I was also pretty sure it was the closest to the city's heart I was going to find. I loped along Castle Street and down Water Street until I got to the Tower Gardens alleyway leading to the back of the church. The iron gates were locked, so I used the stone gatepost as leverage to vault myself up and over the fence, landing softly on the old stone slabs of the church garden. There was a bundle of blankets snoring on the bench, so I walked on past to the church itself and leaned back against the wall. *You in?* I asked. Nothing but silence. I wasn't going to be impressed if the city chose this as one of its rare moments to go awol from the inside of my head. A cat walked out of the dark, its ginger fur glinting in the glow of the streetlamps. It was big—what Izzy would describe as a 'proper chonky boi', and yes, you can hear the spelling—and it glanced lazily up at me as it strolled past. I couldn't remember the last time I'd seen a cat other than Grimm in the city centre. A standard moggy I mean, rather than terrifying huge were-cats. I knew cats existed in town, of course. There are feral cat colonies all over the place, and I regularly see kindly volunteers from the rescue associations wandering around late at night armed with food bowls and metal trap cages, but they rarely came out into the open. Maybe Finn and his cohort of unfeasibly large felines were giving their smaller brethren the courage to stretch their paws a bit. *Come on,* I muttered silently to myself, *you're quick enough to lecture me when you're bored and need company.*

We do not get bored, came the city's reply, **we just like to keep you educated. Have you worked out a better plan yet?**

There isn't one, I said. *Time travel, or nothing.*

It'll be nothing, then, came the sharp response. **We cannot allow such risky behaviour within the bounds of the city.**

Who's above you, I asked the city, *in the rankings?*

Well, it said, **Manchester has big ideas, but it's never going to live up to our standards. Although we'd stick together in the face of anything from the south, obviously.**

Obviously. I rolled my eyes and wondered if it could see me do it. *I meant what's above you here, in Liverpool itself. You say yourself you're only the voice of the people—so who's the voice of everything else?*

Only the voice of the people? Only? It sounded indignant. *We're what this city is built on, Lilith. Blood and toil and tears, for endless centuries and countless generations. And you say 'only'?*

Oh, for fuck's sake, I hissed, *stop being so bloody melodramatic! You know exactly what I mean, and I don't have time to mess around. You've told me before now that you're the spirit of the people of the city—well, right now I need the spiritual embodiment of the city itself. I reckon,* I said, *I need to talk to your boss.*

We don't have a boss, it said. *It's just us against the world. Us and you,* it corrected itself. *Against the world.*

Stop being facetious, I said. *You know exactly who—what—I mean. I want to speak to the big cheese. The head honcho. Commander-in-chief. Big kahuna, toppest of all the dogs.*

Aah, it said. *That one.*

That one, I agreed. *Want to patch me in on a direct call?*

Not really.

Why?

We generally like to stay out of its way. It sounded nervous. *Let sleeping beasts lie, kind of thing. Do not poke the crocodile, for its teeth are sharp and you are tasty.*

Stop being ridiculous and put me through.

It isn't that simple, it said. *It has to want to speak to you. We can't just hail it like an unearthly taxi.*

Well, I've been standing here and thinking very hard about how much I need its help right now, I said, *but it hasn't so much as said hello.* I sighed and looked around me. It was late enough now that even hardened drinkers had given up for the night, and too early for the new day's workers. The Strand was eerily quiet as I gazed across to where the Liver Building stood sentinel at the waterfront. An enormous cruise ship was moored over at Pier Head, all but silent despite the lights visible through its endless tiny windows. I was standing at what I was pretty sure was the epicentre of mercantile Liverpool, with both its spiritual and industrial birthplaces surrounding me, yet something didn't quite fit. *This isn't the right place,* I said eventually. *Is it?*

You made the very human assumption that everything grew from religion, came the response. And I had. Which was interesting, because I'd never been consciously religious in my life (or death). Okay, so I was baptised into the Church of England as a baby. But my parents have always been honest about it having just been down to family tradition, not any personal religious conviction. I suspected my ambiguity towards it all had been helped along by both sides of my family tree having wandered through several different religions across the generations. Kitty and Ivy's side were, unsurprisingly, Catholic. Ivy's house had crucifixes on the wall when I was a kid, but I'd always got the impression it was more for the look of the thing. I certainly didn't recall her ever saying so much as a single Hail Mary in my presence. And Kitty definitely wasn't a believer in anything other than peace and love and possibly the healing power of decent quality weed. Dad's side had, I thought, possibly been Methodists before they gave in and swapped to Protestantism, purely because the churches were more plentiful. That Dad was alive and kicking and I still couldn't be sure about it just went to show how unbothered he clearly was about the whole thing. But yes, I'd automatically thought of the church as the possible birthplace of the city. Perhaps I should have gone to my old workplace instead. Established as the Blue Coat School at the beginning of the eighteenth century, what's now known as Bluecoat Chambers is the oldest surviving building in the city centre and an excellent choice if you're at a loose end and interested in art as well as decent coffee.

Not old enough, said the city. *This place is older than mere bricks.*

Leaning back against the old stone, I considered the options. Liverpool didn't exist as a named place until 1207, and by that point people were already living here in homes that, whilst undoubtedly rudimentary, certainly would have counted as buildings. From before that, then. But when? What constituted the birth of an amorphous being that would one day be transformed into a city? Where would a city spring from in the first place? The answer came to me so abruptly that I almost slapped myself in the face like a cartoon character, so astonished was I by my own stupidity. *Now*, I knew where I needed to be—where the city itself had *always* been. I started running.

∾

If you ever happen to be lost in Liverpool and ask for directions to the Fall Well, you'll be pointed towards an average-looking chain pub that occupies a good chunk of the ground floor level of St Johns shopping centre. Named after a water supply rather than customers' abilities after a full day of discount beer and a range of reasonable food choices, it's actually in the wrong location for its name. The place I was looking for was a couple of hundred metres around the corner. Hidden behind—and below—the large, red-brick vision of Art Deco design that is the Royal Court Theatre, is the Fall Well. Or rather, that's where it used to be, before industry and immigration filled the city with hordes of workers and their attached families, all of whom appreciated a nice bit of old-fashioned entertainment during their rare breaks from physical labour. A circus owner bought the site in the early eighteen-hundreds and converted it into the grandly titled 'Royal Amphitheatre of Arts', a venue which saw performers of all levels of ability and notoriety ply their trade, including the chap who would go on to posthumously inspire the Beatles' song *Being For The Benefit of Mr Kite*. After a tumultuous century of changing owners, bankruptcy and the occasional fire, the theatre reopened as the Royal Court in 1938, in the building that stands facing out onto Roe Street to this day. I knew the Beatles connection from the tourist trails I'd done during my early time in Liverpool, and the building's history via a chatty bloke who'd come into Flora's out of curiosity one day soon after we'd opened, whilst on a break from playing one of the seven dwarves in the Christmas panto. But it wasn't the theatre itself I was interested in now. Somewhere underneath its revolving stage—the largest in Britain outside of London, the enthusiastic thespian had informed me—lay the site of the Fall Well itself. The spot at which fresh drinking water had first been made fully accessible to those laying Liverpool's literal foundations, the Fall Well wasn't the only borehole that had been dug through the sandstone in order to slake the growing town's thirst, but it was the best known and most used. Up until the late sixteen-hundreds, the original seven streets of Liverpool had their water delivered by cart from the Fall Well. It seemed to me that if there was anywhere in the city that could be considered its true heart, it was here. I debated scaling the high brick frontage of the theatre and attempting to get inside, but suspected it would achieve nothing more than causing a racket when the intruder alarms inevitably went off. I might be immortal, but I'm still solid and I still show up on security cameras. No, I decided—if the city really started here, the memories would be strong enough to sense my presence. At least, that's what I was hoping. I leaned back against the bricks and closed my eyes. I wasn't consciously trying to walk through time, but it started happening anyway. It was creeping towards morning now, and the occasional shouts of the last nighttime revellers were slowly being replaced by the clanking sounds of early morning deliveries. I could still feel the wall behind my back, so was reasonably sure anyone walking past would just take me for someone trying to settle their stomach before attempting the final stagger home. I concentrated my mind on what might have been around me hundreds of years ago. Rough ground, well-worn paths, and the sound of pealing laughter coming from the women gathered at the well, as much to catch up on local gossip as to collect the day's water. Slowly, the modern city quieted around me, and the sounds of an unmechanised past took its place. I pressed my hands back against the brickwork, half praying and half trying to keep myself rooted safely in the twenty-first century. The last thing I needed right now was to be dropped into an era when my red hair alone might be enough for the locals to suspect witchcraft. *And for once*, I thought to myself in almost amusement, *they'd be right*. The bricks were reassuringly rough and warm, and I ran my fingers along the mortar lines, feeling my way softly through the veins of the city itself.

YOU'RE HERE. The voice, when it came, was clear and loud and nothing like a voice at all. It was as though the words appeared fully formed inside my head, as real as if I were watching them scroll in front of me on tickertape. It felt female though, somehow. And possibly...Jamaican?

I AM EVERYTHING, it said. The voice was somehow every accent I'd ever known. I got the impression that the City—I decided to mentally capitalise it, to keep it separate from the smaller and frankly more irritating regular city—was thinking carefully before speaking.

"Are you actually talking to me?" I asked. "Or is this one of those weird paranormal batshit things that everyone just accepts because trying to figure out how it actually works only ever leads to a splitting headache?"

I AM OLDER THAN LANGUAGE, LILITH, it added. **YOU KNOW THAT.**

"You didn't exist until the thirteenth century," I pointed out. "So how can you be older than words?"

THE POOL WAS ALWAYS HERE, it said. **THE POTENTIAL FOR A CITY HAS ALWAYS BEEN HERE. SINCE THE BEGINNING.**

"Did you witness the Big Bang?" Silence. "The birth of the world," I persisted. "The first grain of proto-life. That which makes us unique. When a mummy planet loves a daddy planet very—"

I UNDERSTAND THE QUESTION, it interrupted sharply. **AND I FAIL TO SEE HOW IT IS RELEVANT.**

"I just thought maybe I could give Brian Cox a lesson," I said. "*Personal* lessons, if you know what I'm saying. That's more like my idea of a fun science experiment."

I'M SURE HE ALREADY KNOWS. I didn't know whether to be offended by the clapback, or surprised by the City's awareness of scientists in popular culture. **I KNOW EVERYTHING THAT IS RELEVANT**, it said.

"Oh no, no, don't you *dare* start reading my mind!" I growled. "It's bad enough having one of you in my head," I said. "Two is way too much. For anyone."

YOU'LL MANAGE, it said. **YOU GENERALLY DO.** I considered the possibility that I really was just losing my mind. Maybe I'd injured my head in that fall from the fire escape the previous year, and in reality had been lying comatose in hospital ever since. Izzy and my family would be visiting and looking sorrowful as they took turns sitting at my bedside. But the initial shock and heartbreaking horror would have worn off by now, because no one can keep up that level of angst for very long. So they'd perhaps just pop in once a week or so, knowing it was pointless but unable to bring themselves to give up completely. **THIS IS REAL, LILITH**, said the City. **IF IT HELPS**, it went on, **THE BIRDS BELIEVE IN YOU.** A pause. **I DON'T KNOW WHY.**

"Well, thanks a fucking bunch," I grumbled. "Know what would be nice?" I didn't wait for a response. "What would be nice," I went on, "is a tiny bit of appreciation instead of all this snark. You're all quick enough to get me involved when something dangerous happens, aren't you? But in-between times it's all 'Do you even know what you're doing' and 'Are you sure you're up to this?' or 'Would you like us to bring in someone better qualified?' And as I have been repeating to anyone who will listen for nearly a bloody year now, I didn't sodding well ask for this bullshit. But now that I'm neck-deep in it, I'm dealing with it as best I can. And if that's not good enough, then it's tough fucking titties to all of you. So there," I added sulkily.

YOU ARE READING HUMAN INFLECTIONS INTO NON-HUMAN SPEECH, said the City. **MY WORDS ARE LITERAL. I DO NOT KNOW WHY YOU HAVE BEEN CHOSEN FOR THIS PATH, LILITH**. Perhaps I should have found this reassuring, but I didn't. **YOU ARE HERE, AND THAT'S ENOUGH.**

"Why are *you* here, though?" I persisted. "Do all towns and cities have a spirit?"

SOME DO, it said. **OTHERS HAVE YET TO KNOW THEMSELVES.**

"Do you all communicate in garbled psych-speak?"

YOU ARE WASTING YOUR TIME TRYING TO UNDER-STAND ME. I AM OLDER AND YOUNGER AND BIGGER AND SMALLER THAN ANYTHING YOU CAN IMAGINE. I AM INDESCRIBABLE, said the City. **AND YOU ARE RUNNING OUT OF TIME.**

I thought quickly. "How do I get back to the *right* time, then?" I asked. "The time when I can save Billy? I have to help him."

WHY WOULD YOU WISH TO PREVENT THE LOSS OF ONE SINGLE HUMAN AMIDST AN ETERNAL SEA OF DEATH AND DESTRUCTION? it asked. **THERE ARE MILLIONS DYING EVERY TURN OF THE SUN, YET YOU CHOOSE TO SAVE ONE MAN.**

"It's the butterfly effect," I said, "isn't it? If Billy didn't exist back then, my life would be different now, almost two centuries later. He shouldn't have been lost in the time slip—*I shouldn't have lost him in the time slip*. So, my mistake is fucking up the future we would have had. And in turn, that will fuck up the city's future. It might only be in tiny ways, but it makes a *difference*."

THIS MAY BE THE WAY THINGS WOULD ALWAYS HAVE BEEN, came the response. No comment about my choice language, I noted—presumably the City was above worrying about curse words. **YOUR VOCABULARY IS IRRELEVANT**, it went on. **IT IS YOUR INNERMOST THOUGHTS AND BELIEFS THAT I HEAR**. A pause. **AND YOUR DESIRES**.

"There isn't time to worry about my desires," I said hurriedly, mortified at the thought of an entire city knowing all my personal secrets. "I need to know how to save Billy."

YOU MIGHT MAKE THINGS WORSE, it said, rather unhelpfully.

"I don't care about the time slips anymore," I said. "I just want Billy to be okay. I owe him that much. So it's a risk I'm going to have to take. For my friend."

FRIENDS, said the City. **AN INTERESTING CONCEPT. AND ONE I HAVE NEVER FULLY UNDERSTOOD**.

"Maybe you could have a chat with the other version of you," I said. "The one that's got all the people that have ever mattered, but is still too scared of you to introduce me to you directly."

WHY WOULD IT BE WARY OF CONTACTING ME? WE ARE, AFTER ALL, OF THE SAME SOIL.

"Maybe you're intimidating," I said. "Perhaps you should reach out first. Have a catch-up over a cuppa, or something." Jesus H fucking Christ, now I was offering counselling advice to the spiritual embodiment of an infamous human conurbation. If this carried on, I was going to have to buy a much bigger couch. "Anyway," I ploughed on, "how do I find him? Billy, I mean. The city itself is always bloody well with me, I don't have any problem finding that." I could actually feel it scrabbling around in the furthest recesses of my mind, presumably trying to find a table to hide under before the big boss came looking for it. *You fucking chicken*, I hissed at it. All I got in return was a faint shudder, then silence.

THE CURRENT...ISSUES...WERE NOT INTENTIONAL,

said the City, bringing me back to the matter in hand. **SOMEONE DECIDED TO CAUSE MISCHIEF.**

"Who?" I asked. If Liam had been meddling again I would feed him to the sodding mermaids, king or not.

NOT HIM. THE ONE YOU FEEL MORE FOR THAN YOU WILL ADMIT, EVEN TO YOURSELF.

I thought about it for a minute, genuinely confused. "If I wouldn't admit it to myself," I said slowly, "then how do I know who you're talking about?"

THE VIKING.

I screwed my face up and banged my head gently back against the bricks. "Are you fucking *shitting* me?" I hissed into the air. "You think I'm harbouring a crush on Ivo fucking Laithlind? That deceitful, two-faced, hypocritical bastard?"

THERE IS ENERGY IN YOUR VITRIOL, said the City calmly. **IT BETRAYS YOU.**

"Give me bloody strength," I said. "He's even more of a creep than Liam, and that's saying something. Anyway," I huffed a bit to cover my embarrassment, "that's the least of anyone's worries right now. Why did Ivo decide to cause trouble?"

WHO KNOWS THE WAYS OF MAN? said the City.

"Well," I said, "clearly not me. 'Cos right now I'm pretty fucking disappointed in all of them."

MORE PEOPLE ARE KIND THAN ARE CRUEL, it said. **NEVER FORGET THAT.**

"One of the kindest people is Billy," I said. "And in return for that kindness, I went and lost him somewhere in the past."

AND YOU HAVE A PLAN TO RESCUE HIM?

"Yes."

WHY SHOULD THE CITY HELP YOU?

"Because if this works," I said, "maybe everything will reset itself. I'll have changed the future, which will send everything down a different timeline. With any luck, things will go back to how they were. How they *should* have been. Without Ivo bastard Laithlind sticking his stupid Norse oar into my business."

I WAS UNDER THE IMPRESSION YOU WOULD QUITE LIKE HIM TO STICK HIS—

"That is quite enough, thank you!" Amazingly, it shut up. It definitely needed to get out more, because there was no way I was going to spend the rest of eternity with not one, but two invisible city-spirits sitting in my head and taking the piss. "Anyway," I went on, "it's not good for business, having people accidentally walk into different eras. It'll make the sightseeing tours awkward if buses start disappearing halfway down Penny Lane. Your reviews are going to take a hit."

IS YOUR SPEECH ALWAYS THIS LONGWINDED?

"Apparently so," I shrugged. "So we're going to have to work together, whether you like it or not."

I WORK WITH NO ONE. THERE IS ONLY THE CITY.

"There's also a government on the human side of things," I pointed out, "and they're beginning to take an unhealthy interest."

THEY ONLY TAKE AN INTEREST WHEN I'M MAKING THEIR LIVES DIFFICULT, it said.

"Yeah, well, I can't argue with that. But if you don't want them managing your decline again, you're going to have to play ball."

Silence for a moment. Then, **TELL ME YOUR PLAN**. I told the City what I was going to do and, to its credit, it didn't laugh in my face. Actually, it couldn't have laughed in my face, because it was inside my head. At least, that's where I thought it was. **I AM EVERYWHERE, LILITH**, it said. A pause. Then, **YOU ARE CUNNING. IT IS IMPRESSIVE.**

"So cunning, you could put a tail on me and call me a weasel."

FIND JIMMY. I thought I'd misheard it. 'Jimmy' was the sort of name you hear down the pub, or at the garage when you're having your tyres done. It isn't a name often associated with geographical demigods.

"Jimmy?" I said. "Just 'Jimmy'? There's half a million people in this city, and I reckon a good few thousand of them are going to be called Jimmy. Or Jim, or James. Can you narrow it down a bit?"

YOU ALREADY KNOW HIM, said the City. **HE TOOK YOU TO TOXTETH.**

C'MON BILLY

I took off without another word, past caring whether anyone saw me. There'd been so much weird shit going on in the city recently that I was pretty sure no one would even register a speeding runner. Skidding on my heels in order to take a right onto Church Street, I briefly considered investing in a pair of proper trainers. Although Doc Martens are good in a fight—a situation which is never entirely out of the question in my world—they're not so good for sprinting. Left onto Paradise Street, and a hop and a skip over a lone drunk who was groaning over one of the bollards outside Schuh. A curving turn to the right, and I was on Thomas Steers Way, the lights of Albert Dock twinkling brightly in the distance. *One hell of a scenic route*, I thought to myself as I ran across the road to Salthouse Dock. I was just a few minutes meander from my starting point at St Nick's.

The carousel was in darkness, its brightly painted horses monochrome under the street lights. There was a gate in the low fence surrounding it, but at this time of night it was firmly locked with a heavy chain and padlocks, none of which would have stopped anyone but the feeblest of intruders gaining access. I vaulted lightly over the fence and stood next to the carousel itself, wondering what to do next. The horse nearest to me was, apparently, called Simone. She had a purple and pink flower on her bridle, and a glint in her black eyes. I gave her a reassuring pat, just to be on the safe side. "Good girl," I murmured, walking past her to look at the other horses. I found Jimmy in front of Jill, sitting next to a rather sinister-looking Maisie. Considering she'd carried Sean safely around whilst Jimmy dumped me into the old and very cold Mersey, I figured Maisie was just a victim of unfortunate makeup. I put my hand gingerly on Jimmy's neck, half scared he'd either come to life in front of my eyes or give me some kind of horrible shock. Nothing happened. "You okay, lad?" I asked him quietly, feeling stupid even as I did so. Despite all the weird shit that went on beneath Liverpool's—mostly—civilised surface, I'd never heard of anything as weird as a haunted carousel. My money was on the time slip being connected with the spot it stood on, rather than the brightly coloured horses themselves.

"Roll up, roll up," said a voice behind me, "thruppence a ride! Free for the young lady with the red hair! One night only, mind, else I'll be bankrupting myself before you can say give Ireland back to the Irish, you thieving bastards." I spun round to see a man standing on the carousel just a few feet from me. He looked like an old-fashioned fairground worker of the sort you sometimes see in old photos, wearing a patched greatcoat over baggy trousers that were tied down to his heavy boots with ragged strips of cloth. A battered top hat sat incongruously on his head, and I struggled to make out the face beneath it in the gloom. He walked away from me around the far side of the carousel before reappearing next to the horse in front of Jimmy. I jumped, and the man tipped his hat. "My apologies, ma'am," he said, "for I did not mean to startle you. You'll be hopping on, then," he nodded to where my hand still rested on the horse's neck. "We haven't got all night."

"Will he take me where I need to go?"

"I'm not privy to where you're going, ma'am," said the man. "All I knows is how to get you there." He jammed the top hat onto his head and reached in through the window of the carousel's central mechanism. The machinery clanked slowly into life. I climbed onto Jimmy's back as the music began and the horses began to rise and fall around me. I held onto the pole and the music got louder as the horses built up speed. It wasn't the usual generic fairground tune—this was muffled and yearning and unearthly, as though an ancient folk tale had come to life around me. "And so it has," said the man, swinging himself around the pole of the horse in front of me. Suddenly, his face was right in front of mine—manic eyes and a reddened nose, bulbous from drink, loomed out from under the brim of his hat His mouth opened into a wide grin showing stumpy, rotten teeth. I lurched away from him and he laughed. "You don't need to be afeared of me, girl," he said. I took a breath and was assailed by the scent of cinnamon and tobacco, stale sweat and shit and the sharp copper tang of blood pooling on the cobbles. "You just hang on tight and let's see where we can get you, aye?" With that, he swung away and rammed his arm hard down through the window onto the carousel's motor. The music became more insistent, writhing around my head like tentacles trying to find a way in. But despite the cacophony in my skull, I was pretty sure no one else could hear it. If anyone happened to walk down to the river right now, they'd probably see me sitting on the horse and staring at something that wasn't there. Maybe they'd get worried, and I'd suddenly regain awareness as paramedics attempted to strap me down in the back of an ambulance. The horses were moving fast now, up and down and round and round at a speed that would have made me sick had I still been alive. Dawn was breaking, and it felt as though the sun was rising too soon, too fast... Suddenly a loud metallic grinding noise rose from the central column of the carousel, and I wondered if the motor had finally been pushed too hard. In answer to my unspoken question, the music went off-key and slowed, like a clockwork music box winding itself down. The man swung round towards me in another low bow. "Your destination, ma'am," he said. I looked around at the quiet docks and silent roads and the Hilton, shining like a modern-day beacon just up the road.

"We haven't even gone anywhere," I said, as the horse slowed beneath me.

"Can't help that," said the man, backing away as he spoke. "You just gets taken where Jimmy decides to take you."

"Who are you?" I said, as the man wedged his hat tightly back on his head and turned to leave. "Who the *fuck* are you?" The man twisted to look at me and his head turned a little bit too far round to be natural. I was already scrabbling my way off the horse as he spoke.

"My apologies," he said, his dark eyes glinting in the lamplight, "for I did not make the proper introductions. My name," he leered, "is Jimmy." With that, both Jimmy and the carousel disappeared—and I fell headfirst onto the cobbles.

～

"Oi!" said the woman who'd just trodden on my back, "whad'ya think you're doin'?" I scrambled upright, confused by the noise around me. It was daylight and the docks were crammed with people, all hurrying along on unknown errands. Without thinking, I put a hand on the nearest wall to steady myself. When I lifted it away, my palm was black with soot. Looking around, I realised I was still at the Albert Dock—but now it was busy with boats instead of tourists. The air was filled with shouting and clanking, the docks themselves living monsters, sucking in and spewing out life in all its guises. Although I could orientate myself from the buildings around me, my brain was struggling to accept this version of Liverpool. There was vacant airspace where the towers of the Liver Building should have been, Bella and Bertie not yet so much as a twinkle in their designer's eye. St Nick's Church was there on the corner, although my view was obscured by the overhead railway. God, I'd forgotten about the railway. Walking slowly up towards the Strand, I watched a train pass overhead in front of the Custom House that stood where the Hilton would be in all its garish, brash glory many lifetimes later. The original dock that used to lie in front of it was already gone, hidden under rickety-looking buildings that would themselves be pulled down years later in order for the dock's bowels to eventually be subjected to the close inspection of the *Time Team* experts and their geophys detectors.

I had to get back to Billy before he got in Maria's way. If I could just stop him getting close enough for her to attack, maybe that would be enough. And it was absolutely the wrong thing to do. I knew that. I wasn't supposed to even *be* here, let alone trying to change the course of history. But I had to save him—I had to be faithful to my friends, if I was to ever be faithful to something as big as a city. And the city hadn't shut me out, so maybe it was the right thing to do after all. I ducked out of the way of a pair of wealthy-looking gentlemen who were heading straight towards me, deep in conversation. One of them had to move to avoid knocking into me, but neither showed any sign of registering my existence. Things were different back then, though. Maybe they were just trained from birth to ignore anyone who didn't look equally prosperous. Glancing down, I realised my surroundings might have changed, but my appearance absolutely hadn't. I was still wearing pyjama trousers and boots, topped off with the baggy, faded Echo and The Bunnymen t-shirt I'd picked up in a charity shop when I was still at university. I stood in the middle of the street I'd come to know so well more than a century-and-a-half later, and looked around me. If Billy really was here and about to meet his fate, my money was on it happening somewhere near Harrington Street. I rubbed the stones of Gran's ring in the half-hope it might release a helpful genie and was unsurprised when nothing happened. Did Harrington Street even exist this far back? I thought it probably did, but couldn't be sure. My history degree had covered plenty of Liverpool's history, but it had all been to do with the Industrial Revolution and the docks, not the social history of the city itself. It was certainly putting its best face forward towards the world at large, there was no denying that. Ornate buildings sat along the Strand, still beautiful despite the layers of grime disguising their finer features. I automatically patted my pocket, thinking I'd use my phone to take photos, only to realise I must have left it in the flat. Even if I had brought it with me, would the camera have worked? Perhaps it would be like the stories from Bold Street, of phones turning into lumps of useless tech in an era before the tech even existed. So many buildings that wouldn't make it through the Second World War. And so many people, too. How many great-grandchildren of the people walking around me now would end up killed in the Blitz? Or left homeless, their own children growing up in slums as central government carefully forgot about the city on the sea that had brought it so much wealth and prosperity.

Managed decline, said the city, making me jump. *Ha*. It made a spitting noise.

You're here already, then?

We've always been here, it said sadly. *Always here, always alone.*

Looks like you were doing okay at this point, though, I said, trying to sound encouraging. *Everything's busy, there must have been a lot of money coming in. Plenty of work for people.*

Have you ever thought about what this city is built on, Lilith?

That stumped me, and I had to think for a minute. *Sandstone?* I asked, thinking of the walls of Joseph Williamson's tunnels, which would already be snaking out under Edge Hill up at the top of the city.

People, it said. **Those ships might be bringing in sugar and tobacco, but it isn't long since they were used for slaves. Even now, those who work for the people higher up are told they're free, when they're anything but. They might not be in shackles, but they're owned, all the same.**

Yup. There wasn't much else I could say.

The modern version of this country was built on the back of those taken from their own lands and their own lives.

Yup. We stood in silence for a while, me and the sentient city in my head, which currently appeared to be feeling rather tired and emotional. *But surely the important thing is that we remember?* I asked it eventually. *We make sure people remember, so it never happens again.*

Normandy would have us all be slaves.

I was thrown by the change of direction the conversation was taking and it took me a few seconds to catch up. *Liam? You don't seriously think he'll actually try to take over?*

We know he will.

Then I'll just have to stop him, won't I?

That's what we're relying on. Which didn't make me feel any better. **You're going to find the boy?**

That's the plan.

You can't change history, Lilith.

Just watch me, I said, and set off along the Strand.

The streets were narrow and crowded and I was very grateful I didn't have to breathe after I took a small accidental gulp of the fetid air. Even a busy Saturday afternoon on Lord Street had nothing on the nineteenth-century version of the city. It was *loud*. Horses took the place of cars, pulling carts and carriages and occasionally just carrying people.

No one took any notice of me, and I was beginning to wonder if I were really there, when I trod in the horse shit that had spread itself across the road. That certainly seemed real enough. Stopping to knock a particularly vile-looking chunk of excrement off my shoe against an iron lamp-post, I looked around for anything familiar enough to help me get my bearings. Spotting the James Street sign, I dodged people and carts in order to cross over to it, then headed up towards Derby Square. I knew the castle would be long gone by now, its stone used in the building of the docks. But my usually pin-sharp memory had a gap when it came to what filled the space before the Queen Victoria statue was constructed. The sight of a tall spire reminded me. St George's Church towered above the square, its oddly bulky design looming over the people scurrying below.

I stood for a while in a corner of the square, tucked away behind a fruit and veg stall that was currently being guarded by a small child who looked like he was cosplaying Oliver Twist. A blue-eyed dog sat with him, occasionally turning its baleful gaze towards me and growling under its breath. "Pack it in," said the boy, giving the dog a half-hearted kick, "or it's the meat-man for you." The boy's feet were bare, and the dog barely seemed to register the kick, preferring to risk another than take its creepy eyes off me. "What the bloody hell's wrong with you?" said the boy, looking over at me. "There's nothing there except rats," he said to the dog. "Make yourself useful and go catch some, if you're that bothered." The dog didn't move. The boy definitely hadn't seen me, though. I wondered if I was invisible to everyone, or just those too busy to actually look.

"They mightn't be able to see you," said Gran as I stepped out into the square, "but you can still affect them. You be careful, my girl."

"Fucking hell, Gran," I spluttered, turning to where Ivy stood right next to me. "Remember what we said about giving a bit of bloody warning?" She was still dressed in her tweed suit, but there was a transparency to her that hadn't been there before. Here in the past she was more ghost than human.

"No need for that sort of language," she tutted. "You weren't brought up in a barn." A couple walked towards us, the young man's clothes marking him out as a docker. The girl he was with had a tatty, oversized raincoat draped over her shoulders, covering what looked like the anonymously grey and grubby uniform of a domestic servant. Presumably a maid from one of the merchant houses set back away from the river. As they got closer, the man looked straight at me and for a second, I panicked. Then I realised that although he was gazing directly at me, he hadn't registered my presence—he was, to all intents and purposes, looking straight through me. I froze where I stood as he guided his companion around me, his expression completely unchanged. "The absolute cheek," said Gran. "Walked right through me, so they did! Wouldn't have happened in my day." Her familiar grumbling was a comforting anchor to my more usual life.

"How did you get here?" I asked.

"You called me, I expect," she said breezily. "That's what the ring's for." I stared down at the stones glinting up from my right hand. They seemed brighter than they'd been when I first put the ring on. It really had contained a genie, I realised—it just so happened to be in the shape of my mardy grandmother.

"So basically, I've got a bat-phone in the shape of a ring," I said, "but instead of Batman, I get my grandmother?"

"Sounds about right," said Gran. "Used to belong to my great-aunt, that did."

"And did she also appear out of the blue when you needed help?"

"Heavens no," said Gran, "what a ridiculous idea! Honestly, Lilith, you are such a dreamer."

"Gran," I said slowly, "we are both dead. But we're still having this conversation and we're doing so in the middle of nineteenth-century Liverpool. I think that's up in the realms of fairytales, don't you?"

"Depends what sort of stories you read," Gran sniffed. "What are you doing here, anyway?" I explained my plan, and Gran looked just as disbelieving as I'd expected.

"You think that if you stop his original death," she said, "things will go back to normal?"

"That's the plan."

"It's a stupid plan," said Gran. "If you don't mind me saying."

"Got a better one?" She gave it some genuine consideration before replying.

"No," she said finally. "So, we'll have to go with your stupid one. Don't blame me when it all goes wrong."

"I thought you were here to help me," I said, "not shred my confidence before I've even started."

"Just being realistic," shrugged Gran. "You'll be needing to get to Flora's, then. Or rather, where Flora's will be. Up there," she pointed towards Lord Street, "then left, then right. Same as always. What are you waiting for?" she asked, looking at her watch. "By my reckoning, you've got less than a minute. Chop chop!"

I raced across the square and up the main road so fast that a newspaper seller on the corner lost most of his copies of the *Daily Post*, but I didn't dare stop to help. I was in such a panic that I overshot the turning for North John Street and had to turn in at Dorans Lane instead. The alleyway that was quiet and mostly empty in the modern city was now a busy world all of its own, people scurrying back and forth along it like rats through a trap. I walked through as quickly as I dared, ducking out of people's way as I went. None of them acknowledged my existence, not even the bundle of rags on the ground that I trod on heavily by accident, only to discover it was actually a filthy and malnourished woman. Even she looked blank when she stuck her head out to see who the culprit was. Her beady button eyes looked straight at me, but immediately slid off again. It was as though my entire presence was on an opposing magnetic pole to everything else, repelling anything that got too close. What I did know about Harrington Street was that it had a history of being home to brewers and merchants and might well be busy, so I stepped out onto it carefully. The dog on Derby Square had been perceptive enough to make me worry; the last thing I needed was to accidentally scare a cart horse and end up responsible for people getting trampled to death. To my relief, the street was quieter than I'd expected. The only horse I could see was at the far end and travelling safely away from me. Suddenly a sallow-faced man appeared out of nowhere, and ran towards me with fear in his eyes. "Don't risk it!" he yelled behind him as he neatly sidestepped me without pause and disappeared in the direction of the warehouses of Rainford Square and

Mathew Street. Carl Jung's quote about Liverpool being the 'pool of life' had never seemed more apt, despite it currently being about seventy years before the man himself would have the dream that inspired it. I wondered briefly what might currently be at the spot where a sculpture of Jung stood in the modern day, but was distracted by a scuffle breaking out further down the street. A man and a woman fell out of a doorway onto the cobbles. He'd got hold of her arm and was twisting it hard, whilst she screamed absolute blue murder. I was about to yell at him to let her go, when I spotted the knife in her hand.

It was Maria Silverton. And the man she was fighting with was Billy —fully alive, but about to get himself killed for the crime of being in the wrong place at the wrong time. I knew the story only too well. Billy's friend Tom had been seeing a girl who'd helped herself to his pay packet on more than one occasion. Tom also had a wife and kids and they relied on him sending money back home, so he needed to get the money back before Niamh started questioning the drop in income. I knew her name because Billy had told me this story himself, not long after I'd died. The frightened man who'd run past me must have been Tom, who'd been pushed out of harm's way by Billy after they'd realised Maria was carrying a pocketknife. Billy hadn't been so lucky. He'd told me how Maria had killed him right there on the street and walked away without a backward glance. And there Billy had stayed, for the best part of two centuries—until I'd dragged him into the time slips and messed everything up.

This was my one chance to put things right. "Billy!" He turned as I ran full pelt towards him, a look of astonishment on his face. He still held onto Maria, but she was scrabbling like a furious cat in her desperation to get away. "Let her go!" Surprise made him falter, and I saw my chance. I launched myself at him, but overdid it in my panic. Instead of crashing him to the ground out of harm's way, my weight propelled him towards Maria's outstretched hand, and I felt a shudder run through his body as he was impaled on the blade. We tumbled down together, Billy's head smacking down onto the hard ground. I could feel hysteria rising as I clambered to my feet and rolled him onto his back. "Billy, oh god... I'm so sorry—"

"So that's where I knew you from," he said, gazing up at me in wonderment. "Always said you'd be the death of me, Red." But even as he managed a weak smile, the life was fading from his eyes. Maria wiped the knife off on her skirt with a casual air. Giving his lifeless body a sharp kick, she looked down at me.

"You can't change history, Lilith," she said. "You'd do well to remember that." With that, she turned and headed down towards the docks, whistling brightly as she went. I fell to my knees on the ground next to Billy, shaking him even as the tears fell.

"Please, Billy," I said, "please wake up. You don't have to die here. We can change things."

"You can't change anything." I looked up to find Eadric Silverton gazing down at us. "He's dead, Lilith. You need to go home."

"How do you know who I am?" It really was Eadric, a full century-and-a-half before I would officially meet him.

"You've always been here," Eadric said. "Even before you were born. It's a strange world we exist in, Lilith. I learned long ago not to question things too much."

"Why?" I asked indignantly. I got to my feet and glared at him. "Why not question things?" I looked at the street around us—familiar, yet also utterly alien. A small, hairy pony was trudging towards us, pulling a heavy cart past where the bollards should be to stop cars driving onto Harrington Street. The pony was thin and weary, but it didn't stop moving. The man balancing on the back was actually a young boy, I realised. He glanced across as they plodded past, but didn't take any notice of the heap on the ground between us. He winked at me, his blue eyes bright in his grimy face. A large grey cat jumped off the cart and leaped over the wall opposite. Seconds later, there was the high-pitched panicked squeak of a small furry rodent meeting its doom.

"I sometimes wonder that myself," said Eadric. "Perhaps I should question things more. But I'm not sure it would change anything." He looked exactly the same as I'd always known him, his chestnut hair rippling slightly in the breeze coming up from the river. I looked past him to where there was nothing but open sky in place of the tall buildings that lined the docks in my own time.

"Where do you live?" I asked him, and he frowned slightly. "The Liver Building doesn't exist yet," I persisted, "so where do you live?"

"There's plenty of shelter to be had for a man of my status," he said. "When you've been around as long as I have, you learn how to live well. But Billy here," he dropped onto his haunches to look more closely at the body on the cobbles, "all he had to do was survive."

"I killed him," I said hollowly. "It was me all along. It doesn't make sense."

"Since when has anything in this godsforsaken world made any sense?" said Eadric. "You're not even supposed to be here, Lilith. You need to go back home."

"I am home," I said, looking across at the building that would one day become Flora's. The grey cat was sitting on the wall next to it, watching me quietly. When it was sure it had my attention, it blinked once, very slowly. Then it dropped down out of sight behind the wall. "If I give Billy a proper funeral, maybe he'll be free." I looked pleadingly at Eadric. "I can't bear the idea of leaving him here for the next century or more," I went on. "I have to do *something*." I heard hooves on the cobbles and turned to see the little downtrodden pony making its slow way back towards us.

"I told you," said Eadric, "this isn't your time. Go home, Lilith." And then he shoved me under the wheels of the cart.

THE KINDEST WORDS

"Lil! Oh my god, you're awake!" Izzy's voice was right above my face. For a brief second, I considered pretending I was still unconscious, if only to give myself more time to figure out what the fuck had happened. I didn't get the chance. Izzy's arms were already round me and she was sobbing quietly into my neck. My limbs felt as though they were made of lead, but I managed to lift one arm enough to pat her feebly on her back. Finally opening my eyes, I realised I was lying on my own bed in my flat above Flora's. Aunt Kitty was glowing anxiously in the doorway and Izzy was definitely real and solid under my hand, so I was reasonably sure I'd escaped the nineteenth century. I turned my head slowly towards the window, muscles aching more than they'd ever done since the day I'd woken up dead on the car park outside this very building. Grimm was sitting on the windowsill, gazing across at us with an implacable expression on his face. As I tried to formulate the words, he preempted me with a distinct wink before dropping off the windowsill and out of sight.

"How did I get up here?" I croaked. My throat was tissue-dry and my eyes sore.

"Have this," said Izzy, finally sitting up. She reached over to the little bedside table and opened a bottle of water. "Eadric said you might need water when you woke up."

Eadric. I pushed myself upright as the memories started coming back. "What else did he say?" I gulped at the water and nearly choked.

"He said not to let you drink too much water in case you drowned yourself." The man himself was standing in my bedroom doorway. I instinctively looked down to check I was dressed and found I was still wearing the clothes I'd had on when I first set off to rescue Billy. The grime on my hands and knees was proof I hadn't imagined what happened.

"Oh god," I said, "I don't know where Billy is."

"It was absolutely bloody insane," said Izzy, "even more than usual. I got here to open Flora's and Kitty was floating around on the fire escape looking worried. Then Missy turned up and stomped around angrily for a bit, only I think she was just worried and trying to cover it. They told me you'd gone off to save Billy and hadn't come back and now both of you were missing, so I shouted at *them* for a bit, just to make myself feel better."

"I need to get up," I started, but Izzy interrupted.

"Let me finish my bloody story," she said, "because otherwise I might cry with relief, and we've had enough of that today already. Anyway, I was yelling at them and there was a sudden thud against the door to the cafe 'cos I'd latched it closed while I was busy shouting, and when I opened it there you were, lying comatose on the doorstep. We all started yelling at that point, obviously," she shrugged, "but then ol' white knight here," she gestured at Eadric, "came running up the street and picked you up like something out of one of those cheesy romance movies. You know, the sort Hallmark run every Christmas." She stopped to take a breath, and I saw she was shaking. "He started carrying you up the stairs with all of us following behind and when we were halfway up—"

"Like the Grand Old Duke of York," interjected Kitty helpfully, "only without the ten thousand men."

"I haven't *finished*," hissed Izzy. "We were halfway up the fire escape and someone called my name and when I turned round," she paused for dramatic emphasis, "it was Billy. What?" I was staring at her wordlessly, struggling to get my head around what she's said.

"Billy?" I managed finally. "Is he..."

"Dead as a doornail," said Izzy happily, "and twice as ignorant. Clearly has no idea any of this," she gestured vaguely around her head, "even happened. What are you doing?" I'd pulled the duvet off my legs and was already hunting for something to put on my feet.

"I need to go speak to him," I said. "Explain things."

"No," said Eadric, "you need to leave him be." I opened my mouth to speak, but he held up a hand to stop me. "Right now," he said, "only you and I know what actually happened."

"Yeah, Lil," said Izzy, "what *did* happen?"

"And it needs to stay that way," said Eadric. He gave Izzy a warning glare, and she shrugged in response. "If it doesn't stay between us, things will only get more complicated. And I think we can all do without that."

"What did you do, Lil?" asked Izzy. "Was it *really* stupid this time? Oh, come on," this was to Eadric, "you can't say things like that and expect me not to ask!"

"It was really stupid," I agreed.

"But it all worked out in the end," said Eadric firmly. "You're back, Billy's back. The time slips have stopped."

"Really?" I was surprised. I'd fully expected things to have got a million times worse. "How do you know?"

"A little birdie told me," he said, and gave me a very unexpected wink. I gaped at him in astonishment. "That reset button got pushed after all. You might want to pop in on them sooner rather than later," he went on. "They'd feel better for seeing you, I think."

"Aaw," I said, unable to help myself, "I really am their favourite."

The time slips really had stopped, and the birds really were pleased to see me. Billy was back in his usual spot and, as Izzy had said, apparently oblivious to recent events. The only thing that wasn't quite right was the silence in my head. The city—the smaller, lowercase city—hadn't spoken since I'd reappeared back on Harrington Street. It was almost a week now, and the lack of third-party inner monologue was far more disconcerting than I'd have ever expected it to be. I'd got used to having the company, I realised. I was walking home from the Liver Building, having spent the evening sitting with Bella. Bertie didn't take offence, because I'd read him a story first. We were halfway through *Wyrd Sisters* and he seemed to be enjoying it. At least, he occasionally shook with what I chose to interpret as laughter, although I guessed it might just have been horror at my terrible attempts at doing the voices. Bella was just happy in my company, and made little contented humming noises as we watched over the river together.

As I turned onto Harrington Street, I saw Billy in the streetlights ahead of me. He was shaking out his bedding and rearranging things in order to get comfortable for the night. I was pretty sure Billy didn't actually feel discomfort on account of being dead, but maybe I was wrong. After all, I still had working nerves and could get a dead leg with the best of them if I sat in the wrong position for long, so why not Billy? He was certainly solid enough—more living human being than a ghost, despite it all. I stopped and leaned against the wall, watching him from the shadows.

He's doing okay, said the city unexpectedly. **We're all doing okay**. A pause. **We're proud of you, Lilith**.

Why? I asked. *I've done nothing but mess things up. Billy wouldn't have died if it wasn't for me sticking my stupid beak in.*

Billy always died. He was dead when you first got here.

Yes, but—

You've got a visitor.

"Am I interrupting anything?" Jonathan asked. I gaped at him standing in front of me on modern-day Harrington Street, still dressed in the clothes of an eighteenth-century gentleman who'd fallen on what had clearly been very hard times.

"Erm," I faltered. "Not really?"

"You have your friend back," said Jonathan, nodding to where Billy was now settling down on the ground and pulling endless layers over himself.

"Yes," I said, completely forgetting to ask how he knew about Billy. "But he doesn't remember anything that happened."

"Is that a problem?"

"He doesn't know it was me who killed him," I said.

"But you do," said Jonathan. "And you're finding this a heavy burden to bear?" I nodded. "Do you recall our conversation," he went on, "back when we accompanied each other on that delightful wander through the wild beauty of Toxteth?"

"It's the first time I've heard Toxteth described as a wild beauty."

"It's beautiful in its own way," Jonathan smiled. "Everything is, if you know how to look." I noted the use of how, rather than where. "So," he said, "do you remember?"

"We discussed the possibility of everything that could possibly happen, happening anyway," I said.

"And we just choose not to walk down those particular routes," agreed Jonathan. "Yet others would argue that every tiny decision any of us make—from which socks to put on in the morning to whether or not we should attack something or someone who's attacking us—creates another branching universe, within which we live according to each decision we make. And in the meantime, all the other potential results of that decision are also happening in other branches of the same universe."

"But we're in *this* universe now," I said doggedly, "and this is the one I need to fix. Even if you're right and Billy's somehow gone back to a previous, I don't know, bloody save-point of this stupid game of life or something, it doesn't keep me from knowing what really happened. Why hasn't *my* brain reset itself?"

"Who knows?" said Jonathan. "Perhaps this universe only creates the branches you choose, and nothing else exists. It doesn't matter how much you want things to be logical and explainable, Lilith—some things just *are*."

"I need Billy to know the truth," I said. "For his own sake, as well as mine. How am I supposed to live with being his friend now I know it was me who killed him in the first place?"

"Any confession would not be for Billy's sake," said Jonathan, "however much you believe it to be. It would be an unburdening of your own conscience, nothing more. Why cause the boy unnecessary heartache?

No," he shook his head sadly, "if you're any friend to Billy, you'll let him be."

"I was trying to help him," I said, the pleading tone in my voice audible even to me. "I was just trying to be *kind*!"

"You were," said Jonathan. "No one would dispute that. But explaining it won't help anything. Sometimes, Lilith, the kindest words are those we decide never to speak."

"Are you going to tell me who you are?" I asked him. "Who you *really* are?"

Jonathan sighed. "If only I could," he said, "I would tell you everything. You and I are similar in a lot of ways, Lilith O'Reilly. Far more than might currently be apparent." There was such deep sadness in his eyes that I found myself struggling to meet his gaze.

"Will I see you again?" I asked.

Jonathan smiled. "Of course," he said, tipping his head politely, "it would be my pleasure. Perhaps you could visit me in Chester." As I opened my mouth to quiz him about why bloody Chester kept coming up and what the hell was really going on there, there was a scuffle behind us. We both turned to look towards where Billy was disentangling himself from his blanket nest on the pavement and scrambling to his feet to stare at a woman walking out from the darkness of Dorans Lane. Her clothes were ragged, and she didn't look entirely real. But she was clearly real enough for Billy. He was staring at her in astonishment.

"Niamh?" he asked again. The woman smiled and kept walking towards him. Billy stood silently, apparently frozen with shock.

"That's Tom's wife," I said quietly.

"And Billy's lover," said a voice beside me that most definitely wasn't Jonathan's. I whipped round to find Eve standing next to me in the gloom, smiling as she watched Niamh walking confidently towards Billy. "He didn't always tell you everything," she said, "so you needn't worry about keeping things from him. Although I don't think you're going to have to worry about it for much longer, anyway."

"What do you mean?" I said. "I don't want anything to happen to Billy, I've only just got him back!"

"Billy's not yours to keep," said Eve. "He's Niamh's. She's waited an awfully long time for him."

"But," I faltered, "she must have been dead a century or more! Why has it taken her until now to find him?"

"Oh," said Eve, "she's been looking. But she didn't know what it was she was looking for. Just wandering, poor girl. She lost Tom when he came over to the mainland for work, but she didn't mind that so much because Tom wasn't a very good husband. Then Billy went after him with a promise of fetching him back, because he wanted to do right by her."

"But she was married to Tom," I insisted, "not Billy. They had children and everything."

"Niamh had three children," said Eve, "all of whom lived to be a ripe old age and did better than anyone might have expected. But only the older two were Tom's."

"You're not telling me..." I trailed off.

"I'm telling you Billy was the father of Niamh's youngest," said Eve, "and probably came to fetch Tom back out of guilt, because those around them must have known what had happened. Or perhaps he thought he'd just earn enough money for all of them and go back and steal Niamh for himself. Maybe she'd have come over here with the children and chosen him over Tom anyway. Who knows?" Eve shrugged. "Niamh died in her thirties, which wasn't unusual back then. She was lucky, compared to some. But love was her downfall. She couldn't leave without Billy."

"And Billy couldn't leave without her," I said. *This* was what he'd been stuck here for. Not to avenge his own death, or because he was somehow tied to Liverpool itself—he'd just been waiting for Niamh to find him. "Why now?" I asked. "Why not decades ago? A century ago?"

"It needed you to complete the circle," said Eve. "Time had got itself mixed up and was missing a piece. You dropped into place and the cogs started turning again."

"The City told me it was Ivo who'd caused the time slip problems," I said, "not me."

"And the city was absolutely correct." Eve looked at me, her eyes bright and clever. "He knew you'd arrive eventually," she said. "He just had to set things in motion and bide his time. He's been waiting for you a very long while, Lilith O'Reilly."

"How long?" I wasn't sure I actually wanted to know the answer.

"Centuries." Eve smiled. "We've all been waiting for you for centuries, Lilith." Her eyes were...strange. It was like looking into an entire universe, swirling behind her gaze. "No," she said firmly, and I realised to my horror I'd leaned in to kiss her. "I'm not for you, my dear. Which is a shame." Her eyes twinkled with amusement as I struggled to think of something to say through my embarrassment. Izzy was right, I really shouldn't be allowed out unsupervised. "Our paths will cross though, I think. I'm looking forward to it. Look," she nodded to where Billy and Niamh stood slightly apart in the gloom of Harrington Street, staring at each other as though they couldn't quite believe what they were seeing. Niamh's shoulders were shaking slightly, as though she was crying ghostly tears. "Go on, lad," whispered Eve encouragingly, as Billy stepped forward to pull Niamh into his arms. "Sometimes," Eve said quietly, "the world is still a beautiful place." As we watched, a glow formed around Billy and Niamh, like something out of a fantasy movie. I was half expecting sparkles to start falling from the sky. Or at least a bit of snow, to add to the strangely festive atmosphere.

"Where will they go?" I asked, my gaze still fixed on the couple under the streetlight.

"Who knows?" she said. "But at least they'll be going there together." I turned to ask more questions, but Eve had disappeared. The light behind me faded, and I whipped round just in time to see Billy and Niamh disappearing into nothing. I stood alone in the dark, Harrington Street empty in front of me. Then Grimm walked out of the shadows and sat in the middle of the street as if waiting to get my attention. Once he was sure I was looking, he hopped up onto the wall and blinked slowly at me. Then he dropped out of sight. A few seconds later, there was a forlorn squeak as yet another small rodent met its end. And so, the wheel of time turned—again.

WHO RUNS THE WORLD?

"We're out of tuna again," said Finn, coming into the living room.

"So go buy some," I said. "I'm trying to watch Gogglebox, for fuck's sake."

"I'm feeling itchy," he said, "I'm worried I might change while I'm out and it makes me nervous."

"It's your nerves that are making you change all the time," said Kitty, who was sitting next to me with Grimm on her lap. "If you calmed down a bit, maybe your versipellis would be less active." Mapp had recently taught her the Latin for shapeshifting, and she'd decided it sounded far more elegant.

"If I didn't keep changing into a bloody cat without any bloody warning," said Finn, "I wouldn't *be* so bloody nervous."

"Will you both just shut up?" I said, before Kitty could respond. "You need to get used to going out," I said to Finn. "It's not good for you, being cooped up in here all the time."

"I know," he whined, "but that doesn't help me now, does it? I'm hungry and we're out of tuna."

"There's prawns in the freezer," I sighed. It was like having a bloody toddler in the house. "Defrost them first!" I called after him, as he raced back into the kitchen and began hunting through freezer drawers. "You know it gave you belly ache last time." Finn mumbled something that might have been assent, but sounded suspiciously like he already had his face in a bag of frozen shellfish.

It was nearly a month since Billy had gone. We'd left his blankets where they were for a couple of days, just in case he reappeared. On the third day, Izzy had gone out and collected them, put them through the wash in the cafe kitchen and donated them to Finn, who was still sleeping at my place. There'd been no time slips since, which was a very good thing as far as I was concerned. Not that life was boring—it couldn't be, with a fully grown were-cat living in the flat. I'd had to set some house rules early on, mind. Finn was absolutely not allowed to sleep on my bed, under any circumstances. I'd had to enforce this within the first week, after getting under my duvet one night and finding cat hair all over the pillow. Finn had attempted to blame Grimm. Which was a stupid move on Finn's part because not only was the hair involved long and black rather than short and grey, but Grimm was now de facto head of all the shapeshifters in the Liverpool metropolitan region and had a low toler-ance for troublemakers. We didn't know just how many shapeshifters there actually were—or even which species they all were—but it had seemed a good idea to put someone in charge. Eadric had been right in that Grimm was the obvious choice—not only did he put the fear of God up any other animal he met, he was still an actual cat and could go most places completely unnoticed. Anyway, when the human-shaped Finn tried suggesting it was maybe Grimm who'd shed fur all over my nice fresh pillows—I might not need to sleep, but I appreciate a clean bed same as the next person—Grimm had turned and yowled up at him in a manner that seemed not only a fraction too intellectually commu-nicative for my liking, it had also frightened Finn into changing back into his cat form before wedging himself firmly underneath the sofa and refusing to come back out. And Finn's a good bit bigger than the gap under the sofa, so Kitty spent several hours sitting on it at a sharp angle, before he finally relaxed enough to change back into human form and slid sheepishly out onto the rug. Grimm had kept him under close observation for a couple of days and Finn was now too scared to so much as step through the door to my bedroom. Which was why we now had a corner of the living room piled up with Billy's old blanket stash and a couple of spare duvets for extra comfort (and for Finn to cover himself with when he was sleeping, because he often changed form without warning and no one needs to find a surprise naked bloke in their flat unless it's someone they're already willingly intimate with).

"Kitty," I said casually, "what do you know about Chester?"

"Not much," she said, not taking her eyes off the tv. "Why?"

"Nothing important," I said. "I can ask Eadric next time I see him." Finn came back into the room smelling distinctly fishy, curled up on the floor by Kitty's feet and gamely pretended not to be clutching his stomach. We sat in companionable silence for a while—the immortal, the ghost and the world's spookiest cats—staring mindlessly at the scrolling screen of human idiocy. "Actually," I said, getting up from the sofa, "I'm going to nip over to see Bella for a bit. She and I have things to discuss."

"Oh?" said Kitty, finally turning to look at me. "Anything interesting?"

"Yeah," I said with a grin. "I reckon it's about time us birds started running this place."

My phone pinged as I headed down the fire escape. Sliding it out of my pocket, I read the message as I walked down Harrington Street. *'Well, no one can say I didn't try my best.'*

I couldn't help smiling to myself as I typed my reply. *'Better luck next time, Ivo.'*

I hadn't even got to Castle Street before the response arrived. *'Oh, there'll always be a next time.'*

Little dots flashed on the screen as he continued to type at the other end. It seemed to be taking him a very long time to decide what to say. Finally, the rest of the message came through.

'Don't forget, Red—we have forever.'

~THE END~

NEXT IN NETHERWEIRD...

~THE DREAM THIEF~

Netherweird Chronicles, Book Five

COMING MAY 2024

Sign up to my newsletter to be the first to hear about
upcoming releases and other interesting stuff -
and get a FREE short story from Netherweird!
tinyurl.com/netherweirdstory

AUTHOR'S NOTES

As with all Netherweird stories, many of the people, places and events mentioned in these places are real in one way or another. I have, however, taken liberties with some of the finer details and no association with people (either living *or* dead) or places is intended, nor should it be inferred. This is all just strange historical madness, woven out of the tangle of my own mind.

Eadric's first wife was actually called Godda, and Mapp did indeed write a story about them, back in the 12th century. It's included in *De Nugis Curialium*, which, if you can find an English translation, is an excellent—and wonderfully gossipy—read.

Liam's story about the gun boat in the Mersey is true, as is the awfulness of the Liverpool Blitz. You can still work out where bombs hit the city centre by spotting the modern buildings filling gaps between older ones.

'Trumpton Riots' is the song by Half Man Half Biscuit that Lil remembers her dad playing. It's on an EP of the same name (my favourite track is 'All I Want For Christmas Is A Dukla Prague Away Kit', FYI), which is well worth hunting out.

The photo on the cover of this book is of the real Jimmy, on the real Albert Dock carousel. Give him a pat from me if you're passing.

Author's Notes

As always, this book would not exist without the support of people around me. And this particular book even more so, because my beloved best friend of thirty years had the absolute temerity to die unexpectedly when I was halfway through writing it and the bottom dropped out of my world with no warning. So this is for Li Zak, aka (as per the credits in Lark Rising) 'the only reason I still live in the shire' and now the reason I'm finally planning to leave it. And also for those who have propped me up in the aftermath and continue to do so:

Jayne Hadfield, beta-reader extraordinaire and regular one-woman support network; Toni Hibberd, who writes the sort of beta notes that have me crying with laughter at my desk; Sal Geere, whose tolerance of authorial flakiness—and *in*tolerance of overused commas—is legendary; Winston Gomez, who has made everything that tiny bit more bearable (and is always up for debating city centre boundary lines and whether anyone would even notice a shapeshifter prowling Granby Street in the early hours); Tilly Melia, who is somehow still tolerating my endless questions about which street really goes where (hi Pete!); my mum and my kids, who've all been absolute rockstars during this time of awfulness; Sarah Trivedi, who communicates entirely by old-style texts and really needs to join the modern world and get a bloody smartphone; and Lucy Chamberlain, who can still make me laugh (even if it's often only down to our combined idiocy). And the entire city of Liverpool—without whom, etc etc. Love youse.

Printed in Great Britain
by Amazon

42714881R00128